Critical accolades for

The City, Not Long After

"Pat Murphy's newest novel is an indisputable heir to a long and honorable tradition in Northern California literature. Ambrose Bierce, Jack London, Richard Henry Dana, John Steinbeck, Henry Miller, Jack Kerouac, to mention but a few, lived and worked here . . . consider Miller's *Big Sur and the Oranges of Hieronymus Bosch.* Pat Murphy's fog-blessed city occupies the same territory in the geography of the imagination."—*Locus*

"A haunting vision . . . highly recommended."
—*Library Journal*

"Murphy infuses this tale with a type of surrealism often associated with Latin novelists like García Márquez. A major work."—*Booklist*

Ask your bookseller for the Bantam Spectra
Special Editions from Bantam Books
that you have missed:

THE
CITY,
NOT LONG
AFTER

Pat Murphy

BANTAM BOOKS
NEW YORK · TORONTO · LONDON · SYDNEY · AUCKLAND

*This edition contains the complete text
of the original hardcover edition.*
NOT ONE WORD HAS BEEN OMITTED.

THE CITY, NOT LONG AFTER

A Bantam Spectra Book / published by arrangement with Doubleday

PRINTING HISTORY
Doubleday edition published March 1989
Bantam edition / February 1990

ISBN 0-553-28370-7

Published simultaneously in the United States and Canada

---

*Bantam Books are published by Bantam Books, a division of Bantam Doubleday
Dell Publishing Group, Inc. Its trademark, consisting of the words "Bantam
Books" and the portrayal of a rooster, is Registered in U.S. Patent and Trademark
Office and in other countries. Marca Registrada. Bantam Books, 666 Fifth Avenue,
New York, New York 10103.*

PRINTED IN THE UNITED STATES OF AMERICA

KR 0 9 8 7 6 5 4 3 2 1

ACKNOWLEDGMENTS

I would like to thank all my friends for their encouragement while I was writing this book. I wouldn't have made it without them.

I would also like to thank Frank Oppenheimer for founding the Exploratorium, a place where artists of all kinds can find inspiration and assistance. I'm grateful to many members of the Exploratorium staff for sharing their ideas and expertise, particularly Ned Kahn, Bob Miller (creator of the Garden of Light), Pamela Winfrey, Carlye Honig, Brenda Hutchinson, Dave Fleming, Ruth Brown, Gary Crounse, Esther Kutnick, and all the cantankerous artists of the Graphics Department.

Special thanks to Jenefer Merrill, Mark Switzer, and their daughters Sadie and Kate for providing me with a weekly retreat where telephone calls couldn't find me, and to the Virginia Center for the Creative Arts for allowing me two weeks of uninterrupted writing time.

I appreciate the encouragement and constructive advice of my fellow writers: Lisa Goldstein, Mikey Roessner-Herman, Avon Swofford, Cheri Wilkerson, Richard Russo, Lew Shiner, Steve Brown, Mark Van Name, and Richard Kadrey (who had to live with this novel for as long as I did).

Finally, I would like to thank Jean Naggar, Lou Aronica, and Shawna McCarthy for providing the final push required to make me finish.

PROLOGUE

The early morning breeze blew through the vegetable garden in Union Square, shaking the leaves of the bean plants and the lacy carrot tops. The city of San Francisco was asleep. The city was dreaming.

In the Saint Francis Hotel, just off the Square, Danny-boy was dreaming of the color blue. With a paint roller on a long pole, he painted the sky. He had been at work for many hours. At least half of the expanse above him was smeared with paint of a thousand different shades: royal blue, navy, turquoise, baby blue, teal, the fragile hue of robins' eggs, the treacherous blue-gray of the ocean at dusk. Toward the horizon, where Danny-boy's roller had not yet reached, the blues faded to misty gray. But overhead, luminous colors swirled and flowed like the water in a river.

In the middle of the changing pattern, two patches of blue-gray coalesced. Bright eyes watched Danny-boy from the center of the sky. Dark blue shadows defined the angles of a face, the curves of a woman's body. As Danny-boy stared upward, a young woman stepped out of the sky, looking more than a little confused.

The city slept, and its dreams drifted through the minds of its inhabitants, twisting and changing their thoughts.

The man who called himself The Machine dozed on a narrow cot at the back of his workshop. In his dream, he was constructing an angel from objects he had gathered.

The angel's bones were pipes from the plumbing of an old Victorian mansion; its muscles were masses of copper wire, torn from the cables that ran beneath the city streets. On the angel's massive wings, thousands of polished bottlecaps overlapped, making a pattern of scallops like the scales on a fish.

The Machine welded the last bottlecap to the wing and stepped back to admire his work. As he gazed up at the angel, he realized suddenly that his creation was not complete. Its chest was hollow: it had no heart.

He heard footsteps and glanced behind him. A woman was walking toward him, carrying something in her cupped hands. He could not see what she carried, but he could hear the steady pounding of a heartbeat, keeping time with her footsteps.

Dawn broke in the city: gray light shone on the gray stone buildings that surrounded the Civic Center Plaza. The statues on the facade of the public library showed signs of neglect. Over the years, pigeons had adorned the statues' heads with streaks of white and had deposited a clutter of feathers and broken nests at their feet.

In a tree that grew in the Plaza, a gray-muzzled monkey, one of the oldest of the troop that lived in the city, dreamed of the Himalayas. Icicles hanging from the eaves of a temple roof melted in the morning sun. Drops of falling water struck a bell, and the metal rang with a musical note. The water trickled away, whispering and crackling softly as it melted a path through the snow. The monkey stirred in its sleep. Changes were coming.

The sun was rising when Ms. Migsdale stepped from her house on Kirkham Street and headed for Ocean Beach. She wore sensible walking shoes, woolen stockings, a tweed skirt and man-tailored blouse, and an overcoat that would protect her from the wildest storm. Ms. Migsdale believed in clothes made to last.

The delicate watch on her wrist seemed incongruous: a dainty bit of gold with sparkling diamonds set around a tiny watchface. Ms. Migsdale had found the watch in a gutter near a jewelry store, dropped by looters as they fled. Though she would not touch any of the sparkling baubles that grew dusty in the display windows of other stores, she had taken the watch from the gutter, justifying it to herself by saying that she had found it, she hadn't taken it. Finders keepers.

Before the Plague, Ms. Migsdale had lived alone. She had worked as a librarian at a nearby elementary school. After the Plague she continued living in the same small house, dedicating herself to publishing the *New City News* and sending messages out to sea.

Each day, at ebb tide, she walked along the beach, carrying a shopping bag. In the bag were a dozen green glass bottles that had once contained wine. Now the bottles held squares of white paper on which Ms. Migsdale had typed messages.

Each note was different. On some, she wrote proverbs or quotations. ("Opinions are like noses: everybody has one.") On some, she wrote short statements of her beliefs. ("I do not believe in God and I must assume, therefore, that God does not believe in me.") And on some, she wrote poetry—haiku, rhymed couplets, sonnets, and an occasional villanelle.

The bottles rattled and clinked in her shopping bag as she walked down the cement stairs to the beach. Seagulls took flight at her approach, shrieking as the wind caught them and blew them away like dirty scraps of paper. The retreating tide had littered the beach with clumps of seaweed and bits of driftwood. On her return trip, she would fill her bag with driftwood to burn in her wood stove.

When she reached the water's edge, Ms. Migsdale set the shopping bag on the sand and swung her right arm in wide circles to loosen the muscles. Then she selected a bottle and waited until a wave crashed on the beach and began its retreat to the sea. Taking a running step onto the wet sand, she threw the bottle with a graceful overhand pitch, a throwing style she had perfected over the years. The bottle arced high, tumbling end over end before splashing into the water just past the breakers. Ms. Migsdale took a step back so that her shoes were out of reach of the next wave, and watched as the bottle bobbed in a passing swell.

Ms. Migsdale liked this time of the day, when she was

awake but the rest of the city was still sleeping. Sometimes she saw things that emerged from the city's dreams: Once a mermaid with long dark hair sang to Ms. Migsdale in a language she could not understand. Another time she met a wolf loping along the sand. The animal wore a red kerchief around its neck and smiled at her as it passed, a casual greeting between neighbors.

Ms. Migsdale picked up her shopping bag and strolled along the water's edge. A flock of small brown shorebirds that moved like clockwork toys ran just ahead of her, peeping furiously. The flock split to rush around a clump of kelp and reunited on the far side.

Ms. Migsdale hesitated beside the kelp, noticing the glitter of glass among the tangled strands. Sometimes she found her own bottles, washed back to shore. With the toe of one of her sensible shoes, she nudged the kelp aside, revealing an amber-colored bottle that had once held Scotch. Not one of hers. She pulled it from the seaweed. Through the brown glass she could see a ragged-looking scrap of paper.

Her hands shook as she unscrewed the bottle's plastic top. In fifteen years of sending messages, she had never once received a reply. She tried to shake the note out, but the paper wedged in the bottleneck and did not move. Realizing the futility of that approach, she scooped up her shopping bag and hurried toward the seawall, where winter storms had deposited rocks of all sizes.

With her strong right arm, she swung the bottle against a boulder. The brown glass shattered, sending chips flying in all directions. She snatched the scrap of paper from the bottleneck and unfolded it.

The paper had been torn from a newspaper published before the Plague. The message read: "A stranger brings interesting news. Join with like-minded friends to prevent interference in your affairs. Look ahead."

Ms. Migsdale recognized the writing style and the typeface: The scrap had been part of the daily horoscope column that had once been published in a local newspaper. She read the words again, then slipped the paper into her pocket.

Without her usual ceremony, she flung her remaining bottles out to sea and headed for home.

"Join with like-minded friends . . ." the note had said. She wondered what her friend Edgar Brown would think of this.

Edgar Brown, the man most people called "Books," smoothed the scrap of newsprint on his knee and peered at it. Ms. Migsdale waited impatiently. She liked Edgar, but found him exasperating at times. Ask him how to boil an egg, and he would shake his head in puzzlement. A week later he would emerge from the library with a bibliography listing sources that covered every aspect of the operation, from the denaturation of egg proteins at 100° C to the role of the egg in Chinese literature. Before the Plague he had been a research librarian at the University of San Francisco. He approached every problem with the same careful scholarship he had applied to major theological controversies.

"I'd say it was torn from a newspaper," he said at last. "Perhaps from the *Examiner*. I'll compare the typeface, and—"

"I know that," Ms. Migsdale interrupted. "But what do you think of what it says?" She did not give him a chance to respond. "I think it means that trouble's coming. That's what I think."

"That seems like a hasty conclusion, Elvira," Books said.

"It may be hasty, but that doesn't mean I'm not right." She leaned back and looked across the Civic Center Plaza. They were sitting on the steps of the public library, where Books lived. Across the Plaza, Danny-boy and Gambit were constructing something of shiny aluminum reflectors and wire.

"Gambit's building an aeolian harp," Books said. "He's stringing wires from the top of City Hall down to the Plaza. The reflectors will amplify the sound that the wind makes when it blows through the wires."

Ms. Migsdale glanced at his face. "It's no good trying to change the subject."

He frowned. "Well, suppose you're right and trouble is

coming. Remember when the Black Dragons decided to expand their territory into downtown? The city took care of that quickly enough."

"Ghosts," Ms. Migsdale said. "The city scared them off with ghosts. But what if we're up against someone who doesn't scare as easily?"

"I don't see what you're so worried about," Books grumbled. "If something comes up, we'll deal with it."

She shrugged, watching Danny-boy and Gambit. Tommy, Ruby's son, was helping—or, more likely, getting in the way. The sunlight glinted on the aluminum reflectors and Ms. Migsdale suddenly felt sad, as if she were remembering this from some distant future, looking back on happy times.

"I haven't heard from Leon," she said, admitting at last her real concern. Leon was one of the traders who always brought her news of the rest of the state of California. "I expected him a few weeks ago, but I haven't heard."

"He's been delayed, that's all," Books said.

"Maybe." She shivered, feeling a sudden chill. "At night, when I listen to the waves, they seem to whisper warnings."

Books rubbed his hands together nervously.

"You feel it too."

"I suppose I do," he admitted reluctantly. He put his arm around her shoulders and she was glad of that. He was a stubborn man, a stodgy man, but a good friend for all that. Together, they would weather whatever trouble came their way.

PART 1

City of Dreams

CHAPTER
1

Sixteen years before Ms. Migsdale found the bottle, Mary Laurenson had given birth to a daughter. Mary lay on a double bed in an abandoned farmhouse, clinging with both hands to the brass bedstead. With each contraction, she moaned in pain and fear, but no one was there to hear her.

It seemed to her that the moaning came from some external source, only incidentally linked to her body. She could feel the cries vibrating in her throat, but she had no control over them. She could not stop them any more than she could control the contractions that racked her body.

She was alone. When she had run away from San Francisco, she had wanted to be alone, wanted to crawl away and hide. But she had not imagined the consequences of that action.

She had felt the first contractions early in the evening. Her water had broken at midnight. Now sunlight shone through the window. In the almond trees outside, blackbirds sang and flitted from branch to branch. In the blessed moments when her muscles relaxed between contractions, she could hear the birds. But when the contractions came she could hear nothing but her own moaning and the pounding of her heart.

Her body was no longer her own. For hours she had fought for control, struggling to breathe as she had been taught, to relax between the spasms. Now she gave up, let-

ting her body do as it would. She released her grip on the
bedstead and put her hands at her sides, trying to find a
position that would free her from the pain. Another contraction, and she gripped the sweat-drenched quilt beneath her,
tearing the fabric with her hands.

Her mind was as willful as her body. She had no control over her thoughts. She hallucinated, imagining that her
dead husband sat on the edge of the bed, telling her to
breathe the way she had learned to breathe in class. What he
asked was impossible: her body did as it wished and she had
no say in the matter.

"Help me," she sobbed, reaching out to the ghost of her
husband. Her hand passed through empty space. "Goddamn you, help me." He vanished, fading into the golden
sunlight that filled the room.

Not sunlight, she realized suddenly. The golden light
shone from a winged figure that stood beside her bed. She
reached out and felt the warmth of the light on her hand.

"I'll help you," the angel said. She felt the voice in her
body, like the trembling in her legs and the contractions in
her belly. "Let me name the child and I'll help you."

She panted, arching her back with the next contraction.
"Yes," she cried. "Yes, help me. Please help me." The warm
light shone on her face and she closed her eyes against it.

The contractions came closer together, one long unend-
ing rush of pain. She closed her eyes and concentrated on
pushing. She felt the tearing as the baby's head came free.
Again she pushed, seeking relief from the pain that was
ripping her apart.

Relief came suddenly as the baby slid from her body.
For a moment she lay quietly. Then the spasms returned as
she pushed out the placenta.

She felt the movement of a small hand against her thigh
and she reached down for the baby. With a corner of the
quilt, she wiped the blood and mucus from the child's face.
The girl gasped once, whimpered, then opened her eyes and
regarded Mary with an unfocused stare. At last, with her
baby at her breast, Mary fell asleep, waking only when the
night breezes blew in through the open window.

* * *

Mary never gave her daughter a name, calling her "baby" or "child" or sometimes "daughter." She did not know whether the angel would return to name her daughter, but it seemed wisest to wait. Losing her husband and friends to the Plague had made Mary cautious. Naming the child seemed a foolish risk, as if a name would attract the attention of a malevolent universe. Namelessness offered a kind of protection.

When she considered the matter, Mary realized that choosing not to name the child made no sense. But sense did not play much of a role in Mary's life. Besides, the girl really didn't need a name. When Mary called, to her daughter, she simply called, "Come here." The girl knew her mother was calling her. There was no one else around for her mother to call.

The baby grew up to be a wild, skittish, tree-climbing girl. She roamed the open lands around the farmhouse, chasing the feral cattle that grazed in overgrown pastures. She seemed to have no fear, this child. But then, she had no trust either. Somehow the two seemed linked in Mary's mind.

Late at night, when the girl was sleeping, Mary crept into her bedroom. Her daughter lay on her side, curled up like a fox in its burrow, her breathing soft and steady. Mary unconsciously matched her own breathing to her daughter's rhythm. She gently touched the girl's hand, taking comfort from her living warmth.

On nights like that, Mary waited for something that she could not admit, even to herself. She waited for the bright angel to come and name her daughter, then steal her away. Mary guarded her daughter, falling asleep in the chair by the bed.

More often than not, she woke to find an empty bed. Her daughter had slipped away in the early morning, leaving a tangle of empty blankets. The girl was off searching for birds' nests, snaring rabbits, catching crayfish in the creek, scavenging in abandoned houses for things to trade at market.

* * *

When the girl was nine years old, she found the globe
in a nearby farmhouse. It was on a shelf of knickknacks,
wedged between a metal replica of the Empire State Building and a china figurine of Minnie Mouse. With her fingers,
she wiped away the furry layer of dust that covered the
glass. Though the afternoon was cool and only a little sunlight filtered through the dirty window to shine on the shelf,
the globe felt warm to the touch.

The girl peered through smears of dirt at the vague
rectangular shapes inside. When she shook the globe, she
saw flickers of movement through the glass.

She moved to the front porch where the light was better, polished the glass on the sleeve of her shirt, and peered
inside again. Tall buildings with square windows stood side
by side. The tallest of the buildings came to a point, making
a triangle rather than a rectangle. When she shook the
globe, flecks of gold rose in swirls and showered down on
the buildings.

She had never seen anything so beautiful. The glitter
caught the sunlight, sparkling like flames. If only she looked
closely enough, she thought, she might see people in the
tiny cars that stood motionless in the street. She turned the
globe over and over in her hands, liking the feel of it. On
the black base, raised gilt letters read: "Souvenir of San
Francisco."

Her mother had told her about San Francisco. Bedtime
stories always began, "Back in San Francisco, before the
Plague. . . ." The stories were odd and disjointed, fragments of her mother's life. Bright memories of the Chinese
New Year's parade, touched with the scent of gunpowder
from firecrackers. Remembrances of neighbors: the old
woman with twenty-nine cats, the young man who practiced
Tai Chi on the roof.

From her mother's memories, the girl had created her
own picture of San Francisco: a place as exotic as Oz, with
tremendous hills over which cable cars rolled. She had
asked her mother once why they could not go back there.
Her mother had shaken her head. "Too many ghosts there. I
can't go back."

The girl took the globe home with her, along with the other trinkets she had found: a jackknife with an imitation pearl handle, a deck of playing cards decorated with photos of naked women, a set of embroidery scissors in the shape of a stork. When she got home, she put the jackknife and playing cards with the other things she would take to market. She gave the embroidery scissors to her mother. But the globe she kept for herself. That night, before she went to bed, she shook it once more and watched the gold flecks drift around the towers of the city.

When she was still quite young, the girl taught herself to hunt. Not far from her home was a tumble of concrete slabs, where a freeway overpass had collapsed in an earthquake. The rubble provided a maze of ready-made burrows, and the rabbits were abundant. At first she snared them with cunning loops of fishing line, set in faint pathways that the animals had worn in the grass. When she was a little older she made a slingshot with the metal tubing from a rusted bicycle frame and the rubber from the bicycle's inner tube. With slingshot in hand, she would lounge on a sun-warmed concrete slab, waiting in the soft purple twilight for the rabbits to come out and feed. Even in dim light, she rarely missed.

In a neighboring farmhouse, she found a Golden Book Illustrated Encyclopedia. Though her mother had taught her to read, she liked the Encyclopedia mostly for the pictures, and she carried it home, several volumes at a time. After five trips she had the whole alphabet. On winter evenings she lay by the fire, studying pictures of exotic places and things. In the volume marked W she found pictures of weapons. From a picture she got the idea for her crossbow. She cut saplings from the almond orchard until she found one with the right springiness for a bow. She whittled the stock from lumber that she found in the barn. On long summer days she practiced target shooting in the orchard and became an excellent shot.

In the summer the valley was hot; in the winter the rains came. Each spring the almond trees in the orchard bloomed, and each fall she and her mother gathered nuts and hulled them for market. Before she went to bed each night, the girl shook the glass globe. Sometimes she dreamed of San Francisco.

CHAPTER
2

When Danny-boy was eight years old, he learned that art could change the world. The lesson began in an alley off Mission Street in San Francisco. Danny-boy crouched behind a garbage dumpster and watched a man paint a wall.

The man was dancing; his bare feet beat a rhythm on the asphalt. He wore a red kerchief around his neck and a pair of ragged jeans, cut off above the knee. In each hand he held a can of spray paint. His arms moved in sweeping gestures, leaving trails of paint on the red brick wall. As he painted, he chanted in a guttural voice. Danny-boy could not make out the words of the chant—could not even tell for certain that there were words, and not just grunts and nonsense syllables.

A ring of upturned abalone shells surrounded the man. In each shell a clump of herbs burned, sending clouds of pungent smoke swirling through the alley.

Through the smoke, Danny-boy could make out the pictures on the wall. A herd of barrel-bellied horses with manes as stiff as toothbrush bristles galloped toward Mission Street. A stag tossed its rack of antlers toward the foggy sky. A curve of red-brown paint formed the great humped back of a bull buffalo. As Danny-boy watched, the man added a slash of red for the animal's eye.

Without hesitation, the man stooped to discard one spray can and pick up another, making the motion a part of his dance. He reached high on the wall and painted birds—

or rather, pairs of curved lines that somehow suggested birds. Danny-boy recognized them as geese, flying in a V-formation.

Fascinated, Danny-boy crept closer, always ready to dash back to his hiding place. His feet must have made a sound on the asphalt, because the dancing man glanced his way, smiled quickly (a flash of white teeth in a darkly bearded face), and gestured to a stack of herbs by the wall.

Cautiously at first, Danny-boy took bits of sage and *yerba buena* and added them to the abalone shells. The thick clouds of smoke filled his lungs and made him feel a little dizzy. Tentatively, he began to match the man's movements, dancing outside the ring of abalone shells, waving a branch of sage to stir the smoke.

The man painted a meandering blue line. Beneath it, he sketched a school of fish and the enormous body of a whale. His chant changed, growing higher and faster. He painted a herd of deer, another herd of wild cattle. He danced more wildly, sweat glistening on his bare back. He snatched up a can of gray paint and quickly drew a wolf in the right-hand corner of the wall. Without warning, he dropped the can of paint and leaped away from the wall and over the ring of abalone shells, landing beside Danny-boy.

Danny-boy's ears rang in the sudden silence. He stared up at the man, curiously unafraid. Curly brown hair covered the man's arms, his back, his chest. Beneath the hair, his skin was reddish brown, the color of a newly cut redwood. Something about the way he stood—relaxed, yet ready to move—reminded Danny-boy of the wild dogs that prowled the streets of the city.

"My name's Danny-boy."

The man glanced down at him. "Call me Randall."

Danny-boy watched curiously as Randall squatted beside one of the abalone shells and poked at the smoldering herbs with one paint-smeared finger. He picked up the shell, dumped the ashes into his big hand, then rubbed them on his face and body. Glancing at Danny-boy, he said, "Take some. It's good. Purifying."

Danny-boy pulled off his T-shirt and gingerly rubbed ashes on his chest and arms.

"Come," said Randall.

Danny-boy followed him to the stream that ran along Eighth Avenue. Over the years, the flowing water had eaten away the asphalt, exposing the rocks and sand that lay below. Grasses that had taken root between the sidewalk stones grew thick and green beside the water. As Randall approached, a bullfrog leapt from the curb and swam for safety.

Randall splashed cold water on himself and scrubbed his face and chest with a handful of grass. Danny-boy imitated him, shivering a little in the cold. When he had scrubbed off most of the ashes, Danny-boy dried himself on his T-shirt and lay down on the sidewalk, glad of the sun-warmed concrete at his back. Randall sat beside him. Danny-boy studied the man.

"How come you were painting pictures on that wall, Randall?" Danny-boy asked at last.

Randall rested one big hand on the cement and turned to examine Danny-boy more closely. "We need more game around here. Buffalo, deer, fish. We need better hunting."

Danny-boy frowned. "What does that have to do with pictures on the wall?"

Randall plucked a grass stem and nibbled on the end of it. He hesitated for so long that Danny-boy thought he might not answer at all; then he said, "If I did it right, the pictures will bring back the game."

"Yeah?" Danny-boy considered the idea for a moment. "You think so?"

Randall tossed the grass stem aside. "I think so." He shrugged. "I'm only one-sixteenth Cherokee. Raised up in white man's schools. The stuff I know about this—it comes from here." He patted his hairy stomach. "I may not have done it right. But I think I did."

Danny-boy frowned, considering Randall's words. "If you want to bring back those animals, why'd you paint a wolf then? Nobody wants more wolves around."

Randall smiled suddenly, showing his white teeth. "It's a signature of sorts," he said. "Besides, I wouldn't mind having a few more wolves around. Just a few." He grinned

at Danny-boy and Danny-boy grinned back, though he
didn't quite understand the joke.

Danny-boy had grown up in San Francisco. He was
born a few years before the Plague, but his memories of
those early years were hazy. He remembered the plush
rabbit that had been his favorite toy, and his mother's hands
lifting him when he fell on the playground and skinned his
knee. Other than that, his early past was a blank.

After the Plague, a middle-aged woman named Emerald found him wandering in the street and adopted him. His
name came from a song that Emerald liked to sing.

Emerald's grasp on reality was tenuous at best. Sometimes she believed that Danny-boy was her own son, and
claimed that she was a holy virgin and he was the new
Messiah. At other times she remembered who she was and
where she was, and she told Danny-boy stories about the
world before the Plague.

As a child, Danny-boy explored the skyscrapers that
fronted on Market Street, wandering through oak-paneled
conference rooms and offices that smelled of dust. Sometimes he read the papers that he found lying around—
Books, the old man who lived in the library, had taught him
to read. But usually the papers were dull—memos about
mergers and financial statements for companies that no
longer existed.

Most of the ground floor offices had been vandalized:
windows broken, desks upturned, files opened, and papers
scattered. Danny-boy avoided such scenes of violence. He
preferred to explore offices that had remained undisturbed.
There, dust had settled on papers that lay untended on the
desks; mice had deposited turds in the drawers and among
the keys of the typewriters. In dry flowerpots, only the
plastic plants were still green, and even their persistent color
was muted by a layer of dust.

Danny-boy sensed that these offices were still alive
somehow. If someone were to wash the dust away and rinse
the plastic plants clean, he believed that the telephones
would start to ring and the typewriters would hum. People
would rush into the offices, pick up the papers, and take up

where they had left off. Danny-boy prowled the offices, fascinated and terrified by the notion that the old days might come back.

While exploring one office building, he found a red switch marked EMERGENCY GENERATOR. Without considering the consequences, he flipped the switch.

The building came to life around him. From somewhere beneath the floor came a low-pitched rumble that became a steady hum. A subtle vibration traveled through the floor and made him tremble. Overhead, the fluorescent tubes flickered, then glowed with an unnatural blue-white light. There was a clicking sound, like the chattering of teeth. Cold, stale-smelling air blew from a vent, etching patterns in dust that had been undisturbed for more than a decade.

He waited. The cold air made him shiver, but nothing else changed. Cautiously, he began to explore, venturing into windowless interior offices that had always been dark before. He jumped at each unfamiliar sound: the hum of a copy machine, the whispering of the air-conditioning system, the soft click-click-click as the second hand of an electric clock made its rounds, ticking off the seconds of a time long past. He glanced behind him, but the dust was marked only by his own footprints. On a corner desk, a small red light glowed on a cassette player. He ran his fingers over the black buttons, wiping away the dust. Hesitantly, he pressed the key marked PLAY.

Danny-boy watched the tape turn, dimly visible behind the dusty plastic cover. A tinny voice spoke from the headphones that lay on the desk. When he picked them up and held them to his ear, he heard a man saying: ". . . delays caused by the illness of delivery personnel. The following locations have reported shortages: . . ."

Danny-boy threw down the headphones and ran, caught by a primitive terror. He did not fear the voice in the box, but he was caught by the feeling, so strong in this enclosed room, that the past would return to reclaim the city. Emerald had told him of all the people in suits who had worked in the buildings downtown. Suddenly he feared that the gray faceless people who used to sit at these desks would return to find him playing with their things. They would catch him and put an end to all his games. He fled the building and never went back.

When Danny-boy was eight, Emerald tumbled from the window of an apartment building, fell five stories, and died. Danny-boy was never sure what had caused her to fall, but he suspected that she had fallen while reaching for the full moon that hung low in the sky.

CHAPTER
3

When he was fifteen years old, The Machine fell in love with his biology teacher. Of course that was before the Plague and before he knew he was a machine. His father called him Jonathan and he believed he was human, though clearly different from his classmates.

He attended a private high school for gifted students. He did not like it much—the classwork was too easy and his classmates were fools. He knew, from the time he had hacked his way into the school's data base and read his confidential files, that his teachers thought he was antisocial. So did Dr. Ward, the psychologist he visited once a week. He did not participate in class discussions; he hated sports; he avoided group activities. During class he spent most of his time designing and sketching intricate mechanisms: a ball-and-socket joint for a mechanical walking machine, a spiraling digging apparatus for a burrowing machine, rotor blades for a flying machine.

His father was an engineer engaged in robotics research. He was a balding man with a weak chin and brilliant blue eyes. His mother was an engineer of some kind as well. She had left The Machine's father when The Machine was only six. Occasionally, mostly on holidays, she flew in from Tokyo, where she worked for a multinational corporation. On her rare visits The Machine's father treated her with brittle respect, politely inquiring after her latest research project.

21

The Machine's mother seemed uncomfortable around him. She was a sweet-smelling stranger who brought him clockwork toys from Japanese shops. After she left he took them apart in his basement workshop, marveled at the intricate gearing mechanisms, and rebuilt them with minor improvements.

Ms. Bruner, his biology teacher, was slim and dark-haired like his mother. The Machine fell in love the moment he saw her. On the first day of class she had smiled at him and asked him to sit up front. That was enough. In her class, he paid attention. When she perched casually on the edge of her desk and talked about mitochondria, his breathing picked up speed. He still did not participate in class discussions, but he smiled at her and he thought that the smile she gave him back was special, somehow different from the way she smiled at everyone else.

Shortly after school began, he started work on a prosthetic hand for his science fair project. He had originally planned on constructing a six-legged walking machine, and he had been doing research into robotics for months. With Ms. Bruner in mind, however, he shifted the emphasis of his research, reasoning that she would best appreciate the interface between body and machine.

For weeks he did research into artificial joints and prosthetic devices, reading journal articles that he obtained through his father's home computer. Using his father's access codes, he tapped into a bulletin board for robotics researchers and orchestrated a continuing discussion of possibilities for the human/machine interface.

In his home workshop, he worked for long hours on the mechanical parts. He could have opted for silicon/plastic joints, but he preferred working with metal, machining tiny parts that fit neatly together. He liked the look of the metal and the cool feel of it in his hand.

Using his father's credit card, he ordered sensors that would pick up the EMG signals of his muscles and relay them to the prosthetic hand. The science fair came and went, and his project was not done, but he continued working, dreaming of Ms. Bruner's reaction when he showed her the completed hand.

The completed project was elegant: a third hand that strapped neatly onto the side of The Machine's arm. Electrical signals from the muscles in his abdomen controlled the hand's movements. He practiced yoga for hours, regulating his breathing and learning the careful muscular control necessary for dexterity. He could rotate the hand at the wrist, make the thumb and index finger come together in a pinch, grasp something strongly by wrapping his fingers around it. When he flexed the fingers, the joints made gentle clicking sounds that reminded him of the clockwork toys his mother had given him.

On the last day of the school year, he brought the hand to school, carefully packaged in a cardboard box. He did not want to show it in front of the other students, so he kept it hidden in his locker for most of the day. But he could not help smiling to himself whenever he thought of it.

"You seem awfully cheerful today," Ms. Bruner said. He was scrubbing down one of the lab tables, helping with the last day's cleanup. "Looking forward to summer vacation?"

"I have something to show you," he said quickly. "After school, OK?"

She frowned, then nodded. "All right. I suppose."

For the rest of the afternoon, he worried about that frown. But he reassured himself with the knowledge that she would be excited about the hand. He would demonstrate how he could write with it, comb his hair with it. She would be thrilled.

After his last class, he collected the box from his locker. The hallways were filled with kids emptying their lockers and noisily discussing their summer plans. For once, no one had time to bother or bully him. He walked through the corridors, carrying his box proudly beneath his arm.

The science wing was almost deserted. Outside her room the hallway was quiet. He hesitated by her door, anticipating his triumph. From inside, he heard her voice. She was talking to Mr. Pearce, the calculus teacher. He waited for a moment, reluctant to share his creation with anyone but her.

"I'd love to go out for a drink, but I told the Monroe

kid that I'd take a look at something he wanted to show me. He said he'd stop by after school."

A low rumble from Mr. Pearce. The Machine had never liked Mr. Pearce much: he had confiscated some really great designs for a burrowing machine and had torn them up in front of the whole class.

"Yeah, you're right there." Ms. Bruner's clear voice carried well. "He's a weird one. He's always smiling at me in this really peculiar way. I'd guess that he'll grow up to be either a mass murderer or a genius like his dad."

The Machine froze, clutching the box. Mr. Pearce was saying something.

"A crush on me?" Ms. Bruner's laughter chilled him. "Jesus, I hope not. Thank God the school year's finally over. He won't be in my class next year."

A chair scraped across the floor and The Machine jumped.

"Sure," Ms. Bruner was saying. "Let's go. I can't wait around all day."

The Machine escaped into another corridor before they stepped from the room. His father was waiting in the car in front of the school. When he asked what was in the box, The Machine shook his head. "Just some stuff," he said.

That summer, the Plague came. His father came down with the first symptoms while he was at work. His co-workers took him to the hospital and The Machine talked to his doctor on the phone.

The doctor spoke slowly, as if he were very tired. "We'll do what we can," he said. "No, I don't think you'd better come and see him. You sound healthy. Try to stay that way."

The next day, when The Machine tried to call the hospital, the telephone was busy. He set his telephone to redial the hospital's number every five minutes, but the line was always busy. He wandered the quiet house and watched the television news. "The following hospitals have beds available," his local newscaster advised him. The woman co-anchor looked pale.

The next day, the hospital line was still busy. The woman co-anchor was gone, replaced by another woman.

The Machine tried to call other numbers: he called Dr. Ward and got an answering machine.

"Please leave a message at the sound of the beep."

"Dr. Ward, this is Jonathan Monroe." He hesitated, not sure what to say. "My father's in the hospital and I don't know what to do. Could you call me right away?"

Dr. Ward never called back.

The TV news announced that the President had declared a state of emergency. That was just before he died of the Plague. The Vice President took office, then fell ill with the Plague. "The police are advising citizens to stay at home," his local newscasters told him. "Remain calm."

He remained calm. He stayed at home, pacing through the empty rooms. The satellite dish pulled in stations from all over the world. On the news, The Machine watched riots in the streets of downtown New York, Washington, Tokyo, Paris. On the sixth day, the telephone finally got a clear line to the hospital. At the other end, the telephone rang and rang but no one answered.

For a month he lived in his father's house, eating canned and frozen food. After watching the riots on TV, he was afraid to leave. He did not know what he might find out in the world. He stayed in the house where the machines could take care of him. He trusted the machines, relied on the machines. The household computer woke him up each morning and advised him of his bedtime each night. The lights that illuminated the patio switched themselves on and off automatically. A machine washed the dishes and a machine washed the clothes. A cleaning robot, on loan from some lab at Stanford, constantly prowled the halls and rooms, sucking up dustballs and paper clips and bits of food. Sometimes he amused himself by scattering bits of torn paper on the rug for the robot to vacuum up. His personal computer—with its game programs and its teaching software—was his constant companion.

When his stores of canned food ran low, he cautiously ventured out and broke into a neighbor's house. He was not surprised to find that no one was home. He raided the pantry shelves, taking enough canned food for another month. Over time, he worked his way from neighbor to neighbor. In some houses he found decaying bodies. The first time he found a corpse he was sick to his stomach, but he learned to ignore his repulsion, to hurry into a house, get the food, and run away again.

The decaying bodies helped him realize the truth. He was not human after all. That was why he had never fit in with his classmates: he was not like them. His body was whole and healthy, so how could he be human? The humans were dead.

He considered the matter. After much thought he came to realize that his father had constructed him, with the assistance of his mother. In retrospect it seemed obvious. His mother had avoided him because he was a defective machine: he had not lived up to her exacting specifications. It made perfect sense. He decided then that calling himself Jonathan Monroe was dishonest and inaccurate. He began calling himself The Machine. His purpose, he decided, was to build other machines. He was surprised that it had taken him so long to realize it.

CHAPTER
4

When Mary Laurenson's daughter was sixteen years old, her life changed. The changes began, it seemed to her, with a trip to the Woodland market.

She and her mother woke when the sky was still dark. Only a thin line of light at the horizon betrayed the coming day. Her mother loaded the mare with saddlebags that held almonds from the orchard, cured rabbit skins, and home-made apricot brandy. The young woman gathered up trea-sures she had scavenged from surrounding farmhouses: two pocketknives and a sharp buck knife, a set of socket wrenches, a pocketwatch that still kept time, a music box that played "Jingle Bells," and an assortment of jewelry. She wore the jewelry: bangles on one wrist, a silver charm brace-let on the other, a gold wedding band, a dime store ring set with a blood-red garnet, a diamond engagement ring that caught the thin dawn light. The young woman rode bare-back on the mare's daughter, a yearling filly she called Young One for lack of a better name. They left Dog, their Golden Retriever, to guard the house.

It took about two hours to ride to Woodland. The road wound through farmland that had returned to meadow. Barbed wire fences that had once marked property bound-aries had long since rusted away. Here and there the fence-posts remained, dark stumps jutting from the long grass. Wild cattle grazing in the meadows lifted their heads to watch the women pass.

Halfway to market, they spotted a three-wheeled bicycle parked in the shade of a walnut tree. Between the back wheels was a wide bin filled with canvas sacks. A sign hanging from the bin read "Books for Sale or Trade."

A young man called out from the shade of the tree. "Hello there! Can you tell me how far it is to Woodland Market?"

Her mother reined to a stop. "Not so far. About an hour by horse."

The young man grinned. He leaned back against the tree trunk, his hands locked behind his head. He was lean and well-tanned. "Any large hills on the way?"

"Not that I recall." Her mother looked thoughtful. "What sort of books have you got there?"

"All kinds," he said cheerfully. "History, politics, religion, philosophy. A few novels to keep things lively. And some practical books—how to build your own still, how to make a wind generator, cookbooks, first aid manuals. A little of everything."

The young woman watched her mother frown. For a moment, her mother did not speak. The birds sang in the trees by the side of the road; insects droned in the grass.

"You've never been here before," her mother said.

"Never before. This is my first trip out. I've come south from Seattle, trading along the way."

"Your books on politics . . ." her mother began.

"Are you interested in politics?" the young man interrupted. "I have a broad assortment, from Marx to—"

"No," her mother said abruptly. "It doesn't pay to be interested in politics in this part of the country. I just wanted to advise you that General Miles's men might find some of your books a bit controversial."

"General Miles? You mean the fellow everyone calls 'Fourstar.'"

Her mother shook her head quickly. "Around here, you'd best call him General Miles. He's not fond of the nickname. The political climate here is"—she hesitated, then continued—"on the conservative side. You'd be wise to stash your more liberal books and return for them after your visit to the market."

"Oh, nothing I have is very controversial. I've been very well received everywhere I've been so far."

Her mother shook her head. "You may be surprised at what books the army considers controversial."

The young man grinned at her. "I'll take my chances."

Her mother opened her mouth as if to say something more, then shrugged. "Hope to see you in Woodland," she said. "Good luck."

The young woman waved to the cyclist as they passed. "See you in Woodland."

The young woman and her mother were just outside town when a group of men in khaki-colored fatigues hailed them and ordered them to stop. Two men held rifles; the third, a clipboard. "On your way to market?" the man with the clipboard asked, and the young woman's mother nodded. "I have a few questions for you, ma'am. We're gathering information on the flow of goods. Part of the General's efforts to alleviate shortages. Please dismount."

The young woman watched her mother. The older woman's face was very still; her expression, unreadable. "I see," she said calmly, and swung down from the mare. Reluctantly, the young woman followed. Passing the checkpoint was her least favorite part of going to market. She stood by Young One, close enough to feel the warmth that radiated from the animal.

The man consulted his list and began rattling off questions: "Your name? Your permanent address? What will you be trading? Quantity of each commodity? Number of people in your household?" Her mother answered the questions quickly, without hesitation.

One of the other men held Young One's bridle and stroked the horse's nose. The soldier's face was mottled with acne and his hair was cut so short that the young woman could see his scalp. "What's your name?" he asked quietly.

She shook her head and said nothing. She did not like the checkpoint; the men and guns alarmed her.

"You going to be staying in Woodland? There'll be a dance tonight—maybe I'll see you there?"

The young woman shook her head again, trying to look as calm and aloof as her mother.

"You like to dance?" the soldier said awkwardly.

She stared over his head at the distant road.

"Not very friendly, are you?" Out of the corner of her eye, she could see him glaring at her.

"Any weapons?" asked the man with the clipboard. The young woman held up her crossbow and her mother showed them her old rifle. Both were noted on the form.

"Now if you'll open those saddlebags for me, we'll be done." The man searched the saddlebags, pawing through the almonds, sniffing at the brandy, opening the socket wrench set. When he came to the buck knife he examined it carefully, pulling it from the leather sheath and testing the edge. "Nice piece," he said.

The soldier holding Young One's bridle broke in. "The army's short on good knives, ain't it, Sergeant?"

The sergeant nodded, not looking up from the blade. "That's so, Private. Excellent knives like this are in short supply. But I'm sure these ladies are patriotic citizens." He looked up. "I'm certain they'd be glad to make such a trivial donation to the cause."

The young woman glared at him, but her mother spoke first. "Under the circumstances, Sergeant, I'd be glad to make a small contribution."

The sergeant nodded and slipped the knife back into its sheath. "Very good," he said. "Thank you for your time." He held out the clipboard. "Sign here."

Her mother signed and they mounted. The young woman jerked the reins from the grinning soldier and rode off. "Sorry," her mother said when they were out of earshot of the checkpoint.

"It's all right," she said, but her voice was tight and angry.

The market was in the parking lot of an old supermarket. To provide shade, each merchant erected a fabric canopy on tall poles. The canopies of neighboring stalls overlapped to form a kind of tent, a vast expanse of multicolored fabric. When the wind blew, the tent billowed.

They tied their horses at the edge of the tent and went inside. When her mother stopped to barter with a kerosene trader, the young woman wandered away, strolling up and down the aisles, staring curiously at the people around her. Sunlight filtering through the cloth colored the scene below: a patch of red beneath a crimson-colored satin bedsheet, brilliant orange beneath a nylon tarp. The plush ridges of a pink chenille bedspread cast stripes of shadow across a tool-seller's booth.

In the late morning heat, the market had a powerful aroma: a combination of ripe fruits and vegetables, goat droppings, and roasting meat. The tent was a noisy place, filled with the bleating of frantic goats, the clucking of hens, the cries of merchants—"Salt, salt, good sea salt," "Melons, fine melons"—and the constant haranguing of a preacher who read from his Bible at a dead run, never pausing for breath. And over all the commotion was the rustling of the tent in the wind, acres of restless cloth straining to fly away like an enormous kite.

There was a carnival atmosphere, a sense of great excitement that filled the young woman and made her want to fly away with the tent, soaring high above the valley. Everything was bright and alive and new—so many people, so many things. She stared at a black woman who carried a baby on her hip: she had never seen skin so dark and glossy. She stopped to watch the preacher, fascinated by the way his stiff beard jerked when he talked. At one stall, a man played a guitar while a group of people in drab clothing sang songs about God. The young woman lingered for a moment, but moved on when one of the singers called to her.

The stalls were filled with riches. She gaped at shelves crowded with metal buckets and pots and pans; she fingered a fine hunting knife in a booth selling tools; she admired glittering jewelry and wristwatches. People had come from as far away as Fresno and Modesto, bringing their wares to trade.

The smell of roasting meat drew her to a stall where a grimy round-eyed child carefully turned the carcass of a pig over a low fire. The child's mother, a Hispanic woman with a scarlet scarf tied over her dark hair, accepted the garnet ring in exchange for a pork burrito.

From the far end of the tent came the scratchy sound of marching music played through a battery-powered loudspeaker. The young woman wandered in that direction. On the way, she passed a stall selling whiskey and hard cider. A drunken man was speaking loudly to a circle of other men. "Godless perverts, that's what they are," he was saying. "We have every right to go to San Francisco and take what we need. Every right."

In a large open space at the end of the tent, a platform had been set up. Red, white, and blue canopies billowed overhead. At either end of the platform, a teen-aged soldier stood at attention. The young woman stopped at the edge of the crowd that milled around the platform. So many people —almost a hundred, she guessed.

"What's going on?" she asked the man in the stall behind her. He sat on a tall stool, beside makeshift shelves holding herbs and amulets along with bottles of vitamins, aspirin, cold remedies, and the like.

"General Miles is going to speak," he said.

The music stopped abruptly. She waited by the stall, watching a tall, unhealthy-looking man climb onto the platform and speak into a microphone. A hash of static distorted his amplified voice. "I'm honored to introduce"—a series of pops like gunfire drowned him out—"reunify this great country, preserve our way of life, protect our—" A squeal like a dying pig cut through his words. "I give you General Alexander Miles, the man who—" He raised his hands over his head and gestured to the side of the platform. His voice was buried beneath the cheers of the crowd.

A stockily built man climbed to the platform and looked out over the cheering crowd. He had a square face and crew-cut salt-and-pepper hair. Despite the heat of the day, he wore a khaki-colored uniform. There were gold-colored stars on his sleeves and gold-colored braid on the stiff brim of his hat. The sunlight shining through the red canopy overhead gave his face a ruddy tint, making his eyes look impossibly blue. He disdained the microphone, waving it aside along with the man who offered it.

"My friends," he said. His voice was deep and low and the people stopped their murmuring to listen. "I'm glad to see you all here, neighbors gathered together for a day of celebration. I'm glad I'm able to join you on such a fine day." The tent rustled overhead, but the crowd was silent, intent upon the General's words. "It's a wonderful thing for people to come together. In these hard and lonely times, a gathering like this is wonderful and rare, something to be treasured." His voice was compelling. "Alone each of us is weak. But together we are strong. Alone each of us is poor. Together we are rich. Alone each of us is vulnerable and unprotected. Together, we are a nation. Together, we are Americans." His voice lifted, cutting through the rustling of the tent, the distant barking of dogs and bleating of goats. "I dream of true Americans, once again united. I dream of one nation under God, indivisible. A proud nation, a strong nation, with many hands and many voices, joined as one. I dream of a land that is safe for our children and our children's children."

The young woman rubbed at the sweat trickling down her neck. She had heard of America before—her mother had mentioned the name—but she didn't see why the man was so excited about it. His expression reminded her of the preacher at the entrance to the market. He spoke of America in the same reverent tone that the preacher had used in speaking of Jesus. General Miles had the same intensity in his eyes; he scanned the crowd as if he were looking into each person's soul. When he looked in her direction, she shivered.

"We must not forget we are Americans. Each of us is a small part of the glory that makes up the whole. A great gathering is under way, a union forged of many people. Fresno has joined us. Modesto and Stockton are with us. As far north as Chico, they are with us." His voice rose a little and he clenched the hand at his side to form a fist. "But there are also those who would forget our heritage, cast aside our traditions. Those who work against us and seek to undermine our unity, who thrive on division and dissension. A selfish few hoard the resources of the city of San Francisco, scorning our offers of friendship and alliance." His expression was that of an angry father who has been pushed beyond what his patience will bear. "They revel in anarchy, squandering the treasures of the past, delighting in unnatu-

ral acts that are an abomination in the eyes of man and
God."

He went on listing the crimes of San Francisco's inhabitants, implying that these anarchists were responsible for
the chronic shortage of kerosene and good tools, hinting
that their godless ways might have triggered the Plague,
warning that they might choose to descend on the valley.
"We must act for our own protection. We must protect our
land and preserve our proud heritage. We do not seek war,
but if it comes, we will not turn aside." The soldiers at either
end of the platform stood straighter, their eyes fixed on
some distant horizon. The crowd cheered.

The young woman was no longer listening. She imagined General Miles and his soldiers tramping through the
tiny city she saw in her glass globe, and she frowned. Her
mother found her at the edge of the crowd, silent though the
people around her were cheering.

On their way out of town, they passed the checkpoint.
The soldiers were still there, tending a small bonfire. The
cyclist from Seattle stood beside the sergeant, watching the
flames. His face was smeared with dirt; the skin around one
of his eyes was darkening to black. As the young woman
passed, a soldier added another book to the fire.

CHAPTER
5

Danny-boy warded off the past with projects of his own creation. He wanted to change the city so that the gray people from the time before the Plague would not recognize the place. In the beginning, his projects were small. In a sheltered place beside the steps to the library, he built a tiny village of scrap wood. The houses were windowless, thatched with grasses like the African huts he had seen pictured in a *National Geographic* magazine. Paths bordered with seashells and polished stones from the beach led to each miniature doorway. He built several other such villages, tucking them into forgotten corners of the city. Each one had its own style of architecture.

He gathered empty picture frames and hung them in spots where they would capture significant views. On the pavement nearby he painted footprints indicating where the viewer should stand. At the top of the Divisadero Street hill an ornate oak frame, bolted to the supporting pole of a NO PARKING sign, displayed a view of the Golden Gate Bridge. In the financial district a small steel frame, wedged between the iron bars of a fence, set off a view of the Trans-America Pyramid. In the Marina district a simple black wood frame hung from a tree, presenting a view of Alcatraz Island.

As Danny-boy grew older, he realized that he was not the only one striving to change the city. Many others were quietly adding their own embellishments. Now and then, he helped them with their work.

He sat in the sunshine by Saint Monica's Church and listened to Rose Maloney discuss how she would transform the structure through her gardening. "I think the ivy will do well here on the north wall. It doesn't need much sun. In ten years or so it should have covered the wall, I think."

He sat by the fire and listened to Gambit talk about the music that he heard in the city streets. "You know the way the telephone wires sing in the wind, Danny-boy? I'm going to build a harp that the wind can play. If I string wires across the Civic Center Plaza where the wind blows strong . . ."

Danny-boy's own projects grew more ambitious. He took miles of ribbons and laces from the Macy's notions department. Across a narrow street downtown, he wove rope ladders and braids, tangles that mimicked the intertwinings of vines, strict geometric patterns with rigorous repetitions. At noon, when the sun shone down through the ribbons, the light made intricate patterns on the asphalt.

He arranged three hundred pairs of women's shoes on the stairway that climbed from Taylor Street to Broadway. High heels and flats, running shoes and loafers, all of them heading uphill, as if an army of invisible women had paused to rest while climbing.

Danny-boy's inspiration for his biggest project came from a conversation with Duff, an industrious, egg-shaped man with three wives and countless children. In a city filled with artists, Duff was a businessman. On the shore of Mountain Lake, the city's largest spring-fed pond, Duff had established a trading post and a business empire.

His choice of a site proved wise and he did a booming business in barter. Over the years, Duff's trading post had established a reputation. If you couldn't buy it at Duff's, you couldn't find it in the city. Home-brewed moonshine, whiskey from the old times, fresh milk and eggs, cheese from Marin, apples from Sebastopol, caviar scavenged from gourmet shops, dried fish, canned goods, rare gems, welding equipment, methane gas, laundry service, and hot showers —Duff sold it all.

Danny-boy was visiting the trading post one fine spring evening. It was twilight and the luminescent gray-purple of the sky reflected in the still lake. The drooping branches of eucalyptus trees hung low over the water. Now and then, the smooth surface was broken by fish jumping for insects. At the far end of the lake, where the water was shallow, five of Duff's children were netting crayfish. Their shrill voices carried in the evening air, echoing across the water. Overhead, the wind generator that supplied Duff's electricity rattled rhythmically.

Danny-boy was strolling around the lake when Duff hailed him from a marble bench, inviting him to come and sit and smoke a joint. "How's it going?" Duff asked. He rolled a joint from the marijuana in his pouch. "You haven't brought me any trade goods for a while."

Danny-boy nodded. "Yeah. Been busy helping Rose Maloney transplant some of her trees. She had this one rubber tree that must be about fifteen feet tall. We transplanted it into the baptismal font at Saint Monica's."

"Why do you bother with all that?" Duff lit the joint, took a drag, and passed it to Danny-boy.

Danny-boy shrugged. "She likes it."

"It's not going to get you anywhere."

"So? Where would I want to go?" Danny-boy took a long drag on the joint.

The sun was leaving the sky. Down on the beach below them, a campfire burned. A group of artists and scavengers had gathered to sit by the fire and drink whiskey. Danny-boy could hear voices raised in discussion.

Duff gestured at the fire with his joint. "They're always talking. But they never seem to do much."

Danny-boy frowned at the bitterness in Duff's voice. "What do you mean? They do lots of things."

"They live off the remnants of the past," Duff said. "You know, I think you care about all the wrong things."

Danny-boy blew out a cloud of smoke and did not reply.

"Not just you," Duff said. "All of the scavengers in the city. If you only got organized, you could accomplish something. You could get somewhere."

"What would we want to accomplish?" Danny-boy
asked idly. He offered the joint to Duff but the older man
waved it away, eager to make his next point. Danny-boy
smiled slowly and took another hit. The more Duff talked,
the less he would smoke.

"Suppose you wanted some marijuana," Duff said.
"What would you do?"

"I'd see if I could find some wild plants to harvest,"
Danny-boy said. "I know a backyard in the Mission with
plants that are as tall as I am."

"Living off the land like a savage," Duff scoffed. "Suppose someone had already harvested the plants in the Mission. What would you do then?"

"Maybe I'd see if Snake had any to lend me." Danny-
boy was willing to go on proposing solutions as long as Duff
kept asking for them.

"And if he didn't have any, you'd come to me."

"Sure. And I'd trade you for some."

"You'd trade me something you found in the ruins,
right? And why would you come to me? What have I got
that you haven't?"

"Marijuana," Danny-boy said.

"A greenhouse full of it," Duff agreed. "And you could
have a greenhouse too. The materials are there." He waved
a hand toward the city. "A little work, and you could be
self-sufficient."

Danny-boy leaned back on the bench, surveying the
lake dreamily.

"If everyone worked with me," Duff went on, "we
could rebuild this city."

"Why would we want to?" Danny-boy asked. "I like it
the way it is."

"You never saw it before."

Danny-boy shrugged. "I dream of it sometimes. I like it
better now."

Duff was not paying attention; he seemed to be caught
up in his own vision. "All we need to do is work together.
Think about it— one man couldn't have built the Golden
Gate Bridge on his own. One family couldn't have done it.
Hundreds of men, working together, built that bridge. To

accomplish things, you need teamwork. Now if you wanted a greenhouse . . ."

"I don't," Danny-boy interrupted.

Duff shook his head furiously. "OK then, if you wanted to build a wind generator . . ."

"I don't need one."

"It doesn't matter," Duff growled. "It could be anything. Suppose you wanted to paint the Golden Gate Bridge blue. Alone, you couldn't do it. But if you had enough people who would cooperate, you could do it in a week. Cooperation means civilization. Without it, you're alone."

Danny-boy frowned, listening intently for the first time. "I see what you mean," he said. "I never thought much about it before."

Duff eyed him uneasily. "About what?" He seemed startled that Danny-boy was finally listening.

"I've been working on my own. It might be interesting to try a bigger project."

"Like a greenhouse?" Duff suggested.

"I was thinking more of the bridge," Danny-boy said. "Blue's a nice color. Well, I guess I'd best be going." He gave Duff the end of the joint, smiled pleasantly, and sauntered away into the night.

The following week, Danny-boy started accumulating blue paint.

CHAPTER
6

Not long after the young woman saw General Miles speak, Leon arrived. He came on a day in early autumn. The green leaves of the walnut tree that grew near the house hung limp in the heat; the bees droned in the garden, searching for late-blooming flowers. The young woman had been picking cutworms from the last of the tomato plants.

She heard the sound of horses in the distance: the clip-clop of hooves on asphalt and the jingle of harnesses. Dog left the shade of the porch and stared in the direction of the sounds. After a moment, he started barking. The young woman heard another dog, much smaller by the sound of it, yapping in reply. Happy to abandon her task, she ran to get her mother. "Someone's coming!"

She climbed an almond tree so she could watch the stranger approach. The bright mural painted on the side of his wagon looked out of place in the dull dusty landscape. The mural showed the city of San Francisco; she recognized it by the tall triangular tower. She craned her neck, eager to see the driver, and was vaguely disappointed when she caught a glimpse of him through the leaves: he was a middle-aged man with thinning brown hair. His scalp was reddening in the afternoon sun. She had expected something more.

Her mother greeted the trader from the porch. She wore jeans and a faded blue shirt; her dark hair was wild in the summer heat. She held their old rifle.

"Hello, good woman," the man called from his wagon seat, reining his horses to a halt in the yard. "Can I interest you in trade goods from San Francisco?" Dog sniffed around the wagon's wheels, growling at the terrier that rode on the seat beside the man. The smaller dog wagged its tail. "I have nails, screws, tools," the man said, "fancy cloth, seeds, kerosene. . . ."

Her mother stared at the man, squinting into the sun and frowning. "You're from San Francisco?" she interrupted.

"That's right," the trader said.

"From the Haight," she said slowly.

The man looked startled. He scratched his head. "That's right. How did you—"

"I know you," she cried, letting the rifle fall to her side. "You used to run a magazine shop. I bought magazines there." She stepped down from the porch. "I don't remember your name, but I remember your face. Do you remember?"

Through the leaves, the young woman watched the trader climb down from his wagon. Her mother cried as she hugged him. The young woman watched from the tree in amazement. Dog sniffed the man's legs suspiciously.

The trader—his name was Leon—stayed for dinner. After dinner the young woman lay in the hammock on the porch, drowsing in the heat. Through the screen door, she could hear her mother and Leon talking in low voices.

"I feel silly, crying that way," her mother said. "It's just that it all seems so long ago. Like an imaginary world. So far away now."

"How did you end up out here?" he asked her.

"After my husband died, I guess I panicked. I went a little crazy. Got in our old Volvo and started driving, without any idea of where I was headed. Hit a roadblock on my way into Sacramento, turned off the main road and headed toward Woodland. The only reason I stopped here was because I was almost out of gas."

"Alone and pregnant," Leon murmured. "Must have been rough."

"I was acting on automatic. I don't remember much about that time."

"Seems like a lonely spot. Do you have any neighbors?"

"A few. None that are particularly friendly. Most of the people around here blame San Francisco for the Plague. Since I'm from the city, they don't trust us, don't like us much. We keep to ourselves. And what about you? What's happening in San Francisco these days?"

"The city's still there," he said. "A man named Duff runs a trading post on the edge of the Presidio. A handful of people survived in Chinatown. A few families down by Fisherman's Wharf make a pretty good living fishing. And downtown . . . downtown's kind of strange."

"How so?"

"It's been taken over by artists. I guess that's what you'd call them. Painters, poets, sculptors, writers, musicians, and a few that don't fit into any traditional category. They build things."

"What sort of things?"

"Hard to describe, really. They have all the resources of the city at their disposal. Of course, they're all a little crazy. I don't pretend to understand a lot of the stuff they do. I don't know—you really have to see it."

"I'd like to." Her mother's voice was wistful.

"Well, you know, I'll be going back there soon enough. I have room for a couple of passengers. If you'd like to come—"

A long silence. The young woman strained to hear her mother's reply. "I don't know if I could. Too many ghosts. Everyone died—my husband, all my friends. I don't know."

"You don't have to be afraid to go back because of . . ." Leon hesitated, letting his sentence trail off. "I recognized you—not at first, but after a bit. But you don't have to worry. No one blames you anymore. People have forgotten."

"I haven't forgotten," she said.

"The monkeys live all over the city now," he said. "People are going about their lives. They don't live in the past."

Silence from her mother. The young woman frowned, trying to make sense of the conversation.

"Think about it," Leon said. "One way or the other, I understand. I don't spend much time in the city myself, though I always go home to it. I have friends there; I bring them news of the rest of the state. Tell them that the redwoods are coming back up north. Tell them that I saw a mountain lion in the Sierra."

"It must be lonely, traveling all the time," her mother said.

"Sometimes. But I keep busy." A moment's hesitation, then Leon continued suddenly. "I might as well tell you— I'm writing a book."

"A book?"

"Ms. Migsdale, the woman who puts out the city's newspaper, publishes a few books now and then. Some poetry, a few accounts of the Plague, some technical manuals —how to build a solar water heater and that sort of thing." Leon spoke quickly, with a new note of enthusiasm in his voice. "I'm working on a travel book. Nonfiction—mostly advice to travelers. Places to go, places to avoid. A few stories about the people I meet. I've been up and down the coast doing research. Went inland until the mountains stopped me. I have a typewriter and some ribbons, and I've been taking notes as I go. Some of it's pretty good, I think. The chapter about Los Angeles—I think that's good. Down there, it's all places to avoid, near as I can tell. Ms. Migsdale has read that chapter and she thinks it's all right."

Her mother laughed, a sound the young woman had rarely heard. "I can't believe that there's still a publishing industry. That's great. And your book sounds wonderful. So tell me about Los Angeles. What's it like down south?"

"Crazy. Los Angeles always was on the edge. The Plague just pushed them over. The Church of Revelations pretty much runs the city. They preach about what you'd expect: the Plague was God's punishment for our sins and all that. The men wear black and the women wear dresses down to their ankles even when the temperature's over a hundred. Depressing as hell. They're evangelical too. They'll be sending missionaries up here before too long."

"They'll run into opposition," her mother said. "We have our own brand of lunacy."

"I've heard about that. Sounds like you have a nice little military dictatorship in the making. Headed by some military man who promoted himself to four-star General. General Fourstar, I've heard him called."

"Don't call him that around here. Here, he's General Miles, and don't you forget it. He's got big plans. You should warn the folks in San Francisco that he's getting serious about expanding his territory. With so few people, you'd think we'd have given up fighting, but it doesn't seem to work that way."

"I guess human nature hasn't changed."

"I guess not." A moment of comfortable silence. "Would you like some tea? Or I could open a bottle of apricot brandy. I have one set aside."

The young woman heard the pop of a cork. Her mother proposed a toast "to your book," and glasses clinked. Lulled by the murmur of soft voices, the young woman fell asleep. In her dreams, she roamed the streets of San Francisco.

Leon stayed the next day to help her mother repair a leak in the farmhouse roof. The young woman slipped away in the morning, saying that she was going hunting. In the orchard she found a high branch that gave her a good view of the house. She watched her mother and Leon carrying a ladder from the shed to the house and climbing up to the roof. Now and then, when the breeze was right, she could hear their voices: her mother calling up to Leon as she steadied the ladder; Leon calling back. There seemed to be an easy camaraderie between the two of them. The young woman heard her mother laugh in response to something that Leon said. She watched and thought about traveling to San Francisco with Leon and her mother. Finally, when her legs grew cramped from sitting motionless in the tree, she climbed down and went hunting for rabbits.

Leon stayed another day, this time helping her mother split wood from a fallen tree and haul it to the shed for winter firewood. And then another day. The young woman did not mind. Having Leon around changed her mother: she talked more, laughed more, seemed to relax. At night, when they thought she was asleep, Leon and her mother talked about San Francisco—reminiscing about times past.

"So what do you think," her mother said lightly. "Will my daughter and I become a story in your book? Once-famous San Franciscan hides out in the Central Valley?"

Leon said nothing for a moment. Then he spoke softly: "I wish you'd be more than just a story. Why don't you come travel with me? Together we can deal with the ghosts. You don't belong here."

"Maybe," her mother said. "Maybe we could. Maybe you're right."

"I am right," Leon said.

"All right," her mother said. "We'll go."

The young woman lay awake, listening to her mother and Leon plan. They could leave in a few days, her mother said. There wasn't much to pack.

Early the next morning, when the grass was still wet with dew, the young woman went out riding alone. She visited her favorite places: the collapsed freeway bridge where the hunting was good, the creek where watercress grew, the abandoned farmhouse where she had found the glass globe. She was filled with a wild excitement, thinking about San Francisco and the lands beyond it. She tried to imagine what the city would be like. In her mind it was like the Woodland market, only a thousand times bigger.

Just after noon she rode back toward the house. From the far side of the orchard came the sound of barking. Dog's bark was a deep desperate sort of sound, filled with fury and frustration. Leon's terrier was yapping angrily. She heard two gunshots in rapid succession, and the dogs fell silent.

She slipped from Young One's back and tied the filly to a tree. Under the cover of the tall grass, she crept closer to the house. From the edge of the orchard, she could see the yard. The terrier lay by the pump; the blood on his head gleamed in the sun. Dog was sprawled at the foot of the porch steps. The horses tied at the porch rail flared their nostrils and shifted their weight nervously, eyeing Dog's body.

As the young woman watched, two soldiers stepped from the house. One of them, a burly man in his twenties with a blond crewcut, shoved Leon in front of him. The trader's hands were tied behind his back. Blood from a cut on his forehead trickled down the side of his face.

The scene had a crystalline clarity. The young woman could hear the soldiers' boots on the porch, could smell gunpowder and fresh blood. She lay motionless in the grass, scarcely breathing.

Her mother followed the soldiers. A soldier walked beside her. He kept his rifle pointed casually at her head, but she seemed oblivious to him. Her hands had been brought together as if she were praying and bound in front of her with rope. She looked so small beside the soldier. Her expression was calm, as if she were somewhere very quiet and peaceful.

An officer, dressed in a khaki uniform with gold braid on the shoulders, stepped from the house. In the shelter of the tall grass, the young woman clutched her crossbow. The three soldiers were armed with rifles; the officer had a revolver in a leather holster at his side. She would not have a chance against them.

As she watched, Leon started to say something. The officer slapped him hard across the face. "You'll have your chance to speak soon enough," the officer said. "We'll see to that."

They brought the horses around from the corral at the back of the house and hitched them to Leon's wagon. They tied her mother's mare to the back. The burly soldier shoved Leon into the covered section. Awkward because of her tied hands, her mother climbed to the wagon seat.

The young woman ducked her head lower, afraid that the mounted men might look over into the grass and see her. She listened to the wagon wheels creak, smelled the dust raised by the horses' hooves, heard the rattle of the harness fade in the distance. When she emerged from the orchard they were gone. She knew where they were going. Her mother had once pointed out the army's headquarters in Woodland.

The soldiers had ransacked the house. Broken dishes littered the kitchen floor. In the living room, the men had overturned one of the bookshelves. Pages torn from the books were scattered on the floor like fallen leaves. The mirror over the fireplace was shattered, and the knickknacks from the mantel had been swept to the floor.

She was confused and her hands hurt from clutching her crossbow. She was afraid, and she did not like feeling afraid. This house, where she had grown up, wasn't her house anymore. Standing in the living room she felt cold and empty, the way she sometimes felt when she explored houses that had been abandoned since the Plague. Too many shadows at the corners of the room. The air held the scent of strangers, gunsmoke, horse sweat, leather.

She buried the dogs in the orchard and picked her mother's books up off the floor. Then she took a warm jacket, a blanket, and all the jewelry that she had for trade. She mounted Young One and headed for Woodland.

The army's headquarters were in an old bank in the heart of town. The young woman arrived in the early evening. The soldier standing guard at the door would tell her nothing, but she saw Leon's wagon in the street beside the courthouse. She slept that night in a house on the edge of town.

It was more than a week before her mother was released. Each morning, she went to the courthouse and spoke to the sergeant who sat by the entrance. He was a soft-bodied man in his forties, older than most of the soldiers she had seen. The first time she asked about her mother, he questioned her sharply, glancing at the other soldiers who were in the lobby.

She denied all knowledge of a trader from San Francisco. She had been out hunting for a few days, she told him. When she got home, her mother was gone. She said that a neighbor had told her that soldiers had taken her mother away.

The young woman left, but she returned that evening when the sergeant was alone in the lobby. He spoke more softly then and advised her to go home. "Don't you have any other kin?" he asked. She shook her head. When he frowned, she backed away.

Each day she came to ask after her mother in the morning and in the evening. In between times she hunted for rabbits in the surrounding countryside. The weather turned cold, and she woke each morning shivering in her blanket. She spent as little time as possible in the town itself. The townspeople watched her closely, and she didn't like that.

If no one was around, the sergeant would talk to her as she stood by the desk in the chilly lobby. "You know," he said one evening. "I had a daughter once. If she had survived the Plague, I think she would have been about your age."

The young woman watched him, trying to guess what he wanted from her. She did not know what to say.

"I think I can get your mother released," the sergeant said. "She doesn't know anything. Come here tomorrow, and I'll see. I can't promise."

She nodded, her eyes fixed on the sergeant's face. "What about the trader?"

He studied her face. "I thought you didn't know him."

"I don't. I just wondered. . . ." She shrugged.

"They'll be taking him to headquarters. I wouldn't waste my time wondering about when he'll be back. I wouldn't bother waiting."

She nodded. "I'll come back tomorrow," she said. "Thank you."

"Don't thank me yet," he muttered.

Without thinking, she reached out and touched his hand. Then she backed away, and ran from the room.

The next day, the young woman waited by the desk while three soldiers brought her mother to the lobby. The time in prison had aged her. Her skin had a grayish tone; shadows as dark as bruises circled her eyes. She wore only a T-shirt and jeans, the same clothes she had been wearing when the soldiers took her.

The young woman put her arm around her mother's thin shoulders. The older woman was shivering uncontrollably in the cold lobby. "Daughter," she said in a broken voice. "Are you really here?"

"Put this on," the young woman said, draping her jacket over her mother's shoulders and pulling it around her. "I'm really here. It'll be all right now. It'll be all right."

Her mother, ignoring the jacket, lifted her hand to

touch her daughter's face. "You're really here," she said in a tone of great surprise. "I thought you were a ghost."

"You can take her home," the sergeant said. He spoke casually and did not look at her. The young woman knew that he did not want her to speak. She put her arm around her mother's shoulders and led her from the building.

The ride home seemed to take forever. The young woman sat behind her mother and kept her arms locked around the older woman's waist. Her mother had a fever, and she swayed with every movement of the horse. Through the heavy jacket the young woman could feel her mother trembling, as if with the cold. As they rode, the young woman found herself muttering reassurances: "We're going home and you'll be all right. It's not so far. I'll make you some hot soup when we get there and you'll feel better. Really you will." She was not certain whether the words were for her mother's benefit or for her own. Eventually, they reached the farmhouse.

Her mother had always been frail, stronger of spirit than of body. She continued to shiver even when she was wrapped in blankets and sitting by the fire. At night, she coughed with a ragged tearing sound. By day, she huddled near the fire, wrapped in a wool blanket.

The young woman did what she could, clearing away the mess that the soldiers had left, making broth and strong tea for her mother to drink, moving the bed so that the sick woman lay near the stove. But her mother ate little and her fever grew worse. She slept uneasily, muttering and tossing in her sleep. Sometimes, late at night, the young woman believed that her mother was talking with ghosts and tried to quiet her. "Rest, Mother," she would say softly. "Sleep so that you'll get better."

"I'm afraid," her mother murmured one night in her sleep. "Always so afraid." Her eyes opened, staring directly at her daughter. "They can kill you, you know. Blow you up just by pushing a button. Just push a button and the world will burn, we'll burn." She tossed in her bed. "Burning up."

With a damp cloth, the young woman wiped the sweat from her mother's forehead. The fire died to coals and the young woman pulled away the blanket that covered her mother, so that she was wrapped only in a sheet. "It's the fever," the young woman said. "It's the fever that makes you feel hot."

"The fever," her mother repeated. "The fever is killing them all. Burning them up. They're dying. I have to help." Her eyelids fluttered and she thrashed, as if trying to get out of bed. "It's my fault that they're dying. But I didn't know —I didn't know that peace would come like this."

The young woman gently restrained her mother, pressing her shoulders back down onto the bed. "Lie still," she pleaded. "You have to get some rest."

Her mother's talk of death frightened her. The light from the kerosene lantern burning on the mantel seemed dimmer than usual, as if the shadows were pressing close. The coals in the fireplace crackled softly.

"My fault," her mother muttered. "My fault."

"Hush," the woman said softly. "Go to sleep."

"We only wanted peace." Her mother's voice was suddenly strong. "That was all. We wanted peace. No more war. I didn't know how much it would cost." She muttered something more, but the young woman could not make out the words.

She dipped the cloth in the water bucket to cool it, wrung it out, folded it, and laid it across her mother's forehead. Her mother fell silent. The young woman sat by the bed, half asleep herself. Now and then, she would rouse herself enough to wring the cloth out and wet it again with cool water. She was very tired.

The line between sleeping and waking blurred. The lantern burned out, and it seemed too much trouble to adjust the wick and light it again. The only light came from the coals in the fireplace. Sometimes she watched the burning embers, points of light like eyes in the darkness. And sometimes she only dreamed that she was watching the coals, imagining the red glow flickering.

"I'm sorry I never gave you a name," her mother said suddenly. "The angel will name you after all."

The young woman blinked in the darkness, struggling to wake up. Her mother's eyes were open and they reflected the light from the coals. Automatically the young woman reached for her mother's hand.

"I'm going back to San Francisco," her mother said. "There are things I must do there."

"When you're well, we'll both go," the young woman said. "We can take the horses and ride to San Francisco. When you're better, we can . . ."

Her mother was shaking her head. "No, I'll go now. You'll have to follow as best you can." She seemed to be looking past her daughter into the darkness beyond. "There'll be a war, you see, and you have to warn them that Fourstar's coming." She looked at her daughter with fever-bright eyes. She squeezed her daughter's hand. "You must promise me that you'll go to San Francisco and warn them. You understand?"

"I understand." The young woman clung to her mother's hand. "But you'll come with me. You'll get better and . . ."

A flash of golden light filled the house, as sudden as a shaft of sunlight in a darkened room. Squinting against the light, the young woman saw her mother cast off the blanket, get out of bed, and walk away. She heard a sound like the thunder of wings when a heron takes off, only louder. Then the light grew brighter and she closed her eyes against it.

She opened her eyes to morning sunlight streaming through the window. She clung to the hand of a dead woman who looked a little bit like her mother. The blanket was tucked around her body. On the pillow by the dead woman's head was a golden feather that seemed to glow with an internal light. When the young woman reached for the feather, it changed, becoming a bright spot of sunlight reflected from a shard of the broken mirror.

The young woman studied the dead woman's face. The dead woman did look a little bit like her mother, but she knew that her mother had gone to San Francisco with the angel. Those were not her mother's eyes; that was not her mother's mouth. This dead woman was a stranger—much smaller than her mother, much thinner.

For a long time, the young woman sat with the body, waiting for something to happen. She shivered in the chill, but she did not build up the fire. It seemed right that the room should be cold.

Finally, late in the morning, she roused herself, realizing that she had to act. She dressed the dead woman in one of her mother's favorite dresses, knowing that her mother would have wanted it that way. She wrapped the body in a wool blanket to keep the cold dirt from her skin. She tied back the wild dark hair with a blue satin ribbon. The woman buried the body by the vegetable garden and built a stone cairn on top of the grave.

The next day she woke at dawn, touched by restlessness. That morning she wandered around the house, considering what to take with her. She packed her most valued possessions in her leather knapsack and her saddlebags, including her glass globe city, her knives, extra bolts for the crossbow. She collected mustard flowers from the orchard and put them on the grave. She spent one last night in the farmhouse and woke at dawn.

Fog filled the valley, a dense gray cloud that hid the vegetable garden and swirled in the branches of the almond trees. She pulled her leather jacket close around her, threw the saddlebags over Young One's back, took her knapsack, and mounted.

A short distance from the house, she looked back. The fog had swallowed her past: the house was gone, the trees were gone, the vegetable garden and the grave were all gone. She zipped up her leather jacket and turned away, following the road toward I-80, the old freeway that ran between the hills. She had never been there, but Leon had said that he came that way.

By noon the fog had burned away. Soon after, she left familiar territory and looked around with new excitement, studying each farmhouse with sharp interest. Young One seemed to catch her excitement, snorting and pulling on the reins, eager to gallop. She let the horse have her head for a time, then reined her in. She passed herds of cattle that lifted their heads to watch her warily. Twice she flushed coveys of quail, each time bringing down one plump bird with her crossbow.

That night she slept in an unfamiliar house. She found

the remains of one inhabitant still tucked into bed in an upstairs bedroom, but she had made many such finds during her childhood explorations, and was not particularly troubled by the discovery. She closed the bedroom door, built a fire in the living room fireplace, and lay down on the couch. Though the upholstery smelled dusty and the fabric tore beneath her weight, the room was dry and the furniture was free of mildew.

The fire radiated a cheerful warmth, but she felt ill at ease, lonely in a way that she had never been in the old farmhouse. When she heard the distant baying of wild dogs, she brought Young One into the living room, leading her through the front door. She felt more comfortable with the horse near; her bulk and warmth were reassuring. For a long time she stared into the fire, and then she slept and dreamed of wandering through the streets of San Francisco, searching for something that she could not identify.

For three days she followed the freeway. Each night she camped in a different house. Sometimes she shot rabbits. On a day when the hunting had not been good, she found a restaurant where there were still canned goods on the kitchen shelves. The paper labels had been chewed away by mice. She opened five cans before she found one that had not been invaded by rust and mold. The fifth can held chili, which she heated over a small fire.

On the fourth day, she crested a hill and reined in her horse. Below her lay the ruins of Berkeley and the glittering expanse of San Francisco Bay. She could see the ribbon of freeway curving along the shore, leading past dark angular buildings. Far away, hazy in the distance, the tall buildings of San Francisco glistened white in the sun. The triangular building that Leon had called the TransAmerica Pyramid stood above the rest, like a finger raised in warning. Between the city and the dark ruins of Berkeley stretched a white line: the Bay Bridge.

The woman looked toward San Francisco and doubted, for the first time, the wisdom of her journey. Looking at the city in her glass globe, she had not dreamed that it would be so large and so strange. She thought for a moment of returning to the valley, where she knew the best places for hunting, the groves where quail nested, the meadows where deer came to graze. She shook her head and spurred her horse onward, following the ribbon of freeway.

Halfway down the hill, on an old highway sign, some-one had scrawled a new message in red spray paint. "No Trespassing!!!" it said, and "Black Dragons Rule." She won-dered, as she rode by, what trespassing was.

Just inside the city limits, she passed the site of an ancient automobile accident. A black BMW had struck the center divider, leaving a long streak on the cement. From the look of the crumpled fender and hood, the vehicle had struck at an angle, spun around, and ended by smashing broadside into the railing. The driver's side of the car was caved in.

Farther on, other wrecks littered the freeway. A red convertible lay on its back with its wheels pointing to the twilight sky. A pickup truck had driven off the edge of the road, taking a portion of the railing with it. The truck rested on one side at the bottom of the hill, its body blackened by fire.

She was fascinated by the streets and buildings that she could see below the freeway. She had never seen so many buildings packed together so tightly. Some areas had been burned; here and there, charred supports thrust upward through the weeds, and broken glass glittered in the fading light.

She did not like the feel of this place; it smelled of ashes and danger. The sky was the color of bruised flesh: deep purple shot through with crimson from the sunset. It pressed low over the city, a ceiling no higher than the roof-tops. As she urged Young One between the wrecks, the air around her seemed to vibrate with a low, heavy rumbling like distant thunder. The sound grew louder, coming from the streets below the freeway. She urged the horse into a trot.

She was crossing an overpass when three motorcycles appeared on the road below. The rider on the first motorcy-cle spotted her and lifted a bare arm to point her out to the others. She had only a momentary glimpse of them: black motorcycles, bare-chested riders in black leather pants, long hair that streamed behind them in the wind of their passing.

The lead rider wheeled around, heading for a nearby on-ramp. The sound of a siren split the air. She did not have to urge Young One to run. The horse fled the screaming siren, her ears laid back, her neck outstretched. The woman crouched low over Young One's neck, listening to the engines fade as the motorcycles passed under the freeway and then rise in volume as they approached. Glancing back, she could see only bright headlights.

The bridge was ahead; she could see it silhouetted against the sky. The approach was crowded with automobiles, dark shadows that blocked the way. Young One dodged among the wrecks, running full tilt without any guidance. The siren continued to wail. The woman risked a glance back at the headlights. In that moment the horse broke stride, gathering herself for a jump. The woman was off-balance, unprepared; when Young One jumped, the woman lost her grip on the horse's mane and fell to the asphalt below. A sharp pain sliced through her shoulder, but she had no time for that. Instinctively she sought cover, rolling toward the car that the horse had hurdled and squeezing herself into the darkness beneath the chassis, pulling her knapsack with her. She lay motionless, listening as the siren passed her and the roaring of the engines faded. Then pain came and filled her head with hot red light.

She waited, lying still and watching the flashes of pain-light that invaded the darkness behind her eyelids. She did not know how long it was before the engines returned, passing her a second time. When they faded in the distance, she squirmed out from under the car, paying for each movement with a burst of pain. One arm was scraped and bleeding. She bandaged that as well as she could with her neckerchief. The shooting pain that accompanied any movement of her shoulder was internal. She could see no way to bandage that. So she lifted her knapsack onto her uninjured shoulder, and began the long journey toward the city's distant spires.

CHAPTER
7

Tiger was an artist of the skin. With delicate needles and a tattoo rig that purred like a cat on speed, he etched beautiful pictures on anyone willing to have them.

Years ago, just after the Plague, he had tattooed his own face. While tripping on acid, he had looked in a mirror. Sunlight shining through Venetian blinds made patterns on his skin, broad strips that crossed his face at a diagonal. With his tattoo rig, he made the shadows permanent.

He preferred tattooing other people, resorting to his own skin only when he could find no other volunteers. During the year that Lily, the redheaded sculptress, had been his lover, Tiger had painted her back with a riot of wildflowers: buttercups and bluebells and daisies, Indian paintbrush and lupine and wild blue irises. Flowering vines curled around her shoulder blades and forget-me-nots nestled in the small of her back.

From a distance, the individual flowers merged into areas of color and formed a new picture. Two irises formed eyes beneath a blazing mane of Indian paintbrush; two rosebuds were nipples in breasts formed by the curve of the vines. Hidden in the garden was a portrait of Lily, constructed from flowers. In the portrait Lily was naked, standing with one hip cocked, smiling a lopsided and uncertain smile.

Lily had left Tiger when he finished the tattoo. To her friends, she had complained that she could never be sure whether he loved her—or perhaps he just loved the empty stretches of pale skin that served so well as his canvas.

Tiger had not been able to convince her to stay. When Lily had asked him if he loved her or her skin, he had been puzzled. Yes, he loved her skin—and that was a part of loving her. When he looked at her, he saw the tattoos that lingered beneath the surface, waiting to be revealed by his art. Tiger suspected that she had left him because his tattoos revealed that he knew her too well. He saw beneath the surface, and Lily feared that.

In any case, his answers did not satisfy her. In the end, her doubts drove her out.

After Lily had left, Tiger turned to his own body, decorating it wherever he could. Ragged geometrics ran down his left arm; Maori-style tribal patterns decorated one leg. On his belly was a series of lizards that fit into one another like an Escher print. The intertwined reptiles undulated when he breathed.

Since Tiger was right-handed, his right arm had remained clean. He could not tattoo it himself, and he trusted no one else. But one morning he noticed dark lines appearing on the pale soft skin on the underside of his wrist. They were indistinct at first, like bruises beneath the skin. He tried to wash them off, but they remained despite his scrubbing. The skin itched a little, like a new tattoo.

The next day the lines were darker, and he could see a word forming, though he rarely used words in his own work. WAR, it said. As the days passed, the tattoo continued to change. Dark vines climbed the bold block letters, and brilliant red roses grew in the gaps between them. But even so, the message was clear.

Ghosts crossed the bridge ahead of the young woman, pale wraiths that tattered in the night wind and merged with the cold mists that rose from San Francisco Bay. The moon was a vague light in the east, blurred by the fog. Gulls roosting among the metal girders of the bridge stirred uneasily and croaked unintelligible warnings as the woman passed.

In the darkness, she stumbled over a broken place in the pavement, but recovered her balance before she fell. Her head ached and her injured shoulder throbbed with each step. She shook her head to clear it, then started forward again.

Her face was hot and the fog droplets that settled on her skin did little to cool her. Beneath her feet, ghosts whispered in tiny liquid voices. She saw dancing lights in the fog, touches of color, swirling faces that vanished when she turned to look at them. Sometimes white shapes reached for her with vast flowing arms. When she stepped forward, the grasping arms always became insubstantial, only drifting fog. But she knew that the ghosts were more than fog. Her mother had left the city because of ghosts.

She listened to her footsteps, muffled by the dense fog. Then a high, sweet, hollow note rang out in the darkness—a piercing sound that hung in the air like the alarm cry of a frightened bird. In an instant she was crouching by a guardrail at one side of the bridge, holding her knife ready. The note faded.

She waited, listening in the darkness. Moving slowly, she slipped her knife into her belt and took her crossbow from her pack. Favoring her injured shoulder, she cocked the bow with difficulty and slipped a bolt into place. With the crossbow in her right hand and the knife in her left, she straightened from her crouch and took a cautious step forward.

The fog eddied in a light wind, and a low note sounded, followed by a metallic rattling, as if rats with steel-tipped claws were scampering across a tin roof. Another pause, then a stealthy scraping, like a knife being pulled from a metal sheath.

With crossbow and knife, the woman stalked the spectral sounds. They came from farther down the road. After each sound she hesitated, continuing only when silence returned.

Somewhere beyond the fog, the sun was rising. She could see the dark rectangle of a highway sign mounted above the roadway. Strange shapes dangled from the sign, swaying in the breeze. She approached carefully.

The cylindrical tank from a household water heater hung from a heavy metal cable. Its white paint was chipped, and patches of rust mottled the once-smooth surface. The tank was surrounded by a bewildering assortment of other metal objects. A tarnished brass cymbal bumped against a sword etched with foreign characters, producing a high ringing sound. A long metal spring, draped in loops like bunting on a review stand, rattled against the tank, and she heard again the scampering of metal claws. She stepped closer. Tentatively, she tugged on a chain of tuning forks that were hanging from their handles. They clattered together and a faint humming tickled her ear.

The woman stepped back. She wondered why anyone would hang such things to sway in the breeze. A tuning fork bumped against the cymbal and the quavering note made her shiver. She edged around the strange wind chimes and continued trudging toward the invisible spires of San Francisco.

Dawn in the city: gray light on gray stone. Even the red brick buildings looked gray, their color stolen by the light. The breeze from San Francisco Bay toyed with a few pigeon feathers, making them whirl and dance in the gutter.

Weeds and grass had taken root in the cracks between the sidewalk stones. The woman passed an abandoned Mercedes. Its leather upholstery supported an assortment of mosses and tender young weeds, watered by the fog that blew through the broken windshield. A black cat peered at her from a doorway, its whiskers twitching as it tested the morning air.

The woman's footsteps echoed in the silence of the city. She had never seen buildings so tall: tremendous slabs of rock and glass, streaked with bird droppings and crusted with pale green lichen. The broken windows watched her. Fog hid the upper stories. For all she knew the buildings went on forever, reaching up to challenge the moon and the stars.

She was weak and tired; her body ached, and she wanted to rest. But she could not bring herself to venture into any of the buildings, and she could not rest beneath their windows. She trudged down Market Street, half in a dream, knowing that she must keep walking.

As she walked she heard organ music, great hollow notes that echoed through the streets. A machine that looked a bit like a mechanical spider rattled around the corner and passed her, following the streetcar tracks that ran down the center of the street. The round white globes of the streetlights had been painted with the delicate features of women; the faces smiled benignly over the young woman's head.

She passed the TransAmerica Pyramid and stopped to stare toward the top, which was lost in the fog. As far up as she could see, the building's concrete walls had been painted with strange designs. A group of figures with human bodies and animal heads stared back at her. A brightly colored serpent climbed up the wall toward the foggy sky. In her dizziness, it seemed to twist and squirm. She blinked and turned away.

At one intersection, she hesitated. In the gray light she could see a crowd of people, clad in black, standing motionless in the open space where four streets met. The young woman stood by a corner of a building, waiting for some movement that would tell her about these people and who they were. When the breeze blew in her direction, she could hear the murmuring of voices, but she could not make out any words. At last, when the fog had chilled her and she could wait no longer, she approached the people slowly, holding her crossbow ready.

The people were made of black metal; the fog had settled on them in tiny droplets. When the wind blew, their hinged jaws waggled up and down and the muttering of wind-generated voices came from their hollow throats. Their vacant eyes made the woman nervous. She skirted the crowd and continued down the street.

She heard the heavy beating of wings as something flew overhead, swooping low over the street. She looked up to see an angel silhouetted against the fog. The light from the sky surrounded it so that its wings and body seemed to be edged in gold. The angel flew ahead, and the woman followed, hurrying to catch up. If only she could catch it, she felt certain that the angel would lead her to her mother.

The way grew twisted, leading through narrow alleys

where tall buildings shut off the light. Her head ached and the world around her grew darker, as if it were dusk rather than dawn. The buildings pressed close around her. Once she looked back, and the street seemed to shimmer and change as she watched, the buildings shifting to block off the way she had come.

She stopped thinking, stopped wondering where she was going. She followed the muffled drumming of the angel's wings. Each time she thought she had lost the way, she saw golden light ahead, the only touch of color in the gray world.

Ignoring the pain in her shoulder, she hurried after the angel. She tried to run but she stumbled, her legs rubbery with sickness, her head enormous and light, like an unwieldy balloon that she towed behind her body. She turned the corner and the light surrounded her. The angel stood before her. Behind it, the darkness was complete.

The right side of the angel's face was human, a handsome face set in a benevolent smile. But the skin on the left side of the face had been torn away, revealing flat planes of metal. On the curve of the cheekbone, a thin line of corrosion marked where two plates had been welded together. The left eye was a golden light, bereft of eyelid or lash. The light flickered as she watched, threatening to die, then flaring back to full brightness.

The angel was naked, and its skin glowed. It had no genitals, just smooth skin where the genitals should have been. It held its hands out to her. The skin had worn away: she could see the delicate metal joints that formed the knuckles. The seams were edged with rust.

The woman stopped, staring up at the great inhuman face. She was suddenly cold, chilled by the breeze that blew from the darkness. "Where is my mother?" she asked in a whisper. "Will you tell me?"

The angel did not reply. She took a step toward it. "Tell me," she said, her voice breaking. "Where is she?"

The angel held out its metal hand. When it moved, she heard the creaking of ancient machinery.

"No," the woman said and took a step back, out of

reach of the angel's metal hands. But she could not take her eyes from the ravaged face, the glowing golden eye.

She heard a sound in the shadows. A small hairy animal crouched in the darkness just behind the angel, staring at her. She recognized the creature from an alphabet book that she had seen when she was a child: M is for Monkey. The animal studied her with rheumy eyes that seemed to hold a sort of sly intelligence. Then it barked once—a sudden commanding sound—and ran past her.

The woman turned from the angel and ran after the monkey, drawing on her last reserves of strength, ducking around corners like a rat in a maze. She ran blindly, fearing the thunder of wings overhead and the cold touch of metal on her back.

As she ran, the light returned to the world. The buildings no longer pressed close. Her breath came more easily. She reached the abandoned Mercedes. The monkey was perched on the car's roof, idly searching its fur for fleas. It looked up as she approached, then returned to the task at hand, ignoring her. She looked back in the direction from which she'd come. The angel had not followed.

Exhausted from running and from pain, she tugged on the car door and tumbled into the backseat. Sprigs of wild anise had taken root in the carpet and their aroma filled the car. At last she slept.

Danny-boy pedaled his bicycle down Market Street, heading for the warehouse district just south of downtown. His bicycle trailer, an awkward but functional vehicle constructed from the body of a grocery cart and the wheels of a mountain bike, rattled and bounced behind him. On the previous afternoon he had discovered three Coleman lanterns, miraculously unbroken, in the corner of a fire-gutted warehouse. That morning he was returning to see what other treasures might be hidden in the wreckage. As always, he was searching for more blue paint to use on the Golden Gate Bridge.

Jezebel, Danny-boy's mongrel bitch, trotted after the bicycle and trailer. Sometimes she lingered behind to sniff at an abandoned car. The rusting vehicles provided shelter for the cats that prowled through the buildings of San Francisco's downtown.

It was early and the fog had not yet burned away. Gray mist crept through the streets, languidly embracing the lampposts and caressing the buildings as it passed. As he pedaled, Danny-boy admired the patterns that the fog made as it eddied around the buildings. The dark windows showing through tendrils of mist reminded him of a set of old lace curtains that he had noticed in a house in Pacific Heights. He wondered, watching the fog, if he might be able to do something interesting with the curtains—maybe some kind of sculpture that moved in the wind. He filed the notion away—he would have to mention it to Zatch or one of the other sculptors.

On mornings like this, Danny-boy sometimes saw things that he could not explain. A crowd of ghostly people in Market Street, dancing to music he could not hear. A flock of angels, flying just above the buildings. A woman, driving a chariot drawn by flaming horses following the course of the sun. He did not mind these things; they were a part of his life. He knew that such visions came from the city, caught somehow in the asphalt and cement, sprouting up like the weeds that grew in the cracks on Market Street, curling among the buildings like the fog.

Few people lived in the city, but the dreams of many lingered in the burned-out buildings, the abandoned cars, the empty streets. It was these dreams, Danny-boy thought sometimes, that shaped the city. The dreams of the dead, Danny-boy suspected, made Lily collect skulls and display them in the Emporium Department Store window.

Danny-boy stopped pedaling his bicycle as he came to the corner of Fifth and Market and coasted to a stop by the Emporium. Arranged behind the glass of the display window was a neat array of polished human skulls. The clean white anonymity of bone fascinated Lily.

Beside each skull was an object: a pair of wire-rimmed bifocals, an empty whiskey decanter, a naked plastic doll with curly blond hair and baby-blue glass eyes, a hash pipe, a Bible, a lace glove. Each time Lily selected a skull, she also took an object from the skull's surroundings. She polished each skull with floor wax, pilfered from supermarkets and hardware stores, and arranged them to suit herself.

Since Danny-boy's last visit, Lily had added a toothless skull and a set of dentures. Danny-boy admired Lily's skill in selection and arrangement. The bifocals, the glove, the dentures, the Bible—these things changed the array of skulls from something morbid and commonplace to something profoundly human. The window had the look of a memorial, an offering to appease the souls of the anonymous dead.

Danny-boy stood for a moment by the window, studying the display. Then he whistled for Jezebel, who had wandered off among the cars. The dog did not come to his whistle, but began barking from somewhere nearby. Danny-boy whistled again but still the dog barked, an eager baying that clearly demanded Danny-boy's presence.

Danny-boy followed the sound to a Mercedes parked in the middle of the street. A monkey crouched on the roof of the automobile, chattering angrily at the dog. At Danny-boy's approach, the monkey bounded away, disappearing into the open door of a nearby office building. Jezebel sniffed anxiously at the car's closed door and wagged her tail furiously.

Danny-boy peered through the broken windshield. A young woman huddled inside, as far as she could get from Jezebel. "It's OK," he said. "You can come out. Jezebel won't hurt you."

The woman did not speak or move. Her face was very pale and she clutched her worn leather jacket tightly around her, as if for warmth and protection.

"Are you all right?" Danny-boy asked. She regarded him with the fearful gaze of an animal too sick to defend itself. She blinked as if struggling to keep him in focus. Jezebel barked again and scratched on the door of the car.

Strangers rarely made it to downtown. Traders usually headed straight for Duff's Trading Post on the edge of the Presidio. Few wanted to risk encountering the strangeness that lone travelers so often found in the heart of the city. Occasionally one of Oakland's gangs crossed the bridge to scavenge. But a gang would not have abandoned one of its own.

"Are you hurt?" Danny-boy asked. As he watched, she closed her eyes, as if watching him were suddenly too much of an effort. He pulled on the car door, and her eyes opened wide. She lunged forward, leaping past him to run for cover. But a few steps from the car she stumbled and fell, rolled once, then lay curled on the asphalt. The knife in her hand clattered to the ground beside her.

Danny-boy approached cautiously. Her face was smeared with blood from a scrape on her forehead. Her jacket had fallen open and her right shoulder was wrapped in cloth that appeared at first glance to be decorated with a floral pattern in red and brown. Danny-boy looked closer and realized that the red blossoms were fresh blood that had soaked through the cloth; the brown background pattern was old blood that had dried in place.

From the Emporium's bedding department, he took blankets, which he arranged in his trailer, making a sort of nest for her. As gently as he could, he lifted the woman into the trailer. Then he took her home.

On his way to the Saint Francis Hotel, he met Tommy and asked the boy to run and find Tiger. Tiger, who had worked as a paramedic before he took up tattooing, was the closest the community had to a doctor. Danny-boy carried the woman up the stairs to his rooms and put her into his own bed.

Tiger arrived with his medical bag. He studied the woman who lay on the bed, and then shooed Tommy from the room, despite the boy's protests.

Danny-boy supported the woman while Tiger stripped off her leather jacket and shirt. She remained unconscious, for the most part, while Tiger examined her. Occasionally she roused enough to blink her eyes and babble at them, saying something about ghosts and something about angels.

"Looks like she must have taken quite a fall," Tiger guessed. "Mild concussion, I'd say. Broken collarbone. Give me a hand here." Danny-boy supported her in a sitting position while Tiger arranged an elastic bandage in a figure-eight pattern that looped around the woman's shoulders and crossed in the back. "This should keep the break together. I'll need to tighten it up tomorrow or the next day. She's young enough. It should heal fine, but she'll have to take it easy for the next week or so."

"She can stay here," Danny-boy said.

"Good thing," Tiger said. "Doesn't look like she's going anywhere." He sponged off the scrapes on her back and shoulders; then he let her lie back on the bed.

Danny-boy pulled the covers gently over her. He watched her sleep and wondered what had brought her to the city of San Francisco.

Over the years Danny-boy had filled his hotel suite with things that he liked, and the rooms had acquired a peculiar sort of grandeur. The original carpet was buried beneath piles of oriental rugs that yielded underfoot like the leaves and mulch on the forest floor. More rugs hung on the walls, creating a confusion of geometric patterns and rich colors: deep crimson, royal blue, cream, and amber.

In one corner, a trio of cuckoo clocks dutifully kept three different times. Danny-boy told time by the sun, but he liked the clocks for the tunes they played on the hour.

In one window, an array of multicolored pinwheels spun in the light evening breeze. In the other, a chain of diamond necklaces hung. Danny-boy could have traded the diamonds to Duff for blue paint or other necessities, but he liked the way they caught the light on sunny days, and he could always find other things to trade.

The hotel was a comfortable place to live. The carpets provided insulation. A kerosene lantern hanging from a hook in the wall filled the room with soft yellow light.

Danny-boy sat on the floor, leaning back against a tapestry-covered pillow. Jezebel lay curled on the carpet at his feet.

The Machine poured himself a glass of the potent amber-colored brew that Duff called brandy. His third hand, which was strapped into place just below the elbow of his right arm, mimicked the motions of his right hand a fraction of a second later. The Machine made many people nervous, but Danny-boy got along with him well enough.

Just that week The Machine had found an industrial painting rig in reasonable shape. The nozzle was clogged, but The Machine had promised to fix that and give the device to Danny-boy for use on the Golden Gate Bridge. To repay The Machine for his help, Danny-boy had invited him to dinner. On a tray were their leftovers: half a meat pie, two muffins, a few slices of cheese.

"So you know nothing about this woman," The Machine was saying. "Except that she attacked you with a knife when you tried to help her."

"She was scared," Danny-boy said. "I think she was just trying to get away."

"You're too trusting," The Machine grumbled.

Danny-boy grinned. For years The Machine had been telling him that he was too trusting. The Machine trusted no one. "Think of it as a survival strategy," Danny-boy said. "I'm so wide open that no one tries to hit me."

"Bad strategy," The Machine said.

"She's just a kid. Nothing to be afraid of."

"I'm not afraid." The Machine's right fist clenched and his prosthetic hand echoed the motion a moment later. "I just don't think you're acting wisely."

"When have I ever acted wisely?" Danny-boy asked, then grinned at The Machine's silence. "Got you there, didn't I?" The Machine didn't smile. "I don't see what you're so worried about."

"She could be a spy."

"For who?"

"For the Church of Revelations, for the Black Dragons, for Fourstar. For anyone at all."

Danny-boy studied him. "You really are worried."

"According to the traders at Duff's, Fourstar has been talking about an invasion."

"When Fourstar decides to invade, he won't send a spy. He'll figure on walking in and taking over the place," Danny-boy said. "I don't think he's worried about our military might or—"

"Danny-boy," The Machine interrupted. "Your friend's awake."

Danny-boy glanced toward the bedroom just in time to see the young woman dart out and snatch the bread knife from the tray. With the knife in her hand, she backed away

until she stood in the bedroom doorway. She was naked
except for the white bandage that looped around her shoulders. The lantern light tucked shadows beneath her breasts,
between her legs. Her skin looked smooth and polished. She
reminded Danny-boy of a bronze statue of Diana that he
had seen in one of the city's art museums. Diana had held a
bow, ready to fire, and the gaze of her bronze eyes was cool
and steady. This woman's eyes were wild and feverish.

She glared at Danny-boy. "Are you a ghost?"

The tip of the knife blade was trembling slightly, but
her gaze was steady. Her nakedness seemed unimportant to
her; her attention was focused entirely on Danny-boy.

Danny-boy returned her stare. "A ghost?" The words
were slow in coming. He felt trapped by her intensity.
"What do you mean?"

"My mother told me the city was filled with ghosts."

Danny-boy shrugged easily. "There are some ghosts
around. But we're real enough. I'm Danny-boy and this is
The Machine."

"The Machine?" She and The Machine exchanged
looks of mistrust.

"What's your name?" Danny-boy asked.

"Name?" She shook her head quickly. Her grip on the
knife relaxed a little and she lowered the blade. Danny-boy
saw that she was looking at the dinner leftovers.

"You hungry?" he asked. Moving slowly, he leaned forward to pour brandy into a glass. He took the pillow from
behind his back and tossed it so that it landed near the tray
of food. "Sit down," he said softly. "Help yourself."

Her wary gaze reminded Danny-boy of the feral cats
that haunted the city's abandoned buildings. When he offered them scraps of food, they ate. But any truce was temporary. They did not trust him. They did not need him.
They wanted only to be left alone. They were not frightened,
but cautious. Not openly hostile, but faintly contemptuous.
Opportunistic: ready to seize any chance to pounce or to slip
away into the darkness, as the situation demanded.

The woman stepped into the room and awkwardly lowered herself to sit on the pillow. She hesitated, then used the
knife to cut the pie. She ate with great appreciation, chewing

the food slowly, like a person who had been hungry before and who knew better than to bolt the first meal after a fast.

"Where did you come from?" Danny-boy asked.

She swallowed a mouthful of pie and washed it down with a sip of brandy. "Up near Sacramento. Not far from a town called Woodland."

"You came down I-80 and over the bridge?" he asked.

She nodded. Her face was relaxing. She took another sip of brandy. "Came to warn you that Fourstar's coming. He's going to take over San Francisco." Danny-boy glanced at The Machine. So much for her being a spy for Fourstar.

"How did you break your collarbone?"

"Back on the other side of the bridge, men on motorcycles chased me. Got thrown from my horse. I hid until it was dark, then came over the bridge."

"Black Dragons," Danny-boy said. "That's the gang that controls most of Oakland. So you walked eight and a half miles with a broken collarbone?"

She gave him a cool look. "I didn't walk on my hands."

"Oakland's a dangerous place to travel alone," Danny-boy said.

Her mouth twisted in a kind of smile. "Do you know a safe place to travel?" she asked him. "I don't."

"Oakland's worse than most," Danny-boy said.

She did not reply. She had finished the meat pie and was working on the second muffin, but she was slowing down. She yawned, as unself-conscious as a cat stretching. For the moment, she seemed to have decided to trust them. Her eyes were half closed. "I'm a little tired," she said. She set the muffin back on the plate, half eaten. She swayed, her eyes closing. Danny-boy caught her as she fell.

For the second time that day, Danny-boy tucked the woman into bed.

"Real nice," The Machine said sarcastically. "Completely trustworthy, I'm sure."

Danny-boy wasn't listening. He stroked her forehead, pushing back the ragged strands of hair.

CHAPTER
8

Every Wednesday, Ms. Migsdale printed the *New City News,*
San Francisco's only newspaper. Tommy assisted her with
production, cranking the hand-operated press, helping to
fold the two hundred and some copies of the *News,* and
delivering the folded papers to the public library, where
Books distributed them to the city's residents, and to
Duff's, where farmers and traders bartered for copies.

In exchange for Tommy's help, Ms. Migsdale tutored
the boy. Ruby, his mother, thought he needed schooling, so
Ms. Migsdale taught him small things that she thought
might prove useful someday. On sunny afternoons they
studied botany, identifying the wild flowers and grasses that
grew in abandoned yards and vacant lots. Together they
caught tadpoles in the creek that flowed past the library. For
weeks, Tommy kept the tiny creatures in a fish tank, watching with amazement as they grew legs. As the days passed,
their tails shrank down to nothing. Finally Ms. Migsdale
and Tommy released a dozen tiny frogs by the creek. On
summer nights, when Ms. Migsdale taught Tommy the
names of the constellations, they could hear the frogs calling
in high thin voices, barely louder than crickets.

Ms. Migsdale felt vaguely guilty sometimes, because
she knew that she learned as much from Tommy as he did
from her. He knew where edible mushrooms grew and
where watercress floated on still water. When she could not
find her way through the city's shifting streets, Tommy

70

knew the route to follow. He explained to her that Randall became a wolf on nights when the moon was full, and told her about the ghosts he saw in the downtown streets. She had difficulty accepting all the things he told her; he took the city's strangeness as a matter of course, an attitude that she found faintly disturbing. But he was her best source of news. If something interesting had happened anywhere in the city, Tommy would know about it.

On the Wednesday after Danny-boy found the stranger, Tommy could talk of nothing else. "My mom says she's a wild woman," he shouted over the rhythmic thumping of the press. "She said Danny-boy ought to throw her back."

"Seems funny that Danny-boy found her downtown," Ms. Migsdale yelled back. She sat on a stool at a battered wooden drafting table, folding copies of the *News.* "Most people get scared off before they get that far."

Tommy stopped cranking the press and squeezed a little more ink over the rollers. "She didn't get scared off," he said. He seemed proud, as if he had had a hand in the woman's arrival. "She was right in the heart of downtown."

"Did you talk to her at all?"

Tommy hesitated, as if wondering how far he could push the truth. Then he admitted, "Naw. Tiger made me leave. But I asked Danny-boy and he said that she came from Sacramento."

Ms. Migsdale nodded thoughtfully. "That's interesting. I wonder if she has news of what Fourstar is up to. She could be important."

"Sure, she's important," Tommy said, cranking the press again. "The city wouldn't have let her in otherwise."

Ms. Migsdale shook her head, struck by the boy's unswerving faith in the city. His trust seemed, at times, to border on religion. "Don't you think it could just have been an accident?" she suggested.

Tommy laughed. "Naw. The city likes her—that's all there is to it." He cranked the press with increased energy. "She had a crossbow. Do you think she'd show me how to shoot it? Maybe I could make one."

"You can always ask," Ms. Migsdale said.

"She doesn't have a name," Tommy said. "That's what

Danny-boy said. No name at all. Why do you think she came here?"

"I'll ask her," Ms. Migsdale promised. "I'll be interviewing her for the next issue of the *News*. I'll let you know when I find out."

Late that afternoon, when Tommy pedaled toward Duff's with his bicycle baskets filled with copies of the *News*, Ms. Migsdale headed for Danny-boy's, which was just a short bicycle ride from the Mission Street print shop.

The woman sat in an easy chair in front of the Saint Francis Hotel. Three monkeys perched among the carvings on the hotel's stone facade. Whenever they came down to the sidewalk, Jezebel began barking and chased them back up. Now the dog lay panting by the woman's chair, gazing expectantly at the animals and waiting for another game.

The hotel fronted on Union Square. From her chair the woman could look across what had once been a small park. A stone pillar rose from the center of the square, where four curving cement paths intersected. On top, the bronze figure of a young woman stood in a graceful arabesque, one arm reaching out ahead of her, one leg extended behind.

Bean plants surrounded the base of the pillar. Tomatoes, potatoes, and summer squash grew between the curving paths; shiny-leafed chili pepper plants filled wooden boxes that had once held rhododendrons; cucumber vines meandered across the sidewalks, hiding the cement beneath prickly leaves. A few scrawny chickens and a bedraggled rooster scratched among the plants. On the far side of the square, blackbirds squabbled in the apple trees.

The woman noticed a small figure riding a bicycle down the street toward her. She felt for the knife that she had slipped between the chair's cushion and the arm, out of sight but in easy reach. Danny-boy had assured her that she did not need to worry; no one in the city would hurt her. So far, he seemed to be right, but she felt better with her knife nearby.

"Hello," called the old woman on the bicycle. She stopped in front of the hotel, got off her bicycle, and leaned it against a lamppost. Jezebel ran to greet her, tail wagging furiously. "I had heard that Danny-boy had a guest. I'm Ms. Migsdale."

The woman relaxed, releasing her grip on the knife. Ms. Migsdale seemed harmless enough.

"Is Danny-boy around?"

The woman shook her head. Ms. Migsdale smiled, obviously waiting for more. "He's gone to find Randall," the woman said at last. "My horse ran away after she threw me. Danny-boy says that Randall might know where she ran off to."

Ms. Migsdale nodded, settling into the other easy chair. Jezebel laid her head in the old woman's lap with a happy sigh, and Ms. Migsdale rubbed the dog's ears. "If anyone knows, chances are Randall does." Ms. Migsdale smiled at the woman. "You don't mind if I wait a bit and see if he comes back, do you?"

"If you like," the woman said. She studied the older woman curiously. Leon had said that artists lived in the city. She did not know exactly what an artist looked like, but she knew that this old woman did not match her vague imaginings.

Ms. Migsdale stroked Jezebel's head and returned the woman's scrutiny. "I hear you come from Sacramento," Ms. Migsdale said. "You know much about the fellow they call Fourstar?"

"More than I want to," the woman said. "I came here to warn the artists about him. He's planning to come and take over San Francisco."

Ms. Migsdale nodded slowly, but did not show any sign of alarm. "He's been planning that for years, from what I hear. But I'd like to hear more about it. I publish a newspaper, the *New City News,* and I thought I might interview you for it, if you're willing."

The woman nodded, realizing suddenly why the name had sounded familiar. "I've heard of you. I met a trader who mentioned your newspaper."

Ms. Migsdale leaned forward eagerly. "You must have met Leon. How wonderful! I was beginning to worry about him. When did you see him?"

The woman looked down at her hands, wondering

what to say. She did not want to talk about Leon and what had happened to him. One of her hands picked nervously at the stuffing that bulged through a rip in the easy chair's upholstery. The sun had faded the cloth's floral pattern, leaving dark gray patches where roses had once bloomed.

"Tell me." Ms. Migsdale's voice was soft and encouraging. "When did you see him?"

"A week back, I guess." The woman's voice was small and her chest felt tight. "The army took him for questioning." She glanced up, meeting Ms. Migsdale's eyes, then looking away. Her fingers worried at the frayed edges of the tear in the upholstery. "They took my mother too."

Ms. Migsdale laid her hand over the woman's, stopping the busy fingers. "Tell me what happened."

"They let my mother go, but they took Leon to headquarters. I don't think he'll ever come back." She kept her head down, refusing to look up. "My mother was sick when she came back. I nursed her as well as I could." She heard a defensive note in her own voice. Ms. Migsdale's hand tightened on the woman's.

"She died," Ms. Migsdale said.

"No!" The woman pulled her hand away from Ms. Migsdale's. "One night the angel came and took her to San Francisco." She glared at Ms. Migsdale. "I came to the city to find her. And I know she's here. I saw the angel."

Ms. Migsdale nodded slowly. Her hands were knotted in her lap.

The woman straightened up in her chair, watching Ms. Migsdale. "I'm sorry to tell you about Leon," she said. She waited for a moment, but Ms. Migsdale did not look up. The woman reached out and touched her shoulder lightly, a hesitant reassurance. "I liked Leon."

"He was a good man," Ms. Migsdale said. "He always brought me news of the Central Valley." She wiped her eyes briskly with one hand, blinked, and looked up to meet the woman's eyes. "I guess we'll have to start taking Fourstar more seriously now. I suppose the time has come."

"My mother told me to come to the city," the woman said. "Before she went away, she made me promise I would come and warn you."

Ms. Migsdale nodded. She reached into her purse and pulled out a small spiral notebook. "This interview will start people thinking." Her voice had taken on a businesslike tone. "The power of the press, you know. Perhaps you could tell me a little about your journey from Woodland to San Francisco."

Prompted by Ms. Migsdale's questions, the woman talked about the Central Valley, about the farms and the houses she had explored as a child, about the Woodland market and the soldiers who ran the checkpoint. Ms. Migsdale took careful notes. From the hotel's facade, the monkeys watched.

"Hey, dog," Danny-boy said. The black dog looked up from the storm drain grating that it had been sniffing and eyed Danny-boy with suspicion. It was a wolfish-looking animal about the size of a German shepherd. "Look here." Danny-boy tossed a piece of stale muffin in the dog's direction. The animal nosed the food warily, then downed it in one gulp. Sitting back on its haunches, it studied Danny-boy with new interest.

"Listen," Danny-boy said. "I'm looking for Randall. You know him?"

The dog cocked its head to one side and its ears swiveled forward.

Danny-boy frowned, uncertain as to the meaning of the dog's reaction. Whenever he needed to find Randall, he bribed one of the feral dogs that lived in the city to pass on a message. Sometimes his method worked and sometimes it didn't. He figured that some of the dogs were on speaking terms with Randall, and others were not. But he could not distinguish between the two.

"You sure?"

The dog watched him intently, its eyes fixed on his hands, and made an eager noise low in its throat. Danny-boy broke off another piece of muffin and the dog leapt to catch it.

"Tell him I've got to talk to him. He can meet me in Golden Gate Park, over by the big museum. You got that?"

The dog took a step toward Danny-boy, its tail held

high. Danny-boy shrugged and tossed the animal the rest of the muffin, which disappeared in a single gulp.

"That's it," Danny-boy said. "Go find Randall." He held up his empty hands and the dog's tail drooped. The animal trotted away, glancing back only once.

Danny-boy mounted his bicycle and headed for Golden Gate Park by way of Geary Boulevard, one of the city's main thoroughfares. He took his time, figuring it would take the dog a while to find Randall. In a clothes store, he picked through heaps of shirts and jeans, looking for some that might fit the woman. As he examined the clothes, he found himself thinking about the woman. She intrigued him. He had never spent much time talking with anyone from outside the city. The farmers and traders who passed through Duff's were skittish and careful around city dwellers. After some searching, he found a red shirt and a pair of jeans that had escaped the mildew and the moths.

In the storeroom of a hardware store, he found a well-stocked paint department. Most of the graffiti artists in town lived in the Haight or in the Mission district and only occasionally scavenged in the stores off Geary. Danny-boy pried open can after can, checking the contents. More often than not, the cans contained only desiccated paint chips; but he did find five cans of enamel paint in various shades of blue, and three cans of blue spray paint. He added brushes and rollers to the load in his trailer, then headed for the park.

Golden Gate Park stretched from the heart of the city out to Ocean Beach, over a thousand acres of open land. It had grown wild during the years since the Plague. White-tailed deer and horses, descendants of the Golden Gate Stables rental nags, roamed the park's overgrown meadows and groves. Migrating ducks stopped to feed in the small lakes.

The lawn in front of the great, glass-domed Conservatory of Flowers was lush and shaggy. Long ago, grass had overrun the flowerbeds. A herd of buffalo, descendants of animals who had eaten stale bread and sticky buns from the hands of tourists, grazed on the thick grass and sniffed the hardy exotics that had burst through the Conservatory's glass walls to reach for the sun.

Danny-boy checked the snares he had set in the low

shrubs behind the Conservatory and found one rabbit, caught and strangled in his noose. He gutted it quickly, leaving the entrails in the grass, and continued on his way.

Danny-boy cycled around the circular drive that passed the Japanese Tea Garden, the De Young Museum, the Asian Art Museum, and the California Academy of Sciences. He startled a flock of pigeons that had been quietly feeding on the seeds of grasses that grew through cracks in the pavement. "Hello!" he called. "Randall! You here?" A young bull buffalo glared at him balefully from the entrance to the Japanese Tea Garden. The ornamental plum tree that stood by the gate had scattered leaves on the ground around the buffalo's hooves. "Randall!" Three white-tailed deer burst from the shelter of the trees at the center of the circular drive and bounded past the Asian Art Museum. "Hello!"

Danny-boy circled again, calling out to Randall. His voice echoed back to him from the cement front of the Academy. The air was pleasantly cool and the shadows of late afternoon lay thick on the ground. Exhilarated by the beauty of the day, he circled a third time, weaving with wide exuberant arcs around the potholes in the drive and whooping with joy during each sweeping curve. The trailer bumped and rattled, threatening to overturn but remaining obstinately upright.

He was rounding the curve by the Japanese Tea Garden when he realized he was being watched. Randall stood beside the grazing buffalo, watching Danny-boy impassively. Over one shoulder, he carried a set of leather saddlebags.

"Randall," Danny-boy said, braking to a stop by the gate. "Good to see you."

Randall dropped the saddlebags at his feet. "These belong to the woman you found," he said.

Danny-boy frowned. Randall always seemed to know more than he rightly should. "How do you know about it?"

"The monkeys told me."

"Yeah? What do they say?"

"Say there's going to be some changes around here. Trouble coming. The woman's a part of it."

"Part of the trouble?" Danny-boy shook his head. "I don't think so."

Randall shrugged. "Part of the solution to the trouble, maybe. It's not clear yet."

"What kind of trouble?" Danny-boy persisted.

Randall shifted his weight, looking uncomfortable. "Trouble," he said. "That's all I know." He stared at the saddlebags, rubbing his beard with one big hand. Then he glanced up, dark eyes distressed beneath his heavy eyebrows. "Her horse has joined the herd in the park. You can tell her that."

"Okay, I'll tell her."

"Be careful," Randall said.

"Careful of what?" Danny-boy asked.

Randall shrugged again. "When I know, I'll tell you." Then he walked away, somehow finding a path through the mass of trees and shrubs just inside the gate. Danny-boy was left with the buffalo, who shook his head and snorted. The expression in his small reddened eyes was distinctly unfriendly. Danny-boy backed away.

The woman was asleep in the easy chair when Danny-boy came home. Curled up in the chair, she looked frail and vulnerable. At the nape of her neck, her dark hair curled to form little ringlets.

Danny-boy touched her shoulder to wake her. Her eyes opened wide immediately. She reminded Danny-boy of the wild creatures he sometimes encountered while exploring abandoned buildings. The gray fox that slipped out the back door while he walked in the front. The family of raccoons that glared at him for disturbing them. The woman's hands were small and clever, like a raccoon's hands. Her eyes were the eyes of a fox—she knew secrets and kept them.

"I'm back," he said. "I brought you some clean clothes. And I found Randall. He says your horse is in the park."

She started to reach for the saddlebags, then winced and stopped. "Let me help," Danny-boy said. He fumbled with the buckles, conscious of her eyes on him. He slung the bags over the easy chair's broad arm and watched as she sorted through the bag's contents, casting aside a sack of dried apricots, another of jerky, a third of almonds. Beneath the food, she found what she was looking for: a glass globe on a black base.

"It's San Francisco," she said, holding it up for his examination. She shook it, and flecks of gold danced around the towers of the city. "I've had it for years."

He took it carefully from her hand. "Of course," he said. "You can see Union Square." He tapped on the glass, indicating the tiny rectangle of green. "And that's the TransAmerica Pyramid."

She peered into the glass. "I walked by there," she said. "Someone had painted designs on it."

"The Neo-Mayanists," Danny-boy said. "Group of graffiti artists down in the Mission. They've taken over the Pyramid. They're making it into a temple of some sort."

The woman was watching the glitter drift through the city streets. "On my way into the city, I saw a crowd of men made of metal. When the wind blew, they muttered to each other."

"That's a sculpture by Zatch and Gambit," Danny-boy said. "They call it 'Men Talking with Nothing to Say.'"

"I heard music—deep hollow notes that moaned like the wind."

"That's Gambit's wind organ. It plays music when wind blows across the pipes."

"I saw a metal spider the size of a dog. It ran past me down the center of the street."

"The Machine built that. He builds a lot of independent machines. Some people don't like them, but they're all right. They won't hurt you or anything."

He glanced at her face. She wet her lips like a nervous cat, hesitating. Then she said, "I saw the angel that took my mother. Did The Machine build that?"

"An angel? What do you mean?"

She described the angel, her eyes shining with excitement.

Reluctantly, he shook his head. "I've never seen anything like that. The Machine could have built it, I suppose, but I don't think so. I'll ask him for you."

She nodded eagerly and took the globe from his hand, slipping it back into the saddlebags.

"Are you hungry?" he asked her. She nodded. "I usually do my cooking up on the roof. Come on—I'll show
you."

She followed him up the stairs to the third floor and out
onto the roof. Back before the Plague, this had been a sort of
roof garden, joining the old Saint Francis Hotel to the newer
tower. It was wedged between the old structure and the new
one, protected from wind on two sides. Danny-boy used the
area as a kitchen and outdoor workspace. Against the wall
of the old hotel, he had set up a hibachi. On fine days he
cooked in the open air, building a fire with scavenged lumber. He started the fire and skinned the rabbit that he had
snared earlier that day.

The woman sat with her legs dangling over the edge of
the roof, kicking her heels against the side of the building.
Danny-boy sat beside her, waiting for the fire to die down to
coals. Jezebel lay between them, asleep in a patch of sunlight.

The sun was going down, leaving Danny-boy with the
wistful feeling of imminent loss. The air was filled with possibilities. A gull swooped low over the edge of the roof, and
the light of the setting sun tinted its wings with tones of
purple and magenta. The sky was a deep blue. Here and
there, plumes of dark smoke rose to paint lazy question
marks on the blue. The streaks of dirty smoke only made the
blue seem more pure.

"How many people live here?" she asked him.

"I don't know. Maybe a hundred or so."

"How many used to live here?"

He shook his head. "Better ask Ms. Migsdale that. Or
Books—he might know."

The woman rubbed Jezebel's ears, and the dog's tail
thumped against the roof in a steady rhythm.

"You like dogs?" he asked her.

She nodded. "We had a dog back home. He's dead
now."

"I found Jezebel. Her mother was a wild dog. I found
her and her brothers in the basement of a house. They
whimpered and yapped at me, and tried to suck on my fingers."

"Where was their mother?"

Danny-boy shrugged. "Dead, I suppose. I watched for a day, and she didn't come back. So I took the pups and fed them on milk until they could eat solid food. Duff has the other two: he took them in exchange for the milk. But Jezebel was the best of the litter."

Jezebel leaned toward the woman's hand, and she scratched under the dog's chin. "You always take in strays?" the woman asked.

"Sure," he said. "Wouldn't you?"

She thought for a moment. "Dogs maybe, but not people."

"Emerald took me in," he said. "I was only about three when the Plague killed my parents. I remember seeing them lying there dead and I ran away, crying. Emerald found me and she took care of me. People are all right."

"My mother trusted people," the woman said in a low voice. "I remember when I was a kid, a trader came to our house and offered to trade a few pints of kerosene for a sack of almonds. Said he had a craving for some nuts, and we needed the kerosene. My mother went into the shed to get the nuts. He followed her and when she set down her rifle to fill the sack, he grabbed her. I was outside, and I heard her scream." The woman hesitated for a moment, her hand buried in Jezebel's thick fur. "I grabbed the hatchet from the woodpile, and I hit him. Just the way I would have chopped a tree, I hit his legs, and when he fell I hit his head. My mother was crying; her shirt was ripped open. There was blood everywhere. We buried him in the garden with no gravestone. We took his horse and his wagon, and I learned to ride."

Danny-boy made an involuntary move toward her, and she looked up, a warning clear in her eyes. "People aren't all right. They never liked us. We were strangers and they never liked us."

Jezebel nudged the woman's hand, and she continued stroking the dog.

"Sometimes people are all right," Danny-boy said.

She shrugged, but did not reply.

Danny-boy checked the coals and placed the grate over

the fire. He cut the rabbit carcass into pieces and laid the meat on the grate. Juice hissed on the coals.

"Look there," the woman said suddenly. A hummingbird, attracted by the woman's red shirt, hovered a few feet from the edge of the roof. Danny-boy could hear the buzz of its wings. The feathers at its throat were the iridescent blue-green of a dewdrop on a blade of grass.

The woman smiled at the small bird. It circled once, then darted away. "He thought I was a flower," she said. "He got that wrong."

Danny-boy tended the fire, and the meat cooked. After a time, they ate dinner. The rabbit tasted of wood smoke and they ate with their hands from china plates that Danny-boy had taken from the hotel kitchen long ago.

The sun set and twilight breezes played over the roof. The sky had darkened, but the stars were not yet visible. The street below was empty, except for a cat that ghosted along the gutter, heading toward the garden where it might find mice among the vegetables. "Sometimes I feed the cats," Danny-boy said.

The woman scraped the leftover bones onto one plate. "I'll do that," she said. Danny-boy watched without comment as she took the plate and headed down the stairs. From the edge of the roof, he watched her step through the hotel's side door. She seemed a part of the twilight.

The woman set the plate down and sat on the edge of the curb, becoming motionless, a part of the street. Danny-boy watched from the roof. In the doorways and gutters, he thought he saw movement. Cats were gathering: lean shadows with whiskers, sneak thieves, scavengers who were battered like boxers who had seen better days. They slipped like flowing water from the bushes, from the doorways. A black tomcat crept up to the plate, seized the largest bone, and retreated. The woman did not move. A slim gray female moved in, her belly against the ground. Keeping her eyes on the woman, she picked at the scraps delicately. A scrawny calico darted from the gutter to join her.

Danny-boy watched from the roof. Tiger had said of the woman: "She acts like she was raised by wolves." Danny-boy had denied it, defending the woman and saying that she was just shy: it would take her some time to get used to having so many people around. As he watched the woman and the cats, together in the twilight, he doubted his own words.

PART 2

The Mystery and Melancholy of a Street

"A general definition of civilization: a civilized society is exhibiting the five qualities of truth, beauty, adventure, art, peace."

—Alfred North Whitehead

"We are mad in a very different way."

—Max Ernst

CHAPTER
9

The woman woke up slowly, drifting lazily toward consciousness like a hawk soaring on a thermal updraft. She was warm and something soft was beneath her. Her shoulder ached, but the pain was distant, and she had grown used to it. She wondered vaguely where she was.

She opened her eyes and saw a white ceiling. On a carved wooden border where the ceiling met the wall, plump cherubs flitted among wreaths of flowers.

Silently, she slipped from bed and dressed. She peered through the window. The sun wasn't up yet. Union Square was dimly visible in the faint light that preceded dawn. She found her crossbow and knife on a chair in the corner of the room.

In the outer room Danny-boy, wrapped in a blue wool blanket, slept on a pile of Oriental rugs. Jezebel lifted her head to watch the woman go, but did not follow.

Outside, the city was gray with fog. The skyscrapers of downtown caught the first few rays of the rising sun. Reluctant to return to the bleak canyons of downtown but too restless to stay put, she headed away from the tall buildings. It was a good time of day for rabbits, if she could find the right place to hunt.

She walked steadily, glad of the cool air. A few blocks from the hotel, the neighborhood changed—instead of shops and restaurants, houses stood shoulder to shoulder along both sides of the street. She stared at the houses as she

walked. In a way, she found them more disconcerting than
the skyscrapers. People had lived in these houses, but surely
there could never have been enough people to fill them all.
She could not imagine so many people. House after house
after house—each one reflecting a different personality.

From the tiny yard of a red brick house, low juniper
bushes stretched their wiry branches across the cracked
sidewalk stones. Broad-leafed hedges blocked the windows
and the front door of a boxy stucco apartment house. In the
flower bed beside a turreted Victorian, English lavender
struggled for space among the grass and wild mustard. Two
molded concrete lions glared from a riot of roses—great,
bug-eaten, scraggly bushes with long thorns and a few dark
red blossoms.

The woman felt uncomfortable, surrounded by the evidence of so many strangers. As she walked, she found herself glancing up at the empty windows, half expecting to see
faces watching her, noting her invasion of their territory.

She had never minded being alone. She had spent most
of her life wandering alone in the farm country. But this
place was different. She did not feel alone. The street was
crowded with memories that were not her own. She caught
herself looking back over her shoulder, but no one was following.

She skirted a block where a fire had left blackened
beams and twisted wreckage. Wherever she had a choice,
she headed uphill, looking for high ground that would give
her a better view of the city. The streets climbed steeply, and
several times she thought about turning back or finding an
easier route. But the top of the hill always looked so close.
She kept climbing, despite the ache in her shoulder.

Just as the sun broke through the fog, she reached the
top of the hill and looked down on a sea of green leaves. Ivy
blanketed the street. The sturdy vines had enveloped the
cars and overrun the houses. The foliage softened the lines
of the buildings, blurring the hard angles. It had erased all
but the most prominent features: the peak of the roof on one
house, a jutting bay window on another. The lampposts
were towers of ivy; the cars were mounds of leaves. A radio
antenna rose from one such mound, the only visible sign of

the car below. A single strand of pale young ivy climbed the antenna, reaching for the sun.

The woman descended the hill, picking a path through the plants. She could have turned back, but there was something inviting about the leafy canyon between the ivy-covered houses. The air held a cool green scent, like the overgrown banks down by the creek near the farmhouse. The place reminded her of a story her mother had once told her, something about a princess who had slept for a thousand years. The rose garden that surrounded the royal castle had grown wild, making walls of thorns to protect the sleeping princess.

The wind blew and the leaves nodded. They brushed her ankles gently as she stepped among them. The rustling leaves seemed to be whispering softly, telling secrets that she could not understand.

The ivy had sealed the doors to most of the houses, permanently barring entry with networks of interlocking vines. But halfway up the block was a house with an open door. The ivy surrounded the opening, leaving a dark gap, like the entrance to a cave. Somewhere in the ivy a bird sang three high notes. The ivy leaves swayed, as if beckoning.

She was at the bottom of the stairs, looking up into the doorway, when she heard the rhythmic sound of metal on metal, a harsh inhuman noise that grew louder as she listened. She hesitated, then climbed the stairs and ducked inside the doorway.

A four-legged mechanical creature ran past the house, heading uphill. It reminded her of the alligator lizards that had sunbathed on the stone wall near the farmhouse, scurrying for cover when she approached. The creature's hide glistened with moisture from the fog; its legs moved jerkily, carrying it forward at a startling speed. The metal vanes that sprouted from its back rattled against one another. The creature seemed oblivious to its surroundings, hurrying past the house where the woman hid.

She watched the creature pass, then looked around the entryway. The ivy stopped at the doorway, not venturing into the house itself. Just inside the door, other plants had sprouted in the carpet: clover, wild grasses, miner's lettuce, and sorrel. The white walls of the foyer were laced with dark green: algae grew within the paint, spreading along cracks too fine for the eye to see.

Cautiously she stepped into the living room. Sunlight shone through the leaves that covered the windows, filling the room with dim green light. The clock on the mantel had stopped at twenty to three.

A Scrabble board lay on the low coffee table. Words crisscrossed the grid pattern: BLANKET, HELLO, GLOVE, GRAVE. Beside the board, the lid of the game box held wooden letter tiles placed facedown. A layer of mold had grown on the tiles, turning the wood to the color of tarnished copper. The woman studied the game board and wondered about its purpose. She read the words, but they made no sense together. Leaving the board untouched, she explored the rest of the house.

Long ago, rodents had chewed open all the packages in the kitchen, devouring the contents, scattering the wrappings, and defecating on the wreckage. A few rusting cans stood in one cupboard, surrounded by the tattered remnants of plastic bags. In a corner of the linoleum floor lay scraps of fur and scattered bones, the gnawed remains of a cat's feast.

She wandered upstairs. Framed photographs hung on the white walls of the hallway: a smiling man and woman and their two daughters watched the woman stroll through their home. She poked her head into the upstairs bathroom and was startled by a movement within the room. She raised her crossbow before realizing that the person who glared at her from across the room was only her reflection in a full-length mirror.

The bedroom door opened when she turned the knob. Wind blowing through a broken window sent dead leaves scurrying across the hardwood floor. Two skeletons—perhaps the man and the woman from the photos in the hall—lay in the bed. Birds and small animals had picked at the decaying flesh, tearing holes in the blankets that covered the bodies. Ants and beetles had cleared away the bits of flesh, leaving dry bones in a nest of tattered rags. The woman left them alone, closing the bedroom door tightly behind her and returning to the living room.

Outside the living room windows, the ivy rustled in the wind. Shadows swam around the room, wavering on the ceiling and darting into the corners. The patterns on the wallpaper seemed to move, as if they were blown by a breeze that she could not feel. The flickering green light made her think of the patterns of light and shadow that played on the bottom of the creek. Breathing was difficult; the air seemed thick and heavy. The shifting light made her feel dizzy and light-headed, and her injured shoulder ached.

She sat in a wooden chair beside the coffee table. The chair was mottled with the same greenish mold that covered the Scrabble tiles. She could hear a bird singing outside the house, a sweet soaring song stretched thin by distance. She sat quietly and listened. The house spoke: a soft sound like a floorboard creaking underfoot. A windowpane rattled, shaken by the same breeze that stirred the ivy. Wind blew through the open front door, and the house sighed.

Until now, she had been insulated from the city by Danny-boy, by Tiger, by Ms. Migsdale. Alone, she felt the city around her: a fragile and elaborate construction; a maze of streets as complex as the strands of a spider's web; houses in which people had lived and slept and made love, each individual leaving an indelible mark on the place. The city surrounded her, touching her with a subtle pressure, like the pressure of water on her skin when she swam in the creek. She could feel currents shifting this way and that, nudging her, pushing her.

She closed her eyes for a moment. Outside, the bird fell silent. The wind in the ivy sounded like beating wings. In the sudden hush, she heard a tiny click. And another. A third. She waited, but the room was quiet.

Her dizziness passed and the air seemed to lighten. Breathing became easier. She opened her eyes. The moving shadows were simply patterns caused by light through the leaves. The green light played on the lid of the Scrabble box. Three tiles were now face up, exposing pale wood that was untouched by mold. The woman leaned forward to look at the three letters: J, A, and X. JAX.

She said the word aloud and liked the sound of it. "Jax." She took the tiles from the box and slipped them into her pocket. "Jax," she said again, accepting her name. It felt right. She knew that it belonged to her.

When Jax left the house, she closed the door neatly behind her. She stood at the top of the stairs, looking at the ivy-covered houses across the street. The morning sun had burned away the fog. She felt strangely at home here. "Thank you," she said to the ivy and the sunlight. "Thanks for my name." She waited a moment, but nothing happened.

She turned back, climbing again to the top of the hill. From the crest, she could see what had once been a small park, now more like a miniature jungle. She made her way toward it.

Three rabbits dashed for cover at her approach. She slipped a bolt into her crossbow and sat quietly on a park bench that was upwind from where the rabbits had been grazing. One of the braver rabbits ventured out to feed. After a few moments the others joined it. She waited until one was quite close and got it with her first shot. She gutted the dead rabbit there, leaving the entrails for the wild dogs and cats.

Her shoulder had started to ache again. She headed downhill in the general direction of the hotel. At first, the street she followed seemed much the same as any other. Broken glass choked the gutters. Cars rested on the remnants of rotting tires. Through the rust and grime she could see words written in chrome: TOYOTA, DODGE, BUICK. She wondered what the words meant.

She was halfway back to the hotel when she noticed a strip of metal sheeting that stretched across the street, attached to lampposts at either end. Someone had cut through the metal; she could see through the oddly shaped holes. Jax puzzled over the shapes for a moment: they looked familiar somehow. After a moment, she realized that the shapes were letters of the alphabet, upside down and reversed, as if viewed in a mirror. She squinted at them uneasily, wondering why anyone would make such a sign.

She took a step forward, still staring up at the sign. A mirror set behind the metal sheeting reflected sunlight into her eyes, making her glance down. On the pavement at her feet, patches of light reflected from the mirror formed large letters that said: GARDEN OF LIGHT.

Moving cautiously, she continued down the street. No rubbish cluttered the gutters here; no cars were parked at the curb. The buildings on either side gleamed white, as if recently painted.

On the sun-dappled wall beside a tree, she saw a flicker of color: shattered rainbows darted across the white stucco, quick as lizards in the sun. Prisms, crystals, and shards of beveled glass hung from the branches, bobbing in the light breeze. Near the top, a mirror ball spun lazily, sending brilliant spots of sunlight everywhere. Jax held up her hand and colors flickered across her fingers: red as a sunset, green as new leaves, blue as a jay feather. The wind blew and the colors danced away, leaving Jax smiling at her own empty hand.

Farther down the street, sunlight sparkled on oddly shaped structures. A mirrored obelisk reflected her face from thousands of tiles, breaking her image into pieces that did not quite match up. Her reflection had no eyes. She moved her head, and hundreds of eyes blinked at her from the tiles. As she walked past, fragments of red from her shirt and blue from her jeans flickered across the mirrored surface like minnows in a pool.

A red arrow, pointing downward, invited her to duck through the opening in another structure. Cautiously, she peered into the opening, and then ducked inside. The structure's mirrored interior reflected her face endlessly; a crowd of women with ragged black hair surrounded her, all of them staring quizzically at reflections of reflections of reflections. She whirled in the center and the other women spun giddily. She laughed out loud and watched the other women laugh silently.

She ducked back through the opening. Mirrored structures crowded the street ahead of her: cubes measuring several feet on a side; pyramids that stood taller than she did. She walked among the giant shapes, dwarfed by the glittering surfaces. The mirrors took her reflection and distorted it—stretching her body, squashing it, making it ripple in impossible ways. At every turn she met her own reflection.

Feeling a touch of apprehension, she hesitated. In front of her, the structures formed a twisting corridor. She looked back and saw only her own reflection, multiplied a thousand times. From every surface, her own eyes challenged her.

There was a flicker of movement to her right—she caught a glimpse of it from the corner of her eye. She turned to see someone run from between two cubes and dash down the mirrored passageway. She saw only a flash of dark hair and a pale face, but Jax recognized her mother, knew her with a certainty that made words catch in her throat. Of course—the city had led her to her mother. She called out to her mother, "Wait! I'm here!" But the running figure vanished around a bend.

Without thinking, Jax followed, dodging among the mirrors. She listened for the sound of her mother's running footsteps, but heard only her own. The mirrors fenced her in, blocking her way and leading her into blind alleys. She charged into glass walls only to ricochet off and hurry in a new direction. Everywhere she looked, her own image confronted her. She dropped her crossbow and the rabbit carcass but did not stop—she could not stop running any more than she could stop breathing. Her feet kept pace with the wild beating of her heart.

She passed a stained glass window set in one wall of the corridor. The Virgin Mary smiled from the window as Jax rushed by. Jax followed the twisting path: choosing a right fork, then a left, then a right.

Mary smiled with infinite patience as Jax passed her again. A left fork, a right—and Mary appeared around the corner.

Jax leaned against the wall opposite the window, fighting for breath. Sunlight sparkled through the halo that circled Mary's head. Plump children with stubby wings hovered over her. Between her hands, someone had glued a mirror. Jax closed her eyes, unwilling to look at herself.

She took deep breaths, waiting for her heart to slow to its normal pace. Her mother was gone. She was alone, but that didn't matter. She would find a way out and look for her mother elsewhere in the city. She didn't need any help.

Her breathing became steady; her heartbeat slackened. In the darkness behind her closed eyelids, she listened to a bird singing in the distance. Then another sound: shuffling footsteps coming closer. She opened her eyes and put a hand on her knife. She could hear a man talking: "Take it easy now. Just stay where you are, and I'll find you."

A balding man in a worn gray suit shuffled around the corner, still muttering reassurances. "Now everything's just fine. I'll get you out of here." His pale blue necktie (marked in the center with some unidentifiable stain) matched his pale blue eyes, which peered anxiously from behind wire-rimmed eyeglasses.

"I was watching from the roof," he said, gesturing vaguely upward. "You seemed a bit upset, so I thought I'd . . ."

For the first time, he noticed the knife in her hand. He spread his empty hands. "No need for that. No need at all."

"Did you see where my mother went?" she asked.

"Your mother?" He shook his head. "You're the only person I saw."

"I was following her," Jax insisted. "She was just ahead of me." She shook her head, staring at the mirrors around her. "I came to the city to find her. I know she's here."

"Ah," he said, shaking his head. "The city plays tricks sometimes. Leads people astray."

"I know I saw her."

He shrugged. "You may well have. But she's gone now." He held out his hand. "Here now. Come along and I'll take you back to where you dropped that weapon of yours."

Reluctantly, she took his hand and let him lead her back through the maze. At each fork he confidently chose a path, talking all the while. "Back before the Plague, there were mazes like this in amusement parks and fun houses. Well, not quite like this, of course, but similar. People take a certain pleasure in being disoriented, I think. Of course I was trying to capture something of the feeling of the city. Loss of control, confusion, uncertainty."

Jax stared around her, certain she had never been down this corridor before.

"Almost there," he said. "Ah, here we are."

She snatched her crossbow from the ground at his feet, grateful to feel the smooth stock in her hands again. She picked up the carcass of the rabbit and looked around. The spot still looked unfamiliar.

"Surprised?" he said. "Didn't seem like the same spot?" He smiled encouragingly. "You'll get used to it. Good practice for living in the city. Now come along and I'll show you the way out." Over his shoulder, he said, "My name is Frank, by the way. You have a name?"

"Jax," she said. She liked the sound of it. A short, strong, angular sort of name.

"I see. Well, Danny-boy's out looking for a woman with no name. I guess you're the wrong one. Funny—I wouldn't figure that there were two strangers roaming around."

"It's a new name," she said. "Danny-boy doesn't know it yet."

"In that case, Danny-boy was searching for you. He seemed to think you were lost."

The spaces between the mirrored walls grew wider. When Jax saw the empty street up ahead, she relaxed.

"Here we are," Frank said. "I hope you're feeling better." He seemed anxious and concerned.

She nodded. "I'm fine."

"I'll take you through the maze again sometime, if you like. And I'll show you the other things I'm working on. I've made a camera obscura in a house down in North Beach. And I'm building a crystal palace on the other side of town. Danny-boy knows where it is. You should come visit."

She nodded. "Maybe I will."

He smiled at her. "Perhaps I'd best walk you home. You can run into some strange things in the city, if you don't know your way around." He strolled down the street at her side.

For a time, they walked together in silence. She was uncomfortably aware that he was studying her face. "You know," he said at last, "you're not at all as I imagined you would be."

"What do you mean?"

"Tommy describes you as a barbarian, barely civilized." The observation was made in a matter-of-fact tone that blunted the implied criticism. "Of course, he's fascinated by you—but that's mostly because he's met so few strangers. Ms. Migsdale found you quite secretive, a little mysterious. And Danny-boy was worried about you, seemed to think you'd get lost or hurt." Frank hesitated, frowning. "Now don't take all this wrong. I just collect opinions, that's all. Viewing a subject through several opinions is a little like traveling through a hall of mirrors, wouldn't you say? It provides an interesting shift in perspective."

She nodded uneasily, feeling a little dizzy from all his talk. Her shoulder ached even more, and she was suddenly very hungry.

"It's important not to believe too much in the mirror reality," he said. "Can't trust it. It's like the city. Everyone sees it differently."

She trudged toward the hotel, concerned only with the reality of food to eat and a bed in which she could rest. Up ahead, she could see the tall tower of the Hyatt Hotel that stood on one side of Union Square.

"I know the way from here," she said. "Thanks for your help."

He nodded. "All right, I'll let you go on alone. You can find me up by the mirror maze most days. Come back and visit."

"I will."

Jax found Danny-boy sitting in the easy chair on the sidewalk. He was holding her glass globe in his hands, watching the glitter swirl. He looked up at the sound of her footsteps.

"The park up there is good for rabbits." She held out the carcass that she carried.

"I thought maybe you'd left. I thought you were gone for good."

"Why did you think that?" He was silent. She continued, "I have a name now. The city gave it to me." She pulled the tiles from her pocket and held them out for him to see.

"Jax," he read. "That's your name?"

"Sure is." She was tired, but happy to have a name at last. She held out the rabbit. "We can eat the meat for dinner. I'll cure the skin for you too."

"You know, I can show you around the city," he said. "I'd like to. It's a dangerous place if you don't know your way around. You have to be careful."

She frowned at him, surprised at his concern. "I'm always careful," she said.

CHAPTER
10

When Danny-boy had awakened and found the woman gone, he had panicked. He was used to emptiness: empty streets, empty houses, empty city. But the emptiness of the bedroom was different from all that. It was like the sudden silence when a person stops singing halfway through a song.

He had imagined her lost, confused, injured, trapped. She would fall through the rotting floor of a house; she would be bitten by a rabid wild dog. She would be bewildered by the maze of streets, unable to retrace her steps to the hotel. She would leave the city and he would never see her again. He imagined the worst.

"I didn't know what to say when she came back," Danny-boy told The Machine. He was sitting on the hood of a cherry red '67 Chevrolet, watching The Machine work on the industrial paint rig. Back before the Plague, The Machine's workshop had been an auto body shop and a few of the cars remained. The floor was stained with grease and spattered with brightly colored paints. "I was afraid that she'd gone for good."

The Machine fiddled with the rig, aimed the nozzle at the wall, and switched on the compressor. The contraption coughed up a blob of paint, then sputtered, sending drops flying in random directions. The Machine switched it off. Using the delicate pinchers of his third hand, he began to dismantle it.

"She seems so temporary," Danny-boy said. "Like she

99

could vanish any time. Poof, she's gone." He waved his
hands. "I never know what she's thinking. She doesn't say
much."

The Machine shrugged, still carefully disassembling the
nozzle and laying the pieces on the cement floor. The mechanism of his hand clicked softly as it moved. "That could be
an advantage," he said. "Most people around here talk too
much."

Danny-boy shook his head, not really listening. "I
don't know what I would have done if she had gone. Tried
to find her, I guess."

The Machine frowned, but Danny-boy could not tell if
he was frowning at the parts of the nozzle or at Danny-boy's
words.

"You don't like her," Danny-boy said. "Why not?"

The Machine began cleaning each tiny part with paint
thinner. "I don't like most people," he said. "Because most
people don't like me."

"How do you know that she doesn't like you? She
doesn't know you."

The Machine methodically polished a small brass ring
and set it on the floor with the other parts. "Guilty until
proven innocent. I don't trust her."

Danny-boy shook his head. "She's different. I don't
know what it is about her. . . ."

The Machine interrupted. "I know what it is." He
looked up from the nozzle. His voice was heavy with sar-
casm. "Don't you recognize it? It's love. Also known as
hormones. Biological reactions. It's the meat talking, not the
brain. One of many reasons that I'm glad I'm a machine."

"Nothing wrong with biological reactions," Danny-boy
said quietly. "Is there?"

The Machine muttered something but did not look up.
Danny-boy knew The Machine was avoiding his eyes.

"What's the problem?" Danny-boy said.

"You know the problem," The Machine said. He was
breathing faster. "She left and you hurt. A biological reaction. Pain." He glared at Danny-boy. "And this is just the
beginning—you care more and you'll hurt more. A simple
equation."

"But, T.M.," Danny-boy began.

"If I weren't a machine, I would have died with the others in the Plague," The Machine said. "I would have died in the empty house, where only the machines kept running, going about their business as if nothing had happened. Everything was changed, but the machines didn't care. I realized that it was better not to care."

Danny-boy looked down at his own hands. He knew that all the talking in the world wouldn't convince The Machine. "It's not all bad, T.M.," he said. "You can't just look at the pain. You have to—"

"It's dangerous," The Machine interrupted. "Be careful, that's all I have to say. Watch yourself."

When Danny-boy returned to the hotel, he found Jax asleep in the easy chair. A shaft of afternoon sun squeezed between the buildings to spotlight her. She was curled up like a sleeping cat. In her lap, she held the glass globe. She smiled in her sleep, her face relaxed and peaceful. A young monkey that was perched on the back of the chair peered down at her.

Danny-boy had never been in love before, not really. For a while, when he was fifteen, he had courted one of Duff's daughters, a pretty blonde who giggled at everything he said. They had kissed in the shadows by the lake, and he remembered the silky feel of her breast beneath his hand. Apparently, Duff had found out. By the end of the next week she was engaged to a farmer in Marin, a match arranged by her father. Danny-boy had mourned for a while, but it hadn't mattered much.

Jezebel ran up to the chair and the monkey sprang down and then climbed up the hotel's awning. From there, it chattered at the dog.

"Jax?" Danny-boy said softly.

Jax opened her eyes, and for a moment her sleepy smile lingered. "Strange to have a name," she murmured. "Never thought I would."

He sat in the other chair. "The name suits you."

"Yeah?" She straightened up, yawning. "I thought it did. But I didn't know."

"It does." He stopped, not knowing what to say. He wanted to reach over and take her hand, but he was afraid that would bring the wary expression back to her face.

"Ms. Migsdale stopped by," she said. "Asked me to remind you that there's a town meeting at City Hall tonight. She said I should come and tell people about Fourstar."

"Sure," he said. "I can introduce you to everyone. After all, if you're going to stay here for a while, you'd best get to know people."

"I suppose you're right."

He smiled in relief. So she did plan to stick around. "That's great. That's just great."

She looked at him as if he were crazy, but for the moment, he didn't care.

A bonfire burned at the foot of the marble staircase, taking the chill off the evening air. The high arched ceiling of the rotunda was black with the soot of past fires. Beyond the light cast by the fire, candles made puddles of yellow light. The elaborate carvings that decorated the walls of the rotunda were covered with wax drippings.

A crowd had already gathered when Danny-boy and Jax arrived. The sweet smell of marijuana mingled with the wood smoke. To one side of the hall, Gambit was playing a percussion instrument that he had constructed from laboratory glassware. A harmonica player and a guitarist were jamming with him. Around them, people sat and stood in noisy clumps, talking and laughing. Gambit's music bubbled through the conversations like water flowing over polished stones.

"Hey, Danny-boy!" Danny-boy looked up and saw Snake waving to him from a group of people at the top of the staircase. "Come here—we gotta talk to you."

As always, Snake wore his leathers. His left ear was twisted, a knotted fold of flesh that looked a little like a flower bud that had only started to unfold. A scar began at the mangled ear and extended along the line of his jaw. As if to call attention to the scar, he shaved the left half of his head. The tattoo of a rattlesnake writhed across the bare scalp, heading for the protective thicket of his curly dark hair. For once, he was not wearing dark glasses, and his eyes looked curiously naked.

Danny-boy waved back. Jezebel, who did not like crowds, pressed against his leg on one side. Jax stood on the other. Danny-boy glanced at her. Her right hand had dropped to her knife. "I'll introduce you to everyone," he said, trying to reassure her. "That's Snake. He probably wants to talk to me about the Golden Gate Bridge. And you can see Ms. Migsdale over there; you've met her. She's talking to Books—he lives in the library. I'm sure Tiger's around here somewhere. The guys around Snake are all graffiti artists. The folks by the fire are all poets of one sort or another. Everyone will be glad to meet you." Jax's expression did not change. He touched her hand gently. "It'll be all right." She nodded then, but her face did not relax.

Snake called to Danny-boy again, and he made his way toward the group, leading Jax by the hand. En route, he greeted friends, introducing Jax. "This is my friend, Jax. That's right, the woman without a name. She has a name now. Jax, this is . . ." Rose, Mercedes, Zatch, Ruby, Mario, Lily—Jax nodded stiffly at each person he introduced. She kept a strong grip on his hand. It took the better part of half an hour to make their way up the stairs.

As Danny-boy had expected, Snake wanted to talk about the Golden Gate Bridge. He had been convincing some of the artists in the group around him that they should do sections of the bridge. Danny-boy took a swig of homemade wine from the bottle that was passed his way, and he nodded. "That's right. The design is up to you. You can use any shade of blue you want, but it's got to be blue."

"Why blue?" asked a skinny redhead who went by the name of Old Man Hat. "I don't like blue."

Danny-boy shrugged. "It was Duff's idea. He chose the color. If you don't like it, don't sign up."

"Who decides what qualifies as blue?" asked another. "I have a broad definition."

"I decide. I supply the paint."

"I'll sign up," said Old Man Hat. "I guess there are worse colors."

"Me too," said the artist with the broad definition of blue. Several others nodded.

"That's great. Come to the toll booth next Saturday at noon, and I'll assign you to sections. If you want to get started earlier, talk to me after the meeting and we'll work something out." He was noting the names of the artists who wanted to paint, when Books started calling for silence.

"Come to order," the old man shouted. "The sooner we get started, the sooner we'll be done."

Danny-boy looked around and found that Jax and Jezebel had vanished. "Where did Jax go?" he asked the woman nearest him, but she just hushed him and motioned for him to sit so that the meeting could start. Reluctantly, he sat.

"Any announcements?" Books said. Several people made announcements: Mario, a poet who ran a fishing boat, had a supply of smoked red snapper for trade; Frank was looking for a new supply of prisms and would welcome any leads; a new play would be performed on Friday at five, if the weather was good, by the Vallencourt Fountain; Books would be holding a poetry reading in the library on Saturday at sunset; participants should bring candles.

During the announcements, Danny-boy scanned the crowd for Jax. He finally spotted her sitting beside Ms. Migsdale. She had a spooked look on her face.

"Community business," Books called. The first business was a long wrangle between two sculptors. Both of them had chosen to build a major work in the parking lot at the top of Twin Peaks. Bartlett, a bearlike man with a surprisingly soft voice, had begun erecting a replica of Stonehenge, using refrigerators instead of stones. He explained, at great length, that the Twin Peaks location was the only place he had found in the city where the appropriate astronomical events could be observed. Zatch, a lanky black man who lived with Ruby, had planned a kinetic sculpture for the same location. "I need a place with a lot of wind," he said. "That parking lot was just fine."

Danny-boy ignored the discussion that followed. He had heard it all before. Several times a year this sort of conflict came up and generated what seemed like endless discussion. Usually, whichever artist was the most desperate or stubborn stuck it out and got the site. The other gave up and found another.

"I'd put money on Bartlett," Snake said in Danny-boy's ear. "He's a touch crazy, and crazy people got stamina."

"No bet," Danny-boy whispered back. "I think you're right. I heard Zatch talking earlier about the principle of the thing."

Snake shook his head. "He's out of luck. Principles don't count nearly as much as stamina."

After much discussion, the matter was referred to committee. Zatch sat down, shaking his head. "He'll have another site by next week," Snake muttered.

"I'd like to introduce a newcomer to the city," Books was saying. "She has something to say." He beckoned Jax forward into the light. Danny-boy watched her glance at Ms. Migsdale and then step forward. Her eyes were wide and panicky, and her hand rested on the handle of her knife.

A few people in the back were talking. Jax waited without speaking until they fell silent. "My name is Jax," she said quietly. Too quietly, Danny-boy thought. Then he realized that people had fallen silent and were leaning forward to listen. "I grew up in Woodland, a town near Sacramento. I've come here to tell you that a man named Fourstar is going to invade San Francisco." She glanced at Ms. Migsdale, glanced at the floor. For a moment Danny-boy thought she might bolt from the room, but she just paused for a moment, then went on. "In the market, I heard that he's invaded other places. He took Fresno last year; Modesto the year before. I don't know much about it, but I know he hates San Francisco. He blames you for the Plague, he says that you hoard resources. He says that you'll invade Sacramento if he doesn't invade San Francisco. He says he wants to bring the country back together. I don't know much about that, either. I don't know much about this place that Fourstar calls America, but I'll tell you something—if Fourstar thinks America is great, I don't like it. I don't like it at all." She stopped again, her face tight and controlled. "My mother came from San Francisco. She told me to come and warn you. She said you would have to fight. You'll have to

kill Fourstar. You'll have to kill him, or he'll kill all of you."
She looked directly at Danny-boy. "I guess that's all I have
to say."

Danny-boy took no part in the discussion that followed. Books fielded questions and Jax answered them,
mostly with "I don't know." She didn't know how many
men Fourstar had, she didn't know the date of his planned
invasion, she didn't know what type of equipment he would
be using.

"People have been talking about this Fourstar dude for
years," Snake said softly in Danny-boy's ear. "So what's
new?"

Danny-boy watched Jax, standing beside Books. In the
firelight, she cast an enormous shadow that danced on the
curved wall. "Jax seems to think it's going to happen soon."

"You believe her?"

Danny-boy nodded slowly. "I think so. I wish I
didn't."

Snake shook his head. "I'm not convinced."

A few people proposed immediate military action. Others proposed alliances—with the Black Dragons in Oakland,
with the farmers in Marin. Danny-boy leaned back against
the marble steps, knowing that nothing would be resolved
that night. He listened to the artists bluster about what they
would do to Fourstar if he set foot in the city.

Ms. Migsdale and Books were the last to leave City
Hall, lingering to extinguish the coals of the fire and blow
out the guttering candles. Together they crossed the Civic
Center Plaza, heading for the library. The waning moon
touched the trees with silver; the night wind coaxed a few
high notes from the aeolian harp.

"Danny-boy didn't seem like himself tonight," Ms.
Migsdale commented.

"Didn't say more than two words to me all evening,"
Books grumbled. "Practically snatched that young lady
away from me and insisted she had to go home and rest."

"What did you think of the young lady?"

"Very pleasant," Books said. "I suggested that she

come visit me at the library. She seems to be very interested in the city's history."

Ms. Migsdale raised her eyebrows. "I like her, but I wouldn't call her pleasant. I swear she bared her teeth when Zatch suggested we try negotiating with Fourstar."

"Oh, come now. She was just a little tense. Not used to speaking in front of groups."

"Danny-boy was on edge too," Ms. Migsdale mused. "But I expect the tension will ease somewhat after they sleep together."

Books stopped and stared at her. "Elvira, you shock me sometimes."

Ms. Migsdale glanced at him. "Now, Edgar, you might as well admit that you were thinking the same thing."

"I don't believe I was."

"Well, then you're overlooking the obvious, and that's a poor trait for a researcher. Come on now—let's get in out of the cold."

Books followed her across the plaza. "I think you're making some rash assumptions," he said as they reached the library steps. "How do you know that she won't just leave the city? You just said you thought she was rather wild."

"Not wild exactly," Ms. Migsdale said. "Shy, in a wild kind of way. But I'll bet on Danny-boy. He's always had a nice way with wild things."

CHAPTER
11

Mercedes had spent the days of her childhood leaning on the fender of her older brother's 1965 Chevrolet, watching Antonio work under the hood. Antonio was seven years her senior. He had quit high school when she was still in elementary school. When she was in junior high, he had moved out of the family home to share an apartment with two friends, coming home for dinners on Sundays just to keep their mother happy.

Antonio had worked at the corner gas station, pumping gas, fixing cars, tinkering with his own Chevy low rider. After school Mercedes had hung out at the station, watching her brother work. On Sunday afternoons she had helped him wax his car, smearing white paste over the already satiny finish, then rubbing and polishing until she could see her face in the shiny black paint.

A line of grease was permanently embedded beneath each of Antonio's fingernails. On his left wrist was a tattoo that said "Maryann." In his freshman year of high school, Antonio had given himself the tattoo with a needle and the ink from a ball-point pen. The girl, a blonde who was trying out for the cheerleading squad, had broken up with him anyway.

Mercedes's dad hadn't liked her hanging around at the gas station. But then, her dad hadn't liked the boys she dated (tough guys with bad reputations) or the clothes she wore (faded jeans with oversized shirts) or her music, her friends, her constant swearing. So she had hung out at the gas station and told her parents that she was studying at the library.

Sometimes Mercedes had helped her brother with repairs: after years of watching him work, she was quick and knowledgeable. Her small hands could squeeze into spaces where his could not. Her ability to diagnose a car's ailments bordered on the miraculous: she would tilt her head to one side, listen to an engine rattle or wheeze or grind, and then give a repair estimate accurate to the dollar. She had planned to go to work with Antonio at the gas station when she finished high school, and to save her money for a Chevy low rider of her own. But things didn't work out that way.

Her mother had been the first in the family to sicken with the Plague. Then her father. Mercedes had taken care of her parents, bringing food and water, draping cold washcloths over their foreheads, buying over-the-counter remedies that promised to relieve the aches and pains of fever. The hospital emergency room sent her home with nothing. The newspapers were filled with articles on the Plague: they offered warnings, but no hope.

Though she had never had much faith in God or in the Catholic church, she prayed as she took care of her parents, pleading with the Virgin Mary to help her, asking Jesus to make her mother and father well. Late one morning, after a sleepless night, she fell asleep in the armchair by her parents' bed. When she woke in the afternoon, both her mother and her father were quiet, lying still and lifeless beneath a thin blanket. Her mother's head was cushioned on her father's arm.

She went to the gas station to tell Antonio and found him slumped in the backseat of his car. His forehead felt hot and dry. When she woke him, he did not seem to recognize her.

She took the car keys from his pocket and drove him to her family's home. There, she nursed him, even when she fell sick herself. But all the tea and orange juice and cold remedies and prayers made no difference. He died, just as so many died. She stood at his bedside, looking down at him.

His hands were pale, except for the rim of dark grease beneath each nail. The tattoo was dark against his skin.

Wearing her brother's old high school letter jacket, she left her family's home. Though sick with fever, she was overcome with an angry restlessness that made her run through the empty city, screaming in a dry hoarse voice. She carried the tire iron from her brother's car, and she used it to break store windows, reveling in the sound of shattering glass.

On the corner of Valencia and 19th, a group of looters saw her and ran toward her, but she swung the tire iron with great authority and raved in a high feverish voice about the Virgin Mary and the blood of Jesus Christ. They ran, from fear of the fever rather than the tire iron, but she never knew that.

She walked down Valencia Street, smashing the windshields of cars and trucks, until she could walk no farther. Then she found a bed in the back of a furniture store, wandering in through a door that had been broken by other vandals. She collapsed on the bed and slept for a long time.

She woke up thristy but still alive. She got a drink from the water cooler in the manager's office, and then started walking with no destination in mind. The sunlight made her blink, and she had to pick her way around the shards of broken glass that littered the sidewalk. Now and then, she passed a body: a middle-aged man collapsed behind the wheel of a car; an old lady curled in a doorway; a teen-ager —perhaps one of the looters who had threatened her— sprawled in the display window of a jewelry store, among the gems and broken glass.

Antonio walked beside her and talked to her. He was very pale. She could see bits of broken glass on the sidewalk sparkling through his feet. He was dead.

"Aren't you going to talk to me?" he asked her.

"Can't talk to you," she said. "You're dead."

A burning cigarette hung from the corner of his mouth; his hands were stuffed deep in his pockets. "Yeah," he said. "I guess so."

After a moment, she asked, "What's it like, being dead?"

He shrugged and took another drag on his cigarette. "I don't have to worry about smoking too much," he said.

"I want to die," she told him.

"Ah, *muchacha,* you don't want to do that."

"Tony, I do. I want to die. Ma's dead, Dad's dead, you're dead. I want to die too." She ran her hands back through her hair.

He shook his head angrily. "I don't want to hear that kind of talk. That's stupid."

"You sound just like Dad," she said. He turned away from her and she immediately regretted her words, remembering Tony's arguments with their father. "Hey, I'm sorry. Tony, wait! I didn't mean it."

He stopped and waited for her. "Maybe Dad was right sometimes," he said. She had trouble reading his expression; his face was growing more transparent. "Did you ever think of that?"

"Why should I keep on living?" she asked him.

"You got to have a reason?" he asked. He shrugged again. "You can do anything now. Live anywhere. Take whatever you want."

"I don't care about that."

A shadow of a grin crossed his face: he never stayed angry long. "But you got to have a reason? All right then, stay alive so you can take care of my car. I leave it to you. You're responsible for it. OK?"

"Tony, that's stupid," she said. "Why should I . . ."

She was talking to herself. She was two blocks from her home, standing in the middle of the street. She walked home, but did not enter. She took Tony's car and drove around the city, looking for a nice place to live.

That was a long time ago. On the day that Jax got her name, Mercedes squatted in the Union Square garden, picking the last of the tomatoes from the straggling vines. She looked up and saw Antonio standing on the nearest path. She sat back on her heels and stared at him. In the years immediately following the Plague, he had appeared every few weeks, stopping in to chat with her. But she had not seen him for several years.

He was smoking a cigarette and staring off into the

distance. He still wore the same tattered denim jacket, the same grease-stained jeans. "Hey, *muchacha,*" he said.

"I'm not a little girl anymore, Tony," she told him. "I'm older than you are now."

"Maybe so. But I'm still your big brother." He took a drag on his cigarette. "Came to warn you," he said.

"About what?"

"An army's coming," he said. "You'd better get ready."

"That's what the stranger said."

"You listen to that stranger, *muchacha*. She knows what she's talking about."

"Get ready how?" she asked.

He left the cigarette dangling from his mouth and spread his hands, as if there were no words to describe the necessary preparations. "That's up to you. I'm just telling you that trouble's coming. After that, it's up to you." Tony dropped his cigarette on the ground and crushed it with his foot. And then he was gone, leaving a scent of cigarette smoke that filled her with a longing for days past.

Danny-boy courted Jax cautiously, like a man trying to catch a butterfly without injuring it. Or possibly more like a man trying to catch a wasp without being stung. Either way, he was careful; he went slowly.

He watched her surreptitiously, haunted by the wariness that he saw in her eyes. Sometimes, while she slept, he crept into the bedroom and sat by her bed. In sleep, her face relaxed. Her raggedly cut hair curled on her cheeks; her expression was grave and earnest. Her hands, clutching the blanket that covered her, were so small. At odd moments during the day—while fishing for surfperch, setting a rabbit snare, searching a hardware store for blue paint—he found himself thinking about her hands: so small, yet callused by hard work and rough living.

Each evening, he made dinner, and they sat together on the roof and watched the sunset. She did not talk much. She answered questions if he asked them, but her answers were short and matter-of-fact, tossed off quickly.

"What did you do today?" he asked.

"Walked," she said.

"Where did you go?"

She jerked her head to the west but said nothing more.

He offered to show her around the city, and she declined, shaking her head quickly. He let a day go by, then suggested again that he might show her around. Her eyes grew cautious and she seemed to draw into herself, like a cat crouching to spring or flee. He did not make the suggestion a third time.

She did not make small talk, and she seemed quite comfortable with silence. He would begin talking to fill the silence and would find himself rambling on, telling her of his life, his plans, his dreams. Her silence drew him in, an emptiness waiting to be filled. He told her about Emerald; he told her what he remembered of his parents; he told her about growing up in the city.

He brought her gifts: a bouquet of exotic blossoms picked in the ruins of the greenhouse in Golden Gate Park, a paper Chinese parasol painted with herons in flight, a wind-up plastic gorilla that spat out sparks as it walked. She accepted each present politely, but she seemed puzzled, as if she did not know what to make of him.

During the day he left her alone, retreating to his work on the Golden Gate Bridge. On a foggy afternoon a few weeks after Jax had arrived in San Francisco, he was at the bridge, waiting for Mercedes and Snake.

The fog was coming in. To the west, he could see a bank of white mist, rolling slowly toward the city. The first tendrils drifted lazily past the cables of the bridge. Looking eastward, he could see Alcatraz Island and the buildings of downtown, but he knew that the fog would hide them in just a few hours. Somewhere beneath the bridge, a sea lion bayed.

He strolled along the bridge, admiring the work that had been done so far. Danny-boy had made no effort to dictate the style of each artist's section. He provided the materials and assigned a space. After that, it was up to the artist.

Some of the artists preferred the broad surfaces offered by the enormous support cables and the bases of the towers.

Others welcomed the creative challenge offered by the guardrail with its minimal surface area.

One of Danny-boy's favorite pieces was a reclining nude, painted on the thin bars that supported the guardrail. Her toes were at the toll plaza; her head about 100 feet down the bridge. From most positions, the dark blue marks on the pale blue background looked like random lines that did not connect. But if you stood in just the right spot, the connections suddenly became clear; your eye filled in the gaps between the support bars, and the blue nude appeared.

Danny-boy smiled as he passed a section of railing marked with footprints. A dancer had painted the railing turquoise blue, dipped his feet in navy paint, then strolled along the top, leaving his bare footprints along a fifty-foot stretch.

Danny-boy stared across the bridge toward the hills of Marin, aware of the impossible grandeur of the task he had set himself. After a year of work, only the railing was nearly done. The base of each tower was blue, but the rest of both towers and most of the cables were still their original orange. Before Jax's arrival, the interminable nature of the project hadn't bothered him. But recently, he had started worrying. Suppose Fourstar and his army arrived before he finished the bridge? He had not anticipated such an interruption, and he saw no way to finish up quickly.

Danny-boy heard the distant roar of Snake's motorcycle and strolled back toward the toll plaza. As always, Snake made a dramatic entrance, speeding through the toll gate and skidding through a 360-degree turn before he screeched to a halt. He shut off his engine and swung off the bike. "Yo, Danny-boy," he called. "How goes it?" His leathers creaked faintly as he walked toward Danny-boy.

"Not bad." Danny-boy waved a hand at the tower nearest them. "So take a look. You still willing to tackle it?"

Snake looked up at the tower, its top now hidden by the drifting fog. "Sure, man. I've got a dozen guys lined up to help me. One of 'em used to be a rock climber. We got ropes and we've been practicing. I'm a smooth man on a wall these days. Been thinking about changing my name from Snake to Spider, I'm that good."

Danny-boy grinned at Snake's bravado. "All right then, what else will you need?"

Together they strolled toward the tower where Danny-boy stored his equipment. Snake worked exclusively in spray paint, which limited his selection of colors. But after some haggling, they chose three shades of blue that Danny-boy had in abundance. They were heading back to the toll plaza when Snake asked the question that Danny-boy had known was inevitable. "So, who did you con into doing the other tower?"

Danny-boy took a deep breath. "Who else has the balls?"

Snake kept walking, shaking his head. "Don't know anyone, offhand. I . . ." Then he stopped and stared at Danny-boy. "You don't mean you're going to have Mercedes and her *cholos* doing it."

Danny-boy nodded. "Sure do."

"Oh, man, you're crazy. They'll ruin it. You can't be serious."

There had been, over the years, a number of territorial disputes between the Neo-Mayanists that Mercedes headed and the other graffiti artists in the city. Mercedes had once, for religious reasons, painted over one of Snake's murals. When called to task at Town Council, she had apologized for painting over Snake's work, but claimed that it was necessary. The wall on which she had painted was located at the exact geographic center of the city, a spot of considerable religious significance. The new painting was of prime importance to her group. She had been admonished by the Council, but no disciplinary action had been taken. And Snake held a grudge.

"I'm serious," Danny-boy said. He had known the Snake would react badly, but he saw no way around it. "I'm sure they'll do a fine job."

"Forget it," Snake said. "No way we can cooperate with them."

They had reached the toll plaza and Snake's motorcycle. "That's too bad," Danny-boy said. "I figured that tower would be a prime location for your work. Every trader coming into town will see it."

"Don't try to flatter me, man. I know you can't do the bridge without us."

"I wouldn't count on that," Danny-boy said softly. "I could have Mercedes do both towers."

Snake turned away and walked to the railing. Danny-boy followed, saying nothing.

"You'd do that," Snake said at last.

Danny-boy looked down at the waves crashing against Fort Point. "I wouldn't want to. But I guess I would."

Snake shook his head in disgust.

"You could think of this as a trial run. If Fourstar invades the city, you may want to work with Mercedes to keep him out."

"You're just full of comfort, aren't you?" Snake spat over the railing and then turned to face Danny-boy. "Maybe I can work it out. I'll talk to the others."

"Fine." Danny-boy knew that the others would follow Snake's lead.

"You're making a mistake, but I guess you'll find that out when it's done."

"Maybe so."

Snake roared away just as Mercedes arrived on horseback. He accelerated past her, making her horse shy, and sped off without looking back.

"Still an asshole," she said to Danny-boy as she dismounted.

"Yeah, but he'll do a good job on the tower."

She shook her head and tied her horse to the toll gate. Together they strolled toward the nearest tower. Mercedes glanced around her.

"It'll be great when it's done," she said. "But I wonder, will you have time to finish it before Fourstar arrives?"

Danny-boy stared at her in surprise. "What makes you so sure he's coming. At the meeting the other night, you didn't seem convinced."

"Changed my mind," Mercedes said. "Decided that maybe we can trust this stranger after all."

"Of course we can." Danny-boy defended Jax immediately.

"Ah," Mercedes said, grinning at him. "Is that how it is?"

"What do you mean?" He felt his face growing hot, and he looked away.

She put her arm around his shoulder affectionately. "Are you in love with this little wild woman?"

He said nothing, but his face burned.

"Ah, Danny-boy, your ears give you away. They're red as the sunset. You might as well talk."

He kept his face turned away. "I don't know."

"There's nothing wrong with being in love, *chico*. But if you're in love, why aren't you happy? Come on—tell me about it." She led him to the base of the tower. They sat cross-legged on the cement sidewalk with their backs to the metal tower. "Now talk," she said.

He told her his problems. He could not tell how Jax felt about him. He brought her presents, but he didn't know if she liked them. He woke in the middle of the night and tiptoed into the bedroom to check on her, afraid she had left without warning. Mercedes listened patiently.

"You're afraid she'll leave, so you're trying to keep her," Mercedes said at last. "You'd like to lock her up, so you could be sure she wouldn't go."

Danny-boy protested weakly. "That's silly," he said. "I don't want to lock her up. I just don't want her to get hurt, wandering around by herself. It's easy to get lost." But his words carried no conviction. Just the night before, he had caught himself wishing she had broken a leg rather than her collarbone. Then she would have to stay put.

Mercedes nodded in satisfaction. "Exactly," she said. "She might not come back."

"I didn't say that."

"But it's what you meant." Mercedes patted his leg gently. "Face it. The only way to deal with her is to let her go."

Danny-boy shook his head. "How can I let her go? I don't even have her."

"Help her go where she wants to go, then. Give her what she needs."

The next day, Danny-boy gave her a bicycle: a sturdy

blue ten-speed from a bike shop on Haight Street. Jax was out when he wheeled it home. He spent the better part of the afternoon giving it an overhaul: repacking the wheel bearings, checking the brakes, adjusting the gear-shifting mechanism, replacing the tires. Jax came home as he was finishing. As usual, one of the monkeys was following her. When Jezebel barked at the monkey, it sprang to the roof of a nearby car and then ignored the dog.

"This is for you," Danny-boy said. "With this you can get around town faster. You can go wherever you want." He felt sick at heart.

She looked uneasy. "I can walk all over town," she said.

Her reluctance confused him. Having started this project, he was determined to carry it through. "Riding a bike is faster than walking. You can get from one end of town to the other in just a couple of hours."

She looked at the bicycle and wet her lips, but did not say anything.

"I'll adjust the seat to your height, and it'll be ready to ride."

She hesitated, looking fierce.

"What's wrong?" he said sharply. He was torn and confused about this, and she wasn't helping.

"I don't know how to ride it," she said at last.

He could tell that she hated admitting that she couldn't ride. Her back was stiff and her hand rested lightly on her knife. "I'll teach you," he said softly. "It's not hard. Come on. Sit on the seat and let me adjust the height."

Danny-boy held the bicycle upright while she straddled it reluctantly. Her feet did not quite touch the pedals. He had her get off, then he lowered the seat. "Come on. You can try it out."

He showed her how to hold the handlebars and wheel the bicycle as she walked. Wheeling his own bicycle alongside her, he led her to a stretch of street that was relatively free of potholes and debris. A faded brown Toyota sedan had been abandoned in the middle of the block, but otherwise there were no obstacles. The monkey followed, found a new perch on a low wall that had once surrounded a planter box, and began searching for edible shoots in the tall grasses that had taken root in the planter.

Danny-boy demonstrated first, straddling his bicycle and gliding effortlessly down the slight slope. He made a wide turn and pedaled back. "It's easy," he said, and held her bicycle upright as she mounted. "I've got it set in fourth gear to start with. Just leave the gear shift alone for now. Sit on the seat and put your feet on the pedals. I'll hold you up."

She reluctantly took her feet from the ground and placed them on the pedals.

"All you have to do is balance," he said. "If you want to pedal, you could try that, but go easy."

He gave her a push and ran alongside, steadying her by holding on to the back of the seat. Behind them, the monkey shrieked and chattered. Jezebel barked furiously, running alongside them. Jax pumped a few times and the bicycle outpaced Danny-boy, forcing him to let go of the seat.

For a moment, Jax maintained a straight course—a beautiful smooth glide that was as straight as an arrow and as elegant as an aria. Her hands were on the handlebars; the wind whipped her hair back. As he ran alongside, Danny-boy could see that she was grinning wildly, an elated expression that he had never seen on her face before.

Then her front wheel hit a pothole, the bicycle swerved, and she crashed, at full tilt, into the back of the Toyota.

Danny-boy ran to her. "Are you all right? Maybe you'd better not try this yet. Maybe . . ."

Her left elbow was bleeding where she had scraped it on the pavement, but she grinned at him and untangled herself from the bicycle. "It's like flying," she said. "Why didn't you say it was like flying?" She didn't wait for an answer. "It's like the hawk—the way he catches the wind and soars." She waved a hand in the air, demonstrating. "You didn't tell me."

For a moment, he couldn't say anything. She had never said so many words in a row before. She had never smiled at him the way she was smiling now.

"I want to try again," she said.

Again and again he launched her. Each time she went

farther before crashing. He shouted advice that always came a little too late to help: "Straighten up now!" "Don't pump so hard!" "Lean the other way—no, the OTHER way!"

Sometimes she managed to veer around the Toyota. But then she would be unable to recover from the turn and she would lean farther and farther until she finally fell. Each time she fell, she received another scrape or bruise, but she would not give up. "Maybe we should rest," Danny-boy suggested. She shook her head stubbornly and they continued.

At last, late in the day, she successfully avoided the Toyota and kept on riding. The bicycle wobbled when she pumped the pedals, but she recovered, straightening out before she overbalanced, then picking up speed.

Jezebel, who had grown bored with watching, ran after her, and Danny-boy leapt on his own bicycle to follow. He met her five blocks farther on, walking her bicycle up a hill and limping just a little.

"I hit a hole in the road," she said. She was still grinning.

"Your shoulder OK?"

"Fine." She looked up the hill and glanced at his face. "Let's keep going, OK?"

"OK. As long as you're not tired."

Her grin faded a little. "I'm not tired."

He walked beside her in silence for a time. "Pretty soon you'll be riding all over the city," he said at last. "I can show you the best routes. If you're clever, you can avoid the worst hills."

"Why are you doing this?" she asked. "Why are you teaching me how to ride?"

He shrugged, feeling uncomfortable and avoiding her eyes. He could not answer; he had no answer. "Why not?" There was a long silence. He felt her slipping away from him, and he tried to draw her back. "Mercedes suggested I do it."

"Teach me to ride a bicycle?"

"Let you go," he said. "With this, you can leave whenever you want. I won't try to keep you here."

She watched him for a moment. And then looked away.

"Let's ride. Come on." She pushed off awkwardly, but managed to keep her balance. Danny-boy stayed behind her for the first block, then pulled alongside. They had reached the top of a hill, and she was looking down the long straight street that lay before them.

"Oh, let's go," she said breathlessly, and started down the hill. An exhilarated whoop of joy drifted back to Danny-boy, and he followed. Jezebel brought up the rear, racing after him.

Jax led the way through the Richmond District. From there, the street sloped downward slightly. She kept pedaling, calling back every now and then to urge him to follow. He shouted back, pointing out landmarks as they passed them: Golden Gate Park, the University of San Francisco, Saint Monica's Church.

As she crossed 48th Avenue she slowed down, then stopped abruptly, standing astride her bicycle. He pulled up even with her and stopped. Ahead, he could see the waves crashing on Ocean Beach.

"What's wrong? he said. "Why'd you stop?"

"What is that?" When she looked at him, her eyes were enormous. "That water. I can't see the other shore."

"It's the ocean," he said. "The other side is hundreds of miles away."

She stared at him. "Hundreds of miles?" She shook her head in disbelief.

"It is," he insisted. "Books told me about it. Come on."

Taking the lead, he rode to the end of the street. Fine white sand had drifted over the Great Highway, the road that ran alongside the beach. At the edge of the sand, Danny-boy got off his bicycle and walked it to the seawall. When he looked back she was following, still staring at the horizon.

He leaned his bike against the cement wall, then sat on the wall to take off his tennis shoes. "Take off your shoes," he said. "Otherwise you'll get sand in them." He swung his legs over the wall and jumped down onto the beach. He ran toward the breaking waves, stopping only when an incoming wave swept up the beach to lap around his ankles. Jezebel splashed in the surf beside him, snapping at the wave and

barking at the taste of salt. The water was cold and the
retreating wave sucked at the sand beneath his feet. He
looked back.

Jax stood at the edge of the wet sand. When a wave
washed up, she took a step back.

"Taste it," he said, cupping some water with his hand
and touching it to his lips. When a wave returned, she followed his lead and sputtered at the taste.

"Poison," she said.

"It's just salt."

She shook her head, venturing no closer. He left the
water to stand beside her. She was quiet and tense, but it
was a different sort of tension than he'd seen in her before.
She was awed by the ocean. She had forgotten to be wary of
him; she was fascinated by the distant horizon, straining her
eyes to see a faraway shore.

"It goes on and on," Danny-boy told her softly. "Mario
once sailed his boat straight out for a whole day. He says he
didn't see anything but water and more water." She didn't
respond. "Come on. Let's walk along the beach."

He took her hand and she did not resist, following obediently. The tide was coming in, and each wave lapped a
little higher on the sand.

"Look there." Ahead of them, someone had built an
elaborate castle in the sand. Seaweed banners flew from
crenellated towers. A wide wall of sand linked the towers,
dividing the castle's courtyard from the rest of the beach.

Jax squatted in the sand to examine the miniature city
more closely. "It's beautiful," she said. Tiny soldiers woven
of dune grass stood guard on the battlements beside a driftwood cannon. An incoming wave washed through the moat,
passing beneath a driftwood bridge.

Danny-boy watched her study the castle. The setting
sun painted half her face with red light; the other half was in
shadow. Her hands clasped each other loosely. "The waves
will destroy it," she said.

Danny-boy sat on the sand beside her. "You sound
sad."

She shook her head, an automatic and meaningless denial. "It's beautiful. Why build anything so beautiful just so

it can be destroyed? If we hadn't come here, no one would ever have seen it."

"Sometimes you make things that won't last just for the pleasure of making them," Danny-boy said. He watched a wave take a bite out of the castle wall. "You do it for your-self, not for anyone else. When you make something beauti-ful, you change. You put something of yourself into the thing you make. You're a different person when you're done." Another wave washed up against the castle wall, nibbling a little bit away.

"Is that why you're painting the bridge?"

"That's part of it, I guess."

"What's the other part?"

"While you change yourself, you change the world. Make it more your own."

They sat in silence as the waves undermined the tower nearest the sea. When it toppled, Jax stood. "I don't want to watch the rest."

He walked beside her as they headed back. They had almost reached the bicycles when she stopped, staring past him. Her eyes were fixed on the sunset. "The sun," she said in a choked voice. The red disc was flattening and changing shape as it neared the horizon line.

"It's OK," he said. "It does that here."

"It's sinking into the water," she said, and there was a note of panic in her voice.

"It happens like that every night," he said. "It's OK." He touched her shoulder to reassure her and felt her trem-bling. "It's OK," he repeated. "Believe me. I've seen it be-fore."

Then he put his arms around her, surprised even as he did it that she let him. He stroked her hair gently and kept talking in a soothing voice, trying not to break the spell. "Books says that the sun is really millions of miles away. He says that it really isn't anywhere near the ocean. It just looks that way. Don't worry."

She seemed so small, now that he held her in his arms. Her shoulders felt so thin and frail. He could feel her heart beating, hear the whisper of her breath past his face. Her eyes reflected the sunset.

"You've seen this before," she asked, still watching the sun.

"Many times."

She relaxed just a little; he could feel the tension in her shoulders ease. When the sun dipped below the horizon, she looked at his face. She hesitated, just for a moment. He fought the urge to hold her more tightly. She lifted one hand and tentatively touched his cheek, an uncertain movement that was checked almost before it was complete. Then she pulled away from him.

"We'd better ride home," she said. "It's a long way."

All the way home, he kept remembering the warmth of her body against his.

CHAPTER
12

Snake lay on his bed, one arm tucked behind his head, watching Lily unbraid her hair. The windows of the old Victorian house were open, and the evening breeze smelled of wet pavement and growing things.

Lily was tall and lean. He could see her muscles working beneath her thin T-shirt. Here and there, the darker lines of her tattoos showed through the thin fabric: a curve of vine, the brilliant red of a rose.

Lily shook out her hair and combed her fingers through the wavy strands. She lay down on the bed, propping herself up on one elbow and looking down at him. He reached up to toy with a strand of her hair, wrapping it around his finger and admiring its coppery sheen. When she leaned toward him, he kissed her lips delicately. She pulled back and studied his face.

"You seem distracted," she said. "What's going on?"

He shrugged. "Don't know what you mean."

"I think this is the longest time I've ever been on your bed and kept all my clothes on. What's up?"

He ran his hand up her back and tried to pull her down for another kiss. She resisted. "Too late to fake it," she said. "What's eating you?"

He looked away from her face, fixing his gaze on the ceiling. For the past year, they had been sleeping together. Their relationship was casual and playful, and neither of

them would commit to more. Snake liked Lily. Hell, on
dark nights when she wasn't there, he sometimes thought he
might love her. But that thought, when it came, scared him.
She was too different from him. At the time of the Plague,
he had been a street kid, living in the Haight. She had been a
college graduate, working in the financial district.

He had never talked about love to Lily. Love was not a
word or a feeling that he was comfortable with. Still, he
reached up and rubbed her back, a tentative reassurance.

"So what's got you worried?" she asked again.

"I was talking to Danny-boy out at the bridge. He really thinks that Fourstar will be invading the city."

"Traders have been warning us about Fourstar for
years now. You said that yourself at the meeting. So that's
not all of it. What else is new?" She ran her hand over the
shaven part of his head, gently rubbing the smooth skin.

It made him nervous that she knew him so well. He did
not want her to know that he was worried. Sometimes he
thought that she might already know that he almost thought
he loved her.

"Last night, I went by Kezar Stadium. There's a wall
there that's just ripe for painting, so I stopped by to check it
out. The moon was up and when I walked alongside the
wall, I could see my moon shadow, walking along beside
me." He wet his lips. "And then I saw that I wasn't alone.
There was the shadow of a man walking in front of me and
there was another shadow walking behind. The wall was full
of shadows of men, all of them carrying rifles and walking
all around me, like we were in some goddamn parade." He
shook his head. "I was alone except for all these shadows,
all these soldiers that had me surrounded."

Retelling the story, he was suddenly afraid. At the
time, he had watched the shadows calmly. Living in the
city, such things came to seem natural. But afterward, he
realized the implications of the marching men. "Bad times
are coming. Fourstar's coming."

The muscles in his shoulders and back were tense, and
his stomach was knotted in nervous anticipation. He had
not fought for many years. Looking back on his days in the

gang, he remembered the heat of the fight, the tension and the fear.

He remembered the moment of crystalline clarity that had come to him during his last fight, just before the Plague made turf battles irrelevant. The other kid, a young Chicano, had lunged for his face. Snake saw a flicker of light on the knife and twisted to one side. The air around him seemed to shimmer; the world had stood still. He brought up his own knife up and under, catching the kid in the belly and slicing upward to strike the ribs. He felt warm blood on his hand and stepped back. The kid fell forward and Snake was running.

The ringing in his ears was so loud that it competed with the sound of distant sirens. As he ran, he touched a hand to his ear and it came back bloody. His leather jacket was slick with blood: his blood, the Chicano's blood.

Shadows pursued him as he ducked into an alley and he wheeled on them, brandishing his bloody knife. "Cool it, man. Come on," someone said. Friends of his—but he almost didn't recognize them. Their faces were distorted, twisted by the moonlight. "Take it easy." They helped him: they stopped the bleeding from his ripped ear; they threw away his knife and took him to the apartment that he shared with eight others. They treated him with the respect due a killer.

Within a week, they were all dead of the Plague. Within a few weeks, no one cared that the Haight was his gang's turf. Everyone was dead. And the death of the Chicano kid was swallowed up in the thousands of deaths. But he remembered washing the blood from his hands and wondering how much was his and how much belonged to the Chicano kid.

"Why can't they leave us alone?" he growled.

Lily shrugged. "Because we're different from them," she said. "Isn't that always why people fight?" She was beautiful, lying there with the last light of the day gleaming on her face.

"It's another turf war. I thought I was too old to fight turf wars." He stared at the ceiling. "I've got to talk to some people about this. We've got to figure out what to do."

She leaned over and kissed him. "Later," she said. "They're not here yet. We have a little time."

They took advantage of the time they had.

Jax felt Danny-boy's attentions as a steady pressure. She did not know what to make of him; she did not know how to respond. Sometimes she caught him watching her, his gaze as tangible as a touch on her skin. When she returned his stare, his eyes slipped away, as if he had just glanced in her direction by accident.

She knew about sex. The farm animals had never been shy about fucking. Her mother had explained how men and women made love. But that clinical knowledge had little to do with the tension that she felt when Danny-boy touched her arm.

When their eyes met accidentally, she looked away quickly, confused and unsure. She was afraid. She was not often afraid, but she was afraid of him. Or maybe she was afraid of herself, of the confusion that came when their eyes met. She wanted something that she could not identify or define. She felt restless and dissatisfied.

Whenever Danny-boy went to work on the bridge, she explored the city on her own. On foot and by bicycle, she roved the streets with no destination in mind. Alone in the city, she sensed a gap, a break in some internal rhythm, an omission of some kind. As if one tile were missing from a mosaic, one piece from a jigsaw puzzle. If anyone had asked, she might have said that she was looking for her mother, and that was part of it. But only part. She was searching for a sense of completion, for a feeling that she belonged.

Sometimes, when she passed a shop window, she thought she saw her mother's reflection from the corner of her eye. The specter vanished when she turned to examine it more closely. A flicker of movement—that was all. But she knew that her mother was there.

Sometimes she felt a sudden sensation—as startling as an electric shock—and she would realize that her mother had walked where she was walking, stood where she was standing. Her mother had sat on this bench; her mother had waited at this street corner; her mother had lingered by this shop window, admiring the rhinestone brooch that still hung on the dusty black velvet stole worn by a mannequin.

Such moments were rare and unrepeatable. When she tried to return to a place where her mother had been, she could not find the way. The streets looked different, the stores had changed. She searched without success for the ivy-covered house where she had received her name, for the dark alley where she had seen the angel. But the streets refused to take her to these places, leading instead to new neighborhoods, where she had never been.

In the end, she let the city direct her wanderings. She did not choose a path. Each day she set out in a new direction, paying little attention to her route. She let the city lead her.

And she found things, though not what she was looking for. Under the reception desk in the lobby of a downtown office building, she found a tiny village built of mud bricks and pebbles. The huts were thatched with eucalyptus leaves that had long since lost their pungent smell. In an alley off Mission Street, she found a red brick wall decorated with running buffalo and deer. In a vacant lot south of Market, she found a tower constructed of crystal doorknobs, clear glass bottles, window panes, wine glasses, and crystal tableware of all varieties. The ground surrounding the tower was littered with rainbows, broken shards of colored light that shifted position with the movement of the sun.

Sometimes she met people. On a chilly afternoon when the sun had just broken through the clouds, she walked along Haight Street, going nowhere in particular. Halfway down the block, she noticed that someone had painted a series of footprints on the pavement. Two sets of footprints: one in pink paint and one in pale blue. Jax studied them for a moment, then stepped in the pink prints. She tried to follow their path, though it seemed rather odd. To put her feet in the prints, she had to take a big step, then two small ones, then another big one. Following the prints, Jax found herself moving in a peculiar spinning path. She stopped, staring down at the pavement in puzzlement.

"You need a partner," a man said.

She looked up. Snake was watching her from the side-

walk. She recognized him from the meeting at City Hall. He
wore the same leather jacket, the same arrogant smile.

"I'll show you," he said. He came toward her and stood
in the blue footprints. In a reflex action, one hand dropped
to her knife. "Oh, lighten up," he said in a faintly contemptuous tone. "I'm not going to hurt you. You want to learn to
waltz or not?"

Feeling foolish, she released her hold on her knife.

"Just relax," he said, putting one hand on her waist and
taking her other hand in his. "Put your hand on my shoulder. Now follow my lead—take a step with each count. One,
two, three; one, two, three; one, two, three."

She stepped in time with his counting. "Just go with
it," he said. "Don't resist." The pressure of his hand at her
waist made her turn, and her feet naturally took the small
steps painted on the pavement. The pattern of footprints
began to make sense. Snake stopped counting and hummed
a lilting melody that kept the same beat.

She muttered the numbers under her breath: "One,
two, three; one, two, three." She found herself smiling as
they spun down the block, forgetting her initial distrust.
"One, two, three; one, two, three."

He stopped, releasing her, and she twirled for three
more steps. ". . . two, three; one, two, three."

"You're out of footprints," he pointed out.

She stopped and grinned at him. "Maybe we should
paint some more."

"I'll tell Lily you said so. She's the one who painted
these and taught me to waltz."

"I like that," she said.

He raised an eyebrow. "I wouldn't have figured you for
a waltzing type."

"I'd never tried it before."

"I suppose you didn't get much of a chance back where
you came from." He shoved his hands in his pockets, looking over her head. "So where are you going, anyway?"

She studied his face and decided that maybe he wasn't
so bad after all. What she had taken for arrogance was an
automatic sort of protection, a barricade that he erected

against the world. She waved her hand in the direction she had been walking. "This way."

"Looking for anything in particular?"

"Whatever the city wants to show me."

"Mind if I tag along for a while? I'd like to ask you about this Fourstar."

He strolled beside her, his thumbs hooked in the belt loops of his jeans, his shoulders slouching. He asked her about Fourstar's speech, and she repeated all that she could remember. He asked her about Woodland, about the market, about the army. And he nodded as she talked.

"You see, the way I figure it, Fourstar is scared of us," he said at last.

She looked at him and shook her head. "Have you been listening? He didn't sound scared to me."

"Damn straight he's scared." Snake's boot heels clicked on the pavement, matching the rhythm of his words. "We don't fit into this nice tidy new world he's building. And he doesn't like that."

Jax considered this for a moment. "Why don't we fit? Seems to me we fit just fine."

Snake seemed to take no notice. "I was around before the Plague, so I know damn well I don't fit. You and Dannyboy—you're so far out of it, you don't even know that you don't fit. You don't know what fitting is. And that makes people like Fourstar real nervous. That's why he wants to wipe us out."

"He talked about the resources here," she said, remembering Fourstar's speech.

"Bullshit. Just a way to get people behind him. Take my word for it. He wants to wipe us out because we're rebels, we don't fit. People like Fourstar don't like people like us."

Jax frowned. She didn't agree that Fourstar was afraid of the people in the city, but she liked being included in "people like us." She had never been one of a group before. She had always been alone, and the hint of communal identity was appealing.

"I never thought of it like that before," Jax admitted tentatively. "I never thought that I was part of a group."

Snake glanced at her face. "Sure, you fit in here. You're just as odd as the rest of us, I'd say. The city takes all kinds. Of course, you've got to work on your attitude a bit."

She frowned at him, puzzled. "What do you mean?"

He stopped walking. When she paused beside him, he turned her shoulders so that she faced him. Startled by his sudden scrutiny, she glared at him.

"Not bad," he said. "You look pretty tough. But you need some props. Come on."

He led her down the block and into a corner drugstore. The glass door had been shattered years before. They stepped through the wreckage. Snake made his way through the dimly lit interior, stepping over piles of fallen packages and broken glass. "Here they are," he said, reaching a rack of sunglasses in the back of the store. He selected a handful. "These might make it," he muttered. "Come on."

On the sidewalk outside the store, he had her hold still while he put a pair of sunglasses on her face. Through the tinted glass, the world looked dim and cool. "Look here," he ordered her, gesturing toward the store window.

She stared at her reflection in the glass. The mirrored lenses reflected her image.

"Like it?" Snake asked.

"I don't know." She found her new appearance both attractive and faintly disturbing. She looked like a stranger that she wouldn't have trusted.

"Try them for a while. They'll grow on you."

That evening, when Danny-boy returned from the bridge, she greeted him wearing mirror shades and a new leather jacket.

CHAPTER
13

Late at night The Machine heard metal claws scratching at his window. He moved the kerosene lantern from his desk to the windowsill, so that light spilled out into the alley.

Through the dirty glass, he could see a face of sorts: sickle-shaped mandibles beneath multifaceted eyes. Jointed legs ending in crude metal pinchers gripped the windowsill, supporting the rounded metal torso and lifting the head to the window. The rest of the body was lost in the shadows.

As The Machine watched, the head swayed to and fro. Lantern light fell on one faceted eye and then on the other, glittering on the photoreceptors that made up the facets. Mandibles rattled against the glass.

She wanted the sun—The Machine knew that. Her photovoltaic cells converted the sun's rays to electricity, which powered her movements. His kerosene lamp was a pale substitute, but the best that she could find in the darkened city. "Be patient," he said to her. "It will be daylight soon enough. Sleep now."

She scraped her mandibles against the glass. The wooden windowsill began splintering under the pressure of her pinchers. The Machine took the lantern from the sill, blew out the flame, and crawled into his narrow bed. He smiled as he listened to her retreat, and he imagined her raising her head to the feeble light of the moon. Reassured by the sound of metal on asphalt, he fell asleep.

The Machine's bedroom had once been the office for

the manager of Cole Street Auto Body Shop. In the adjoining garage, The Machine built metal creatures, which he turned loose to prowl the empty streets of the city. Some, like his late-night visitor, took their energy from the sun, storing the feeble current in banks of batteries that they carried in their bellies. Torpid and slow-moving, they basked in the sun like reptiles. Others were equipped with wind turbines that converted the breezes into power. Still others were wholly battery-powered, scurrying along the city's gutters throughout their brief and unproductive lives. The Machine had experimented with a breed that ingested organic matter and fermented methane gas, but that proved too volatile, and after a few explosions he had stopped building that species.

He called his creatures "Children of the Sun." Though he built their bodies, he felt that he did not truly create the Children. It seemed to him that the Children already existed in some other place or time. He assisted them by building bodies that they could inhabit in this world.

He searched the city for metal scraps that he could shape into abdomens, torsos, mandibles, legs. He recognized the hubcaps or metal pipes or oil drums or auto fenders that belonged to the Children. He could lay his hand on a set of vise grips and know immediately that this tool would become a claw, manipulated by an intricate set of gears. He could run his hand along the smooth metal surface of an industrial light fixture and know without question that the metal shape would become a head, set with photoreceptors that would guide the creature to light. The Machine gave the Children bodies, and set them free to prowl the city.

Sometimes he dreamed of the Children's home: a hot desert world with a blazing sun. There were gray rock walls and canyons through which Children shaped like centipedes scrambled. Wasp-winged Children, able to fly in the world's low gravity, buzzed overhead and landed on wind-etched turrets of stone. Ant Children clambered up the steep walls, clinging with their pincers to the rock.

The sun warmed The Machine, and he felt a surge of power as the light charged his batteries. He lifted his wings and took flight, rising to join the circling Children above him.

Morning: the double garage doors were open and sunshine made a golden parallelogram on the cement floor. Just outside the doors, a metal centipede basked in the sun, recharging its batteries.

The Machine pushed his gyrocopter from the garage. The dream of flight had made him eager to fly the small craft once again. The cockpit was about the size of a go-cart, riding high on outsized wheels. When the gyrocopter was on the ground, the blades of the overhead rotor drooped a little, giving the craft a mournful look. In the air, the rear propeller pushed the craft forward, and the forward motion kept the overhead rotor turning, providing constant lift.

The design was based on the autogiro, invented in 1923 by Juan de la Cierva. The Machine's gyrocopter was a highly maneuverable craft, suitable for flying low over the city. He had built the small craft as a prototype, hoping that its design and construction might lead to the development of Children that could fly. But the control mechanisms required for a flying Child had proven too complex. Though the gyrocopter itself was quite functional, he had had no luck in extending its principles to the construction of Children.

The Machine pointed the vehicle down Cole Street. He had a straight run of several hundred feet, more than enough to get airborne. He strapped himself into the bucket seat, taken from a high performance sports car. When he turned the ignition key, the Volkswagen engine that powered the craft caught with a throaty roar. Carefully, he set the pitch on the rotor blades to zero and shifted the clutch, connecting the engine to the rotor. The blades began to spin, straightening under the influence of centrifugal force. He watched a dial that registered rotor speed as he adjusted the throttle.

With a sudden movement he slipped the clutch, disengaging the rotor linkage. At the same moment, he adjusted the pitch of the rotor so that the blades caught the air, jerking the craft aloft. At the top of the ascent, the rear propeller kicked in, pushing the small craft forward.

He relaxed. Without thinking, he adjusted the rotor pitch, leveling out his climb and flying over Haight Street, past the Golden Gate Park, and out toward the bay. He circled Alcatraz Island once and headed toward the Golden Gate Bridge. He could see Danny-boy in the center of the span, far below him. Danny-boy waved and The Machine waved back. Then he headed back toward his workshop.

He had no reason for making the morning flight. He just wanted to feel the wind on his face; he wanted to rise above the buildings and see the city from above. He felt guilty about indulging himself, but there were times that he could not help giving in to the desire. This weakness and lack of control on his part, he felt, was simply another indication that he was a defective machine. If his father had been a better designer, the urge to fly for no purpose would not overwhelm him.

Late in the morning, he returned to the ground, landing on the four wide lanes of Fell Street and motoring back to his workshop. When he turned off the engine, the world seemed suddenly silent. He pushed the vehicle into the garage and was taking off his helmet when a woman called to him. "Hey!"

The Machine looked toward the doorway. Jax stood on the sidewalk just outside the garage door. He stared at her, uncertain of how to react. She was a small woman, but she carried herself with insolent grace, as if she owned the sidewalk beneath her feet, the street behind her, and the sun in the sky above. She wore mirrored sunglasses that hid her eyes.

"Hey," she said again. "I've been waiting for you to show up. There's something trapped in the alley."

"Something?"

"Like that." She gestured at the centipede Child that was still sunbathing on the sidewalk. "Sort of. I'll show you."

Reluctantly, he followed her down the block.

As they approached an alley he could hear the rhythmic scraping of metal on asphalt. From the entrance to the alley he could see the trapped Child. She was one of his favorites: she had the body of a wasp with a thorax as big around as a strong man's chest. Attached to her thorax were batlike wings, membranous structures braced with metal struts. On sunny days she spread these wings to expose twin arrays of solar cells.

Somehow she had caught one wing in the gap between a metal drainpipe and a cement wall. As she walked forward, lured by the sunlight that shone into the end of the alley, the wing had bent, twisting around the pipe until it halted her forward progress. But she had kept trying to walk. The asphalt at her feet was streaked with white where her feet had persistently scraped against it.

The Machine ran to her, stripping off his T-shirt and tossing it over her head to block the photoreceptors. Blindly, she turned her head from side to side, searching for the light. The pulleys that controlled the movement of her head wheezed and chattered. When she turned her head to the left, he fumbled at the back of her neck. He found and flipped the switch that cut off the power from her storage batteries, and she froze with one foot lifted to step forward. The Machine removed the shirt from her head and stepped back to survey the damage.

The wing was a total loss: the metal struts were hopelessly twisted; most of the photovoltaic cells were cracked and broken. He tugged gently at the twisted metal, trying to work it free.

"Here," said Jax, and it was only then that he realized that she was still nearby. "If I pull here and you pull there, it'll come free."

He nodded and she grabbed the strut. He could feel the heat of Jax's hands beside his as they pulled. The metal gave way with a creaking scream, bending under their united pressure, and the wing came free. The Machine stepped back, grateful to put some distance between himself and the woman. The warmth of her hands made him uneasy.

"Is it dead?" Jax asked.

"She," he corrected.

"Is she dead?"

He shook his head. "I can fix her," he said. "In the shop."

He moved to her torso, undid the fastenings that held the metal casing closed, and removed the auto batteries. He could return for the batteries later; without them, the body would be considerably lighter. Jax watched, and when he started dragging the body in the direction of the workshop, she helped. Together they lifted the Child: The Machine supported the head and the woman lifted the abdomen and held it on her shoulder.

When they reached the garage he thanked her abruptly, but she still didn't leave. She stood in the doorway and watched as he found a wrench and began to remove the bent wing. She held the wing steady as he worked and caught it so that it did not clatter to the floor.

He ignored her and continued working, detaching the cable assemblies that controlled the expansion and contraction of the wing, then spreading the broken wing on the floor and salvaging the parts that were worth saving. She left the garage, and he felt relief that she was going. She returned a few minutes later, carrying one of the auto batteries. She made five more trips, bringing back all six batteries. Then she perched on the fender of a car and watched as he dug through the scrap steel to find pipe that would replace the bent wing struts.

"You don't talk much," she said at last.

He didn't say anything.

"It's kind of nice," she said after a minute. "Most of the people around here talk all the time."

He kept working. She did not leave.

"How come you're called The Machine?" she asked after a bit.

"Because I'm a machine."

"You look like a regular person."

"I'm not."

"A machine like a clock or something?"

"More delicate than a clock. I was built before the Plague. People were much more skilled with intricate machinery then. But that's why I survived the Plague. Because I'm not human."

Jax frowned. "Does that mean that everyone who survived the Plague is a machine?"

"Of course not," he said impatiently. "But some of them may be machines and not know it."

"Yeah? You think Danny-boy is a machine?"

"No, he's too disorderly. But I would guess that Fourstar is a machine."

Jax shook her head. "I don't think so. He sweats just like a regular person."

"That doesn't matter," The Machine continued calmly. "I appear to sweat, but I'm still a machine. Fourstar is a small part of a larger military machine, set in motion before the Plague. Now that he's moving, he won't stop."

"You're right there."

She didn't say anything more. After a time, he grew used to her presence. When he stopped to rest, she was still there. He sat down in the shade just outside the garage door, and she came to sit beside him.

"You'll be able to fix her?" she asked.

He nodded.

"That's good." She sat with one leg stretched out comfortably and one bent. Her hands were clasped easily around the bent leg, and she was looking out into the distance.

A moment's silence. The shadow of a lamppost had shifted so that it fell across the back of the centipede that lay in the street outside the garage. As they watched, the centipede Child lifted its head and slithered forward until its entire body was in the sun. Then it lowered its head and was motionless again. He understood the Children: they reacted to certain stimuli in predictable ways. People made him nervous.

"What are you doing here?" he asked her abruptly.

"I just came to see you."

"No one comes to see me."

"I did."

"Why?"

She didn't speak, and he glanced at her. The hands that were clasped around her leg had tightened. She seemed smaller and less sure of herself. She shrugged. "I wanted to ask you something."

He waited, saying nothing.

She drew her other knee in, as if for protection, and locked her hands around both legs. She spoke hesitantly. "When I came into the city, I saw an angel. Instead of skin, half its face was metal. And its hand . . ." Out of the corner of his eye, he saw her hold out her hand as she spoke. "Its hand was metal, with joints like those." She pointed to the centipede's legs. "And I wanted to know—did you ever make anything like that?"

He shook his head, remembering the dream that he had had months before. "I make nothing," he said finally. "I only help the city think its thoughts. These . . ." He waved a hand to take in the centipede and the other Children in the garage. "These are thoughts of the city. So, I think, is the angel."

"I think the angel I saw was the same one that took my mother," she said.

He looked at her. Her confidence was gone. She seemed much smaller than before. "Your mother must have belonged to the city," he said. "The city came and took her."

"But where is she now?" Jax asked. "I can't find her."

"I don't know."

"Sometimes I think I'll be able to find her soon," she said. "Sometimes, when I walk down the street, I know that just around the next corner I'll find what I'm looking for. I turn the corner, and the street is empty. But the feeling is still there. The next corner. Or the next. Do you know what I mean?"

"I know." He had felt the subtle pressure of the city surrounding and containing him.

The warmth that came from her did not seem as objectionable as it had. He remembered a time that he had found a sick kitten in the street. He had offered it things to eat, but it hadn't taken them. Finally he had taken it to Danny-boy, who fed it with milk from a bottle. But it died anyway. He preferred the Children. He knew how to fix the Children. He did not like this feeling of confusion. He resented her presence, but he could not tell her to go away.

"Fourstar is coming," she said. "He wants to destroy the city." She rested her head on her knees. "Sometimes I want to run away, but I can't. I told my mother I would help. And Danny-boy . . ." She let the sentence trail off, saying nothing about Danny-boy. She looked sad and broken.

He tried to think of things that might help her. "Are you thirsty?" he asked suddenly. "Here—I have cold drinks; I have a refrigerator. Here." He rushed to the refrigerator and brought back a cold Coca-Cola. "Here, this is for you."

She accepted the bottle. "It'll be all right," he said, not knowing where the words came from. Somewhere in the past, back before the Plague, back before he knew he was a machine. "I'll help."

She smiled at him and he immediately regretted his words, but it was too late to call them back.

Long after she left, the air of the garage held the scent of her: a touch of sweat, a hint of wood smoke. He tried to work on the solar array for the new wing, but he kept dropping the tiny components. His patience was not up to the task. He began cutting pipes for the wing struts, but the first cut he made was wrong, spoiling a length of pipe. He set that aside as well.

He washed his hands in cold water, but he could still feel the warmth of her touch, where his fingers had brushed hers when he handed her the Coke. He stood in the doorway to the garage, looking out into the street. The sun was setting, and the lampposts cast long shadows.

In the twilight, he felt that something was going to happen. The air was blue and cool and pure and the street seemed to be waiting for a signal of some kind. He waited with it, but all that happened was the sunset.

CHAPTER
14

Books was surprised and pleased when Jax came to visit him in the library. He offered her mint tea and Danish sugar cookies from a metal tin. "They're a bit stale, but otherwise they've kept remarkably well," he said. 'I've salvaged dozens of tins from the gourmet department of Macy's. Help yourself."

Jax accepted a cookie and nibbled a corner of it, perching uneasily on a wooden chair.

"I had hoped you would stop by," he said.

Jax nodded. "The city brought me here," she said. "I just started walking and ended up by the library steps. I thought I should come in."

"Whatever brought you, that's fine with me. Have you been enjoying your time in the city so far?"

She looked noncommittal. "I keep meeting new people."

"Nothing wrong with that, is there?"

"I guess not. They all want to talk and ask questions."

"I think you'll find most of the people around here are pretty friendly," Books said.

Jax looked thoughtful. "I wouldn't know much about that, I suppose. I've never had any friends. My mother and I lived alone." Her voice held no trace of self-pity. She was stating a fact, nothing more.

"You and your mother must have been friends," Books

said. He found her quiet acceptance of a solitary life faintly disturbing.

She shook her head. "I don't think so. She took care of me, but we never talked much. It may take me a while to get the hang of this friends business."

"I'm sure you'll do fine." Books studied her. Ms. Migsdale was right—the woman had a feral quality: a little shy, a little dangerous. "Being friends is simple enough. Friends do things like this—sitting around and drinking tea and talking."

"Yeah?" She took a sip of tea and regarded him steadily across the table. "Does this mean we're friends?"

Books rubbed his beard, considering his answer carefully. "I guess it means that we could eventually be friends. I don't think we're there yet. But you don't have your hand on your knife all the time, so we're much closer."

She glanced down at her knife. When she looked back up he thought he saw a hint of embarrassment in her expression. "I guess so." She took another sip of tea. "Danny-boy told me that you could tell me a lot about the city."

"That's true. I've been working on a book that gives the history of the city since the Plague. So I suppose I know a fair amount."

He watched her glance toward the window. On the ledge outside, a pair of monkeys were grooming each other.

"What can you tell me about the monkeys?" she asked, jerking her head toward the window. "They follow me around sometimes." She watched the animals, an uneasy expression on her face. "Sometimes they try to talk to me. But I don't know what they're saying."

"Oh, yes, I can probably tell you more than you want to know about the monkeys. They figure in my history of the Plague. They brought it to the city, you see."

Jax was watching him intently. "Tell me about that."

Once a week, Books held classes for the children who lived in the city. After teaching reading or math, he always told a story, something about the city. He had told the story of the monkeys before and he slipped into it easily.

"Back before the Plague, the monkeys lived in a country called Nepal. It's far away from here—across the ocean and half a continent. High in the mountains of Nepal there's a monastery, a place where holy men live. For hundreds of years the holy men have lived in the monastery, and for hundreds of years the monkeys have lived with them."

Books took a sip of tea. Jax was leaning forward, her eyes on his face.

"The monastery was a peaceful place, even in times of war," Books continued. "And the people in Nepal had a legend that the monkeys were what made the monastery so peaceful. According to the legend, peace would come to the world when the monkeys left the monastery. Back before the Plague, the world was not a peaceful place."

Books hesitated, wondering whether to try explaining the Cold War to Jax. The posturing of nations, the threats and counterthreats, the nuclear deterrents and summit talks —they all seemed so distant, like a book he had read as a child. He remembered the constant fear, the awareness of death. But he could not begin to describe the reasons for it and he generally left it out of the story.

"Everyone was afraid that we would all die in a war," he said at last. "And many people banded together to try to do something about it. An international peace effort grew up —a coalition of dozens of groups from dozens of countries. Somewhere along the way, the monkeys became a symbol of peace. The Coalition for Peace wanted to bring the monkeys from Nepal, and every zoo in the world wanted to have a pair. Schoolchildren donated their milk money to help build monkey enclosures at the zoos; rock-and-roll producers arranged benefit concerts. It seemed like the whole world was ready for peace.

"The monkeys came to San Francisco, to Washington, D.C., to Moscow, to Tokyo, to Beijing, to Paris, to London. All over the world, people welcomed them as harbingers of peace. At the San Francisco Zoo, hundreds of thousands lined up to see them. The mayor declared a city holiday."

Books fell silent for a moment, remembering the feelings of hope and joy that had attended the monkeys' arrival. He had taken the day off from work and joined the crowd that waited to see the monkeys. Though he had known that importing a few monkeys could not bring peace, he had wished it were otherwise. He wanted to believe in the monkeys.

"What happened?" Jax's question brought him back to the story. She was listening closely, her teacup cradled in her hands.

"The monkeys brought peace," Books said. "But not the way we expected. Everywhere they were, the Plague broke out. People died. Hundreds of thousands of people died. The disease spread from the cities into the countryside, and more died." He discovered that his hands had clenched into fists, and he tried to relax them. He did not like remembering those days. At first, the dead were buried with proper funeral services. But by the end, overwhelmed with the number of bodies, public health officials had resorted to burning the dead. The smoke had mingled with the city fog and drifted through the streets. "They figured out quickly enough that the monkeys were the source and that fleas were the carriers. But it was already too late. In humans, the disease could be passed by an airborne virus, like a common cold. The Plague resisted all efforts to contain it. And after the Plague, there was peace. There had to be—no one was left to fight."

Books looked up. Jax was staring out the window, watching the monkeys. She glanced at him. "But why are the monkeys in the city?"

Books shrugged. "I suppose someone let them out of the zoo. After all, it wasn't their fault. They brought peace, just as the legend said they would. It just wasn't the sort of peace we expected."

Jax nodded, still looking out the window. "I wonder why they follow me around."

"They're curious beasts. They probably just want to know what you're up to."

"Maybe so," she said. "Maybe you're right."

After talking with Books, Jax returned to the hotel and waited for Danny-boy to come home. She sat in the easy chair by the hotel door. The sun was going down, and the streets near the hotel were already in twilight, shadowed by the skyscrapers of downtown. To the east, the sky was a luminous blue; a crescent moon was just rising. The air was filled with anticipation of the coming night.

Not far away, two monkeys were playing in an abandoned car. The windows had been broken long ago, and the animals chased each other in and out through the openings. Then the larger of the two stopped to bang on the hood with a stick, while the other clung to the steering wheel, making faces at its reflection in the rearview mirror.

Jax watched them idly. Books's explanation had not helped her understand the animals any better. They watched her and they followed her. It seemed sometimes like they knew something that she should know, but they wouldn't talk.

In her lap, Jax held the glass globe that contained the miniature city of San Francisco. Every now and then, she shook it and watched the golden flecks dance.

On her way back from the library, she had visited Tiger. He had finally removed the figure-eight bandage and declared that her shoulder was as good as new. She was relieved to be free of the constraining bandage at last, but its removal made her aware of how long she had been in the city. For weeks she had been exploring the city's streets, meeting its inhabitants.

She studied the city in the globe. The miniature had helped bring her to the city, but it was not enough to hold her there. The city itself did that. She could not run away. She felt that she was a part of this place, and that feeling surprised her.

She leaned back in the chair, looking out at the tall buildings around her. When she heard Danny-boy's bicycle bell in the distance, she set the globe down on the curb and stepped into the street to look for him. She waved at him as he approached.

She heard a monkey chattering behind her and looked back to the chair in time to see the animal rush up and snatch the glass globe from the curb.

"Hey! Put that down!" She started to run toward the monkey, but it dashed away. As the animal leapt for the safety of the hotel awning, it dropped the globe.

The glass shattered on the cement sidewalk. The water

splashed in all directions to make a dark starburst on the cement. The monkey shrieked at her from its high perch.

Jax picked the tiny city from the shards of glass. The buildings were molded plastic with painted windows. A few bits of glitter were caught in cracks and irregularities in the plastic. The city was much smaller than it had looked through the glass. It wasn't what she had expected. It wasn't what she had expected at all.

CHAPTER
15

The next morning it rained flowers. Tiny stemless golden blossoms, each about as big as the nail of Jax's smallest finger. She woke to the gentle sound of flowers tapping against the window. They formed small drifts on the sill.

She opened the window, stuck her head out, and twisted her neck so that she could look at the sky overhead. Bright motes of yellow fell from the featureless gray, dancing as they descended.

Danny-boy stood in the street below her, knee-deep in flowers. Tommy and his sister were having a flower-fight just down the street, throwing great handfuls of blossoms at each other. Jax called out, and Danny-boy looked up to see her in the window. "Come on down," he called to her.

She brushed the flowers from the windowsill and watched them flutter down to land on Danny-boy's head. "I'm going up to the roof," she shouted back, and she ran through the halls and up the stairs.

Flowers filled the hibachi and blanketed the gravel. The sun was breaking through the clouds, but the flowers kept falling, spiraling like snowflakes on a windless day. Jax peered over the edge of the roof. Specks of gold filled the gaps between the rows of bean plants. A dusting of yellow capped each building, each car, each lamppost.

She craned her neck to watch the flowers fall, then lay down among the blossoms. They smelled sweet and green, like new-cut grass. When she heard Danny-boy's step on the stairs, she called to him, and when he came she gestured urgently toward the sky. "Look at how they catch the light," she said.

He lay beside her, looking up at the flowers that fell from the sky. "If we lie here long enough, do you think they'll cover us completely?" she asked.

He didn't answer. She felt the warmth of his body beside hers, felt the warmth of the sun on her face. His hand found hers among the flowers and when he touched her, she did not pull away. The flowers touched her face like kisses, each one leaving a pollen mark and the smell of spring. Danny-boy brushed the blossoms from her face. Where his hand passed, warmth seemed to linger. Gently, his hand swept petals from her neck, her breasts, her belly. He stroked her neck, tracing the line of muscles that led down to the collarbone, tracing the edge of the collarbone.

The flowers fall from the sun, she thought. The sunlight and the flowers and Danny-boy's hands on her body were all part of the same moment. She responded to the sunlight and the flowers and Danny-boy's hands. In this moment, there was none of the tension that had once made her stiffen when he took her hand or watched her too intently.

He unbuttoned her flannel shirt and caressed her breasts. The sunlight was touched with urgency and the warmth came from within her, as well as from the sun. They fumbled with clothes and at last they were naked in the mound of flowers. Danny-boy's bare skin was dusted with pollen and stray blossoms were tangled in his hair.

He was looking down at her, and for a moment, he hesitated. "Am I hurting you?" he asked, touching her shoulder. She shook her head and pulled him down to kiss her. He kissed her mouth, her breasts, her belly, her crotch. He lingered there until the warmth that came from within her pulsed and glowed with a dangerous heat. She cried out in a small, high-pitched, broken-sounding voice that rose and fell.

He pressed his body against hers. She felt each touch so intensely that the sensation was near pain: the flowers falling on her face, the warm rooftop against her back, Danny-boy's hands on her breasts, his body moving against her. He entered her, and she cried out. The warmth moved in waves, surrounding her, enveloping her. He cried out too, a choked sigh that was scarcely louder than his breathing.

They lay together in the flowers. She could feel the beat of a pulse between her legs. She closed her eyes and watched the patterns that the sunlight made on the inside of her eyelids. She could feel the city around her, like an extension of her own body. The beat of her heart was the pulse of the city. The wind flowed through the city streets like the breath flowing into her lungs. Her nerves reached beyond her skin and into the rooftop, the streets, the buildings around her. The sun warmed the pavement and she felt safe and content.

Half asleep, she heard a sound, like the rush of water in a river. As she listened, she realized it was the rustle of wings, and she was frightened. By the sound, she knew that the angel was swooping low over her. She wanted to run but she could not move. The city had captured her: the network of streets twined around her legs; the concrete weighed her down. She could not breathe. Panicked, she opened her eyes to look for the angel.

The flowers had stopped falling. The sky was blue and clear and empty. She lay with Danny-boy beneath a blanket of yellow blossoms that were already starting to wither and brown at the edges. Danny-boy slept, one arm serving as a pillow beneath his head, the other arm flung across her waist. She slipped away from him and stood. For a moment, she watched him. He was smiling in his sleep.

She could still feel the city around her, but it was more distant now. She wanted to lie back down beside Danny-boy. She wanted to stroke his arm and waken him, so that he would pull her close to him. She knew that if she lay back down, she would stay beside him until he awoke. She knew that if he woke up and looked at her and asked her to stay with him, she would. And for some reason, that knowledge frightened her.

She gathered her clothes and pulled them on. As Danny-boy slept, she hurried down the stairs into the street. She didn't know where she was going, but she knew that she had to go somewhere, had to do something. She took her bicycle from the hotel lobby and rode toward the Civic Center Plaza.

Books was sitting on the library steps, examining a single blossom with a magnifying lens. He hailed her as she passed, and she stopped beside him. A book was propped open on his knees and several more were on the steps beside him. "Can't find them in any of the books," he said, waving the flower that he held. "Could be a completely new species. I wonder where they came from. Here, have a look."

She propped up her bicycle with the kickstand and sat beside him on the steps. Through the lens, the flower was enormous. She could see darker gold veins in the delicate golden petals; the grains of pollen were the size of boulders. Her fingers were blobs of pink, marked with ridges.

"Where are you off to?" Books asked her.

She shrugged, wishing that he hadn't asked. She kept looking at the flower though she knew that he was looking at her. Why wouldn't these people just leave her alone? She didn't know what to say. She crushed the blossom between her fingers and dropped it onto the steps.

"You're worried about something," he said, peering into her face. "What is it?"

She shrugged.

"You know, Danny-boy has been afraid since the day that he found you that you'd vanish any day. But you're still here. That's good. I hope you stick around."

"The city gave me a name," she said. "I never had a name before."

He nodded, as if he were waiting for more. She stood abruptly and handed him the magnifying lens. "I've got to get going," she said.

She rode away on her bicycle and did not look back. She headed up Fell Street, toward the ocean. Her bicycle wheel scattered drifts of flowers. Outside the downtown area, the flower fall had been lighter, just a few blossoms here and there.

She rode to Ocean Beach and sat on the seawall, watching the waves crash against the beach. She took off her shoes and strolled by the water's edge. The waves rushed in, then returned to the sea, hurried back, then retreated again in

eternal indecision. The cold water lapped around her ankles.
When the waves retreated, they sucked sand from beneath
her feet.

She felt soothed by the steady rhythm of the waves, by
the endless stretch of blue horizon. The air was filled with
the briny scent of dying kelp. She watched a line of pelicans
flying single file over the water.

She squatted in the wet sand at the water's edge and
began shaping the sand with her hands. A long diagonal line
became Market Street. She used a flat piece of driftwood to
smooth the sides of mounds of sand, forming the skyscrapers of downtown. With a stick she etched streets in the sand,
creating the Mission District, the Western Addition, the
Richmond District, the Haight, the Sunset District. She
piled up sand to make Nob Hill and Mount Sutro. She collected blackened sticks from an old bonfire near the seawall
and scattered them over the burned sections on Nob Hill.
With bits of broken glass, she made an intricate pattern
where Frank's Garden of Light stood.

The sun climbed overhead, but she did not notice.
When the sand dried so that she could not sculpt it, she
found a rusty can and carried water to moisten it again. She
gathered seaweed for the greenery of Golden Gate Park and
constructed boxy apartments in the Western Addition. Just
beyond the Sunset District, she dug a trench to mark the
edge of the city, smoothing the trench walls to form the very
beach on which she worked. The waves flowed into the
moat, lapping at the beach.

The fear that had overwhelmed her on the hotel roof
had retreated. It was not completely gone: she could remember the panic that had made her breath catch in her throat
and her heart beat faster. But now, squatting in the sand, the
panic was far away.

She sat back on her heels and straightened her shoulders. Her back ached from stooping, a pain that she had
been feeling for hours but had refused to acknowledge. Her
stomach rumbled, reminding her that she had not eaten
breakfast.

When she stood, she heard a flurry of wings. Her sudden movement had startled a seagull, which had taken

flight. She grinned at the bird. A tiny city was spread at her feet and the sounds of wings did not frighten her.

"Hello, Jax!"

Jax looked over her shoulder and saw Ms. Migsdale, hurrying along the beach toward her. "I'm glad to see you. I just got back from the library. Books says that Danny-boy is looking for you."

Jax stretched, relishing the twinges of pain from reawakening muscles. Ms. Migsdale was studying the city in the sand. "How lovely," she said. "You must have worked on it for hours."

Jax glanced at the sun, which was low in the sky. "I guess I did."

Ms. Migsdale shifted her gaze to Jax's face. "What got you started on such a project?"

Jax shrugged. She spread her hands, unable to explain the feeling that had compelled her. "The city's too big for me," she said at last. "I wanted something more my size."

Ms. Migsdale nodded. "I see. Sympathetic magic. By making something, you gain control over it. Makes sense."

Jax stared down at the city. If Ms. Migsdale wanted to try and find an explanation, she was welcome to it. Jax felt free of the constraints of the city, and she was content with that. She thought about Danny-boy and smiled. "I guess I'd best be heading home."

That night, when Jax undressed and crawled under the covers on the big double bed, Danny-boy came and lay down beside her. He put his arms around her and kissed her gently.

He made love to her again, and the warmth that had come to her on the roof returned, moving through her body with an inexorable rush. The feeling, she realized, had nothing to do with the sunlight and the flowers. It came from within her, in response to Danny-boy's touch.

Afterward, she lay awake, listening to him breathe softly and evenly in the darkness. He slept on his back with one arm touching her thigh, the other relaxed at his side. She did not understand how he could sleep like that—so open and vulnerable. When she turned restlessly in the bed he did not wake up, as she would have. Still asleep, he merely adjusted his body to hers.

More than once that first night she woke up, startled when he moved in his sleep or changed the rhythm of his breathing. For no reason at all she touched him as he slept, caressing his shoulder or stroking his arm. It was good that he was sleeping with her, she decided. If a threat arose, she would wake up. He obviously needed to be protected.

Even in her sleep, she was aware of the warm body beside her. She dreamed, as near as she could remember, of happy times.

Danny-boy woke at dawn, when the first light crept in the window. Jax slept in a fetal position, with the curve of her back protecting her vulnerable belly, her arms held tight by her head. He wondered, watching her sleeping face in the pale light, if she ever relaxed.

She needed him, he decided, watching her unsmiling face in repose. He would show her that she did not need to be always on guard. She could relax with him. He curled his body around her, fitting himself to the curve of her back. He would protect her. She would learn that she was safe here.

CHAPTER
16

Morning sunlight filtered through the library's dirty windows. On his cot in the history department, Books yawned and blinked his eyes. He had been up late the night before, attempting to pinpoint a mistake on an ancient Chinese scroll. For the past few years he had been studying both Chinese lettering and the Siddham alphabet used to transcribe Sanskrit in the seventh century.

The text that had kept him up was the "Heart of Perfect Wisdom" sutra. After hours of comparing the Chinese characters with the original Sanskrit, he ascertained that a Chinese translator had transcribed two syllables incorrectly, rendering the Chinese text meaningless. Only after he discovered this could he finally go to sleep.

Books rubbed his eyes, stretched, and wandered out into the reading room. Light flooded through the windows. On the central table, beside Books's scroll and set of dictionaries, there was a neat stack of books. It had not been there last night. Beside the stack, a single slim volume lay open on the table.

Books glanced around the room. Nothing else had been disturbed. Three cats slept peacefully on top of the card catalog.

The old man approached the table and inspected the open book. It was a collection of essays translated from the Chinese. The open page was headed "The Art of War, by Sun Tzu." Books glanced at the other volumes in the stack:

The Selected Writings of Mao Tse-tung, Mini-Manual of the Urban Guerrilla, A Short History of Guerrilla Warfare, The Anarchist Cookbook, and *Guerrilla Warfare* by Che Guevara.

The air in the room was warm and stuffy. As always, it smelled faintly of cats. But Books felt a sudden chill, as if a cold wind had blown through the library. Must it come to this? He was not a violent man. Certainly he had fought in a few barroom brawls in his youth, but that had been long ago. He had never picked a fight; he had always tried to leave when one started. Besides, he was an old man, not ready to lead a war. At best, he might serve as an advisor for some younger leader.

He turned away from the table, picked up the metal bucket that he kept by the reference desk, slung a towel over his shoulder, and went downstairs. Outside, he squatted beside the stream that ran past the library. The water chuckled quietly to itself as it curled around the marble stones of the library's side steps. A frog jumped into the stream, disturbed by Books's presence. Minnows darted for cover as his shadow crossed the water. Out here, Books could forget what he had found on the table.

He pulled off his shirt and took a bar of soap from his improvised soap dish, a niche in the ornate carvings that decorated the lamppost by the steps. He washed his face and splashed his chest, gasping when the cold water touched his skin. He ducked his head just below the stream's surface, then dried himself and combed his long white hair, taking his time and letting the sun soak into his bones.

When he could delay no longer, he filled the bucket with water and carried it back up to the reading room, where he filled the kettle and lit the flame on his kerosene stove. When the water boiled, the kettle whistled softly, a homey comforting sound. He made a cup of mint tea and ate a breakfast of bread and cheese. Then he could think of no other way to postpone looking at the books. Ever since Ms. Migsdale had brought him the message in a bottle, he had feared it would come to this eventually.

Carrying his second cup of tea, he reluctantly returned

to the books on the table and sat down in front of the open book to read:

All warfare is based on deception.

Therefore, when capable, feign incapacity; when active, inactivity.

When near, make it appear that you are far away; when far away, that you are near.

Offer the enemy a bait to lure him; feign disorder and strike him.

When he concentrates, prepare against him; where he is strong, avoid him.

Anger his general and confuse him.

Pretend inferiority and encourage his arrogance.

Keep him under a strain and wear him down.

When he is united, divide him.

Attack when he is unprepared; sally out when he does not expect you.

These are the strategist's keys to victory.

It was good advice, Books thought. He continued reading, pausing occasionally to sip his tea. One of the sleeping cats relocated to his lap. There was a certain grace to the writing, an elegant logic that elevated warfare from brute struggle to something closer to philosophy or poetry. And that wasn't so strange. After all, a Chinese general had to be a poet as well as a warrior.

Books finished the essay and picked up *The Writings of Mao Tse-tung.* It would take some study, but perhaps he could be ready for war.

Jax slowly brushed baby-blue paint onto a section of railing. Earlier that week, Danny-boy and The Machine had sandblasted the railing to remove the loose and peeling paint. The newly exposed metal was pitted from the salt air, and the paint went on unevenly, sticking in the crevices.

The weather was clear and fine, the perfect day for a work party. Danny-boy had a good turnout—thirty-five people had come to help paint. A light breeze blew toward her from the north tower, carrying bits of conversation and laughter. Jax knew most of the helpers. They were friendly enough; they joked with each other and shouted across the bridge, shared food and wine when they broke for lunch, talked continuously about projects and plans. Gambit kept calling down to people, telling them about the music that the wind played in the cables: "That's a perfect fifth. Can you hear it?" Ms. Migsdale recited poetry as she dabbed paint onto the base of a tower. At the far tower, Mercedes and her two helpers chattered in Spanish. But Jax didn't get the jokes, and the constant discussion made her head hurt.

Over the course of the day, she had drawn away from the others, choosing a place to paint that was as far as she could manage from the other people. She was working in a spot midway between the two towers. There, in the center of the main span, the cable dipped down to the roadway, then rose in a graceful arc to the tower tops. A monkey chattered at Jax from a perch on the bridge's cable. The animal had followed her out from the city and throughout the day had watched her paint.

In the distance, she could see the others. On the south tower, Mercedes and her helpers were painting an elaborate design of overlapping triangles in royal blue and turquoise and navy. On the north tower, Snake dangled from a rope. Jax could see the outline of a tremendous dragon; its massive coils encircled the tower. The body was outlined in pale blue. Some twenty feet above the roadway, Snake was working on the head. Danny-boy stood below him, calling out advice and instructions. The words, blown to Jax by the wind, were as meaningless as the cries of the seagulls or the baying of sea lions from beneath the bridge.

On the far side of the bridge, Gambit was methodically working his way up the main cable with a can of spray paint; he carried four spare cans, tied together with rope and slung around his neck. Lily was using an industrial rig to spray a coat of vivid turquoise on the base of the north tower.

The monkey chattered at Jax again. She had grown used to the monkeys and did not mind their noise. They seemed friendly enough, and their chatter was often easier to bear than the conversation of people. The animals did not expect her to chatter back, or to laugh in the right places, or to be polite.

"I'm a little tired of all this painting too," she said to the monkey. It tilted its head to one side, watching her, and then spoke to her again. "Can't make out a word of it," she said, and then dipped her brush and dabbed blue paint onto another foot of railing.

When she looked up again, the monkey had started climbing up the cable, walking on all fours with its butt in the air. About fifteen feet up the cable, the animal turned and looked back at her. Its expression was encouraging.

Jax glanced in the direction of Danny-boy and the other artists. No one was looking her way. She balanced her paintbrush on the edge of the paint can, climbed over the railing onto the cable, and followed the monkey.

The cable's surface was ridged, providing a purchase for her sneakers. Two wire ropes ran on either side of the main cable, offering fragile handholds. Ahead of her, the monkey bounded up the cable. Drawn by the promise of the deep blue sky overhead, Jax kept climbing.

It was a long walk up to the sky. The wind shook the main cable and tugged at Jax's jacket, as if it wanted to pick her up and carry her aloft like a kite or a cloud. She could see whitecaps on the water below. The monkey always stayed a little bit ahead of her, stopping now and then to look back over its shoulder.

Halfway up, she stopped. She had not intended to climb so high, but she liked the feeling of the wind on her face. The people on the bridge below were tiny. When they waved to her she lifted a hand and waved back, but she felt no urge to return to the roadbed.

The slope of the cable steepened as she approached the tower. The paint that covered the cable's ridged surface had peeled. It crackled under her feet as if she were walking on dead leaves. Whenever she took a step, the newly broken fragments blew away in a flurry of orange chips.

Once, her feet slipped and she had to cling to the wire rope to keep from falling. The monkey stopped and watched in silence from a few yards above her. Her hands were numb from the cold, and she could scarcely feel the wire rope, even though she gripped it tightly. A seagull, caught by the wind, called out to her as it blew past. She could not make out the words, but it sounded like a warning.

The top of the tower had been blasted clean by the wind. The cable ran through a saddle in the center. She sat down beside the cable and drew her knees up, hugging them for warmth. The monkey huddled beside her, leaning against her. "Long ways up," she said to the animal, but the monkey didn't reply.

To her left was the Golden Gate, the opening that led from San Francisco Bay to the Pacific Ocean. To her right was San Francisco, shrunken by distance to the size of the city in her glass globe. She could have cupped it in her two hands.

She was alone. She could not hear the artists or the gulls or the sea lions, only the steady rush of the wind past her ears. She looked out toward the city and tested the hollow place that she had found within her. It was not really a pain, but an emptiness. She had noticed it when she was listening to the artists joke amongst themselves.

She had been in the city for almost two months, but she had not found her mother. The city led her to one place or another, but never to where she really wanted to go.

She lay back on the tower top. The sky overhead was precisely the color of the satin ribbon that she had buried with her mother. Her eyes suddenly ached with tears. Her mother was dead. She had known that all along, but she had locked the knowledge away, hiding it from herself. Even if she found the angel, the best she could hope to find was her mother's ghost.

A gust of wind whipped the tears from Jax's eyes. But once the wind caught them they were not tears at all, but tiny blue butterflies that fought the wind to fly back to her. They hovered close to her body, sheltering from the wind in the folds of her clothing. They crept across her hands, tickling her cold flesh with delicate legs. Heat spread from each tiny pinprick where a leg touched.

She could not stop weeping. She was not sure why she wept. For her mother? For the city? But the tears came, and she could not stop them. She lifted her hands to wipe her eyes, and butterflies fluttered on her fingertips. They surrounded her, soft wings and velvety bodies gently brushing her face. She watched them creep on the bridge itself, flattening their wings against the orange surface and trembling just a little when the wind blew. They pressed themselves so close that they merged with the metal, covering the orange paint with their iridescent wings.

Her tears came more slowly. The air was filled with butterflies and her eyes hurt with the dry gritty feeling that follows tears.

"Jax?" Danny-boy's voice echoed from somewhere below her. "Jax?" His anxious tone was amplified and distorted by the echo. She heard the rattle of metal and a trapdoor opened. Danny-boy climbed out.

He did not call again, but came to her and put his arms around her. She did not pull away. He was warm from the long climb up the tower's interior and he smelled of sweat and paint. Beside her, the monkey grumbled at the intrusion. The last butterfly landed in Danny-boy's hair, its wings trembling.

"Are you all right?"

"I'm all right." She nodded and looked down at the bridge. Everywhere she looked it was blue, the color of her mother's satin ribbon, of the sky at twilight, of butterfly wings.

A Marin farmer, on his way to Duff's trading post to trade fresh produce for tools, stopped his wagon at the first tower of the Golden Gate Bridge. "I'll be damned," he said. "Will you look at that. They painted it blue." He stared at the dragon that coiled around a tower.

His ten-year-old son had already jumped down from the ox cart. He ran over to examine the tower more closely. "It's butterflies, Dad," he called back.

"What do you mean—butterflies?" The farmer climbed down from the wagon and followed his son to the tower. Up close, he could see the gaps in the blue paint. It did look like someone had painted thousands of butterflies on the metal surface. Flecks of orange showed where the wings had not quite covered the surface; the blue was darker where wings from two insects had overlapped. The blue shimmered in the sunlight, slightly iridescent.

The farmer scratched at the surface with a work-hardened fingernail. The blue did not scratch off.

"Look, Dad," the boy said. He had found a living butterfly, sunning itself on the railing, and had captured it in his cupped hands. "I got one of them."

"Doesn't make sense," the farmer grumbled. "Come on, let's go."

Reluctantly, the boy let the butterfly go and returned to the cart with his father. The insect, a straggler who had been blown away by the wind, found a butterfly-sized patch where the orange paint still showed, opened its wings, and flattened itself against the surface. The ox cart moved off in the direction of San Francisco.

"The people who live in that city are crazy," the farmer muttered, more to himself than to his son. "It's always been that way." But his son smiled, thinking of butterflies; and the farmer, for reasons that he could not name, felt a little happier too.

CHAPTER
17

Rose Maloney had grown up in the Richmond district, just a few blocks away from Saint Monica's Church. Each Sunday her mother took her to Mass. Her father was a building contractor who drank too much and was always generous in his inevitable repentance. Maloney & Associates repaired the church's roof, fixed leaks in its plumbing, improved its wiring.

Rose's childhood memories were filled with polished wooden pews, perfumed holy water, stained glass windows in which every bit of glass shone like a jewel. When Rose was old enough to enroll in kindergarten, she went to the parish school and spent her weekdays under the watchful eyes of black-clad nuns. During recess the students played on the blacktop that doubled as a parking lot on Sundays. Games of four-square, Chinese jumprope, jacks, and dodgeball were conducted beneath the shadow of Saint Monica's steeple.

Rose was thirty-nine years old when the Plague struck. She had never married, and she had always lived in her parents' house. When she graduated from high school, she had taken a job as a secretary. She was a thin woman with a square face and mousy hair that her mother's hairdresser cut in a style that matched her mother's. At the time of the Plague, Rose had been working for many years in a small insurance office: typing forms, filing forms, removing forms from the files. She assisted with Catechism class each Saturday and played the organ for weddings.

Then the Plague came. Her father was an early victim: half the parish attended his funeral. Her mother's funeral, held just two weeks later, was sparsely attended—by that time, death had become commonplace and every family had funerals of its own to attend. The priest had comforted Rose and murmured platitudes about the will of God.

After the Plague, when Rose was the last remaining member of the congregation, she continued to walk to the church each day. She sat in a wooden pew, gazing at the effigy of Christ on the cross and admiring the colored light that poured in through the stained glass. She missed chatting with her friends after the service; she missed the Sunday afternoon potluck dinners. But she felt quite at home in the empty church.

She took good care of the church. Every morning, she swept the congregation hall's marble floor. She filled the fonts with water—it wasn't holy water, but she could not help that. She watered the plants that grew in planter boxes just inside the door. This last was her favorite chore; she had always been an amateur gardener.

One Sunday, three months after the Exodus, she sat in the empty church and looked at the altar. It seemed awfully bare. She wondered if God would mind if she dressed it up a little with flowers and plants. Surely He wouldn't, she thought.

As she was thinking about it, a warbler flew in through the open door of the church, perched on the altar, tilted its head back to release a burst of song, then flew to perch on Christ's head. It was, Rose thought, a sign from God.

She started slowly, with a few pots of geraniums beneath the crucifix and baskets of English ivy beside each station of the cross. She took the plants from the nursery, stilling a pang of conscience by tallying up the cost of the plants and leaving an IOU at the register.

She opened the church's windows to let in more light and air. Finches and sparrows came to explore the cool interior. She took to feeding them—scattering bird seed on the marble floor beside the altar. Each day, she added something: a window box filled with the soft-leafed house plant known as creeping Charlie, a plaster replica of a Grecian urn in which a glossy-leafed olive tree grew, a potted palm that she rescued from someone's living room.

After a year or so, she moved to the rectory to be closer to her garden. She set up a system of barrels to catch the rainwater, so that she would have irrigation water during the summer months. She planted ivy at the base of the steeple, bamboo in the baptismal font. When a minor earth tremor broke three of the stained glass windows, she tore out all the colored glass to let in more light. The plants flourished; the birds sang in the foliage and nested on the outstretched arms of the crucifix.

Danny-boy watched Books flip through a field guide to butterflies. "What about this one?" Books said, holding the book out to Jax and tapping his finger on a photo of a pale blue butterfly. "It's about the right size. And it's a uniform blue, as you said."

Jax examined the photo and shook her head. "Wrong color. You can see if you go look at the bridge. These were a darker blue."

Books continued leafing through the book. For the past few hours he had been writing down Jax's account of the incident at the bridge, noting the details for his history of the city. He was determined to identify the precise species of butterfly, and he was having little luck. "Are you certain they weren't moths?" he muttered.

"I suppose they could have been," Jax said. "Butterflies and moths aren't that different, I guess."

Shaking his head, Books pulled another book from the stack on the table. Danny-boy wandered away, leaving the two of them poring over a field guide to moths. He strolled down the broad stairway that led to the foyer and stood in the doorway, looking out across the Civic Center Plaza.

It had been drizzling on and off since morning, and the sky was a sodden gray. He felt restless, tired of being indoors. Ever since the butterflies had made painting the rest of the bridge unnecessary, he had been feeling at loose ends, in need of a new project.

He heard a bicycle bell ringing and saw Ms. Migsdale riding her bicycle down McAllister Street toward him. Her orange poncho flapped as she rode, like a tropical bird desperate to escape this earthbound mode of transportation. She pulled up at the curb and leaned her bicycle against a lamppost.

"Hello," she called to him as she climbed the library steps. "Glad to find you here. I came to tell Books that Fourstar's sent a scouting party to Duff's place. This is more than the usual spy masquerading as a trader. Looks like he's getting serious."

Danny-boy felt a touch of excitement, which he tried to suppress. It seemed wrong to be glad that the long-promised invasion was finally materializing.

In the foyer, Ms. Migsdale pulled off the poncho, scattering drops of rainwater on the marble floor. She draped the wet garment over the check-out counter and left it dripping. Danny-boy followed her upstairs where she interrupted Jax and Books to tell them her news.

"Ten men, headed by a short dark fellow called Rodriguez. Seems like they came the long way around: over the Richmond Bridge and then over the Golden Gate. According to Duff, Rodriguez claims he wanted to avoid a skirmish with the Black Dragons in Oakland. But Duff thinks he wanted to avoid a direct route through the city. A cautious man, I'd say."

Danny-boy noticed that Jax's expression was grim. He rubbed her shoulder gently, but she seemed to take no notice.

"Duff says he's been asking about the city. Says he wants to talk to some representatives of the local government."

"I'll talk to him," Danny-boy said, just as Jax said, "I'll go."

Ms. Migsdale looked at Books. "I thought we might all go. Together we represent a good cross-section of the city, wouldn't you say?"

As always, the asphalt courtyard in front of Duff's trading post bustled with farmers, traders, scavengers, and city dwellers. Farmers were selling vegetables from wagons and makeshift stalls. The drooping awnings that sheltered the produce steamed in the afternoon sun as the last of the rain evaporated.

With the others, Danny-boy followed Ms. Migsdale through the market. The old woman greeted many of the traders by name, inquiring after their families and promising to stop and chat after she finished her business with Rodriguez.

"Ms. Migsdale knows just about everybody who trades at Duff's," Danny-boy told Jax. "That's one way she gets stories for the *New City News*."

Jax nodded, but didn't reply. She held her crossbow in her right hand, and her left kept straying to touch her knife.

"You doing all right?" he asked, touching her arm.

"I wish I'd been wrong." He could barely hear her voice over the noise of the market. "I thought maybe they wouldn't come after all."

He squeezed her arm in an effort at reassurance. "You don't have to talk to them. You can go back to the city."

She shot him an incredulous look. "Go back? Not likely. I have to stay. These guys would eat you three for breakfast and look around for more."

"You're underestimating us," Danny-boy protested. "You'd be surprised at—"

"Right," she said in a tone of disbelief. She straightened her shoulders and whistled to Jezebel, who was delicately sniffing at an unattended basket of dried fish. "I'm coming."

On the front porch of one of Duff's houses, they found a barefoot soldier leaning against the wall and polishing his black boots. "Excuse me," Ms. Migsdale said. "We're looking for a man named Rodriguez."

The soldier, a Chicano no older than Danny-boy, looked up from his work, studying them with eyes as black and expressionless as his polished boot. "You mean Major Rodriguez?"

"I suppose so," Ms. Migsdale said.

"What's your business?"

Danny-boy noticed Jax stiffen, but she said nothing. Ms. Migsdale ignored the soldier's hostile tone. "We under-

stand he wanted to speak with some representatives from
the city," she said mildly.

"You represent the city?" The soldier eyed the group—
taking in Ms. Migsdale's orange poncho and Books's stained
gray suit—and laughed. "You've got to be kidding. This
place must be even worse off than we thought. Is the dog a
representative too?"

"There's really no need to take that attitude," Books
began. "I don't see . . ."

Danny-boy glanced at Jax and saw her lift her crossbow. "Soldier, we don't have time to waste on your bullshit," she said, and fired the bolt into the wall just a few
inches above the man's head. The bolt penetrated the wood
with a sharp crack. Without taking her eyes from the soldier, Jax slipped another bolt into place and lifted the bow
again.

Danny-boy noticed that the traders nearest the house
had fallen silent and were watching the soldier. He saw the
soldier's eyes dart to the traders, then back to Jax. The
corners of her mouth lifted in a kind of smile. "Just wanted
to get your attention," she said softly.

"Why don't you try being polite, son?" a trader suggested.

"Don't know if he knows how," said a farmer standing
nearby.

"There's no need for all this," Ms. Migsdale broke in.
"If you would just let Major Rodriguez know that we're
here, I'm certain that he'll be glad to see us."

The soldier backed away, abandoning his boots on the
porch and vanishing through the front door. Danny-boy laid
a hand on Jax's shoulder. "Take it easy," he murmured. She
was trembling, ever so slightly. "It's okay."

The curtain at an upstairs window moved, as if someone were glancing out. A few minutes later, a different soldier—this one with his boots on and his rifle in hand—came
to escort them into a small living room.

Major Rodriguez was a clean-shaven man with a military haircut. He smiled when Books introduced the members of the group, but the expression was just a movement of
the lips. It never reached his eyes. "My apologies for the

incident at the door. I wasn't expecting a citizen's delegation." He sounded more annoyed than apologetic.

He shook hands with Books, Ms. Migsdale, and Danny-boy. Jax hung back, remaining in the doorway. The soldier who had escorted them to the room held his rifle ready and kept his eyes on Jax. The Major gestured to the couch, and Ms. Migsdale, Books, and Danny-boy sat down.

"Please make yourself comfortable," he said to Jax.

She didn't move. "I am comfortable," she said.

Major Rodriguez's smile vanished for an instant, then reappeared quickly. He shrugged. "As you like." He turned his attention to Books, the person he clearly regarded as the leader of the group. "Now, what portion of the city's population do you represent?"

Books wet his lips, frowning. "We represent ourselves, of course. And we can talk to the others. But you see, we don't have a representative form of government. We follow more of a town council model. When we want to decide something, we all get together and discuss it. But you'd be surprised at how few things really affect everyone. Most decisions can be made in smaller groups."

"I see. But you've been appointed to talk for the other people who live in the city?"

"Not at all," Books said. "We just thought we'd come and find out what you wanted."

Rodriguez frowned. "Then you aren't an official delegation?"

Books looked at Danny-boy and Ms. Migsdale. "As official as you'll find anywhere in the city, I'd guess. Wouldn't you say?"

Danny-boy shrugged. "I suppose."

"You won't find anything more official," Ms. Migsdale said. "I'd say you're lucky to find anyone who wants to talk to you at all."

"You might as well talk to us," Books said. "We can let the others know what you say. So why don't you just explain what you're doing here?"

Rodriguez shifted uneasily in his seat, then straightened his shoulders as if determined to proceed under such irregular circumstances. "I'm sure that you're aware of

Sacramento's efforts to reunify our nation," he said. "Under
the leadership of General Alexander Miles, the citizens of
the Central Valley are reaching out to their neighbors.
Wherever we find pockets of survivors, struggling to make a
new life in the ruins of the old, we join with them, add our
strength to theirs. I've come to invite you to join us."

Danny-boy studied the faces of his companions during
Rodriguez's speech. Books looked noncommittal, Jax
looked hostile, and Ms. Migsdale's expression grew distinctly sour. When Rodriguez finished, they sat in silence for
a moment. Finally, Ms. Migsdale spoke.

"I wouldn't say we were struggling," she said dryly.
"In fact, I'd say we were doing quite well." She stared at
Rodriguez steadily. Danny-boy had seen her use the same
kind of look on Tommy when he misbehaved. "And from
what I hear, General Miles's invitations are difficult to de-
cline. As I understand it, the folks in Fresno chose not to
accept the invitation—and yet somehow they're now part of
the General's empire."

Rodriguez leaned back in his chair. Danny-boy had the
feeling that he welcomed Ms. Migsdale's objection. "In
Fresno, a minority faction attempted to prevent the city
from joining our alliance. The General's army assisted the
legitimate government in overcoming this resistance." He
smiled, showing a thin line of yellowing teeth. "If you visit
Fresno today, you'll find that the citizens are proud to be
part of our alliance."

"I find that difficult to believe," Ms. Migsdale muttered.

"Could you be more specific, Major?" Books asked
calmly. "What exactly do you want from us?"

"We want to join forces with you," Rodriguez said.
"Our forces will protect you from your enemies. In return,
the resources of San Francisco will assist our efforts. Both
parties will benefit."

Danny-boy spoke for the first time, genuinely puzzled
by Rodriguez. "I don't understand. Who are you going to
protect us from? The only people who ever bother us much
are the Black Dragons, and they haven't been on this side of
the bay for years."

Rodriguez glanced at Danny-boy, obviously annoyed by what he perceived as an interruption from a minor member of the delegation. "I'm sure you're aware of the fanatics to the south and the bigamists to the east," Rodriguez said. "The fabric of our society is threatened by gypsies, who wander from place to place, spreading infection, stealing. General Miles seeks to restore order to a nation sorely in need of it."

Danny-boy scratched his head. "I've always liked the gypsies and traders. They've got some interesting ideas. How would we get our news if they weren't around?"

"I agree," Books said. "Why, I had a fascinating conversation just the other day with a Mormon who had stopped for the night here at Duff's. Quite an intelligent man, though I felt his views on the Bible were rather narrow. Still it was an interesting interchange."

"It seems we have a very basic disagreement," Ms. Migsdale broke in. "You seem to think that joining together into a larger and more powerful nation is automatically good. We don't necessarily agree. Personally, I've always thought that nations were tremendously overrated. I can't say I was particularly proud to be an American; I never cared much for America as a whole, though I liked my neighborhood well enough. I've always favored a somewhat looser structure, more like the city-states of early Greece."

Danny-boy spoke up, trying to explain their position more clearly. "I don't really like this business of wanting to restore order," he said. "I think disorder works just fine. There's a lot to be said for chaos. It's a much more creative environment. So I guess we don't have much to say to each other. It doesn't seem like we have all that much in common." He hesitated, watching the expression on Rodriguez's face. The man seemed so distressed. Danny-boy groped for a suggestion that might comfort him. "But maybe you could send some of your artists here. Just a few, maybe. That'd be fun. They'd bring in some new ideas, and it might be interesting."

"Not a bad idea," Books said. "Sort of a cultural exchange program. A few poets and painters. And sculptors— we have a very active group of sculptors."

"Sculptors," Rodriguez echoed in a choked voice. "Poets and painters." He shook his head slowly. "You don't seem to understand your position." He hesitated for a moment, taking a deep breath. "General Miles wants an alliance with San Francisco. It would be in your best interests to agree. Since you admit that you have no central government, we would help you institute a provisional government immediately. After that . . ."

"What if we refuse General Miles's offer?" Ms. Migsdale interrupted.

Rodriguez shrugged. His face had returned to a carefully pleasant expression, but his smile held a suggestion of threat. "I strongly suggest you accept. One way or the other, the General will have San Francisco."

Danny-boy heard Jax's feet shift on the carpeted floor. He shot her a warning look. She wet her lips and remained still.

"I don't agree," Ms. Migsdale said. "I don't agree at all." She stood. "Perhaps we'd best be going. I think we've heard enough."

Danny-boy took a firm grip on Jax's right arm as the soldier escorted them to the door. It seemed that there would be trouble soon enough. He did not want her to begin it prematurely.

CHAPTER
18

The next morning Rodriguez consulted his map and took a party of five men into the city. They rode down Geary Street, heading toward what had once been the business district. He was confident that they would have no trouble here. If the odd bunch who had visited him were representative of the city's population, then taking the city would be easy. No central government, no organization—resistance would be minimal.

The sky was overcast, and tendrils of fog drifted through the city. The street was quiet except for the horses' hooves against the asphalt and the jingle of their harnesses.

Initially, Rodriguez found the city to be unremarkable. He had explored abandoned cities before. San Francisco was larger than any other he had visited, but otherwise it was much the same.

A few miles from Duff's place, Rodriguez first noticed evidence that this was not quite like Fresno or Modesto. At one intersection were hundreds of identical baby dolls who watched the soldiers with wide blue crystalline eyes. The dolls sat on the curbs, on the sidewalk, on the green wooden bus benches. Over the entrance to a store was a metal structure that had once supported an awning; the canvas had long since rotted away to tatters. Hundreds of dolls perched on the framework, their pudgy legs locked around the metal tubing. When the breeze blew, the canvas tatters fluttered, tickling the naked plastic bellies.

The hoof of a horse brushed against a doll and knocked it over. A strange mewling came from within the doll: "Maaa-Maaa." The horse shied, but the soldier brought the animal back under control.

It made no sense, but the unwinking stare of the pale blue eyes made Rodriguez uneasy. Who would go to the trouble of collecting so many dolls? Why would anyone bother? It looked like something from a bad dream. Not quite a nightmare, but a vaguely disturbing dream in which nothing is quite right. "Waste of time," he muttered to the man riding at his side, and the soldier nodded nervously.

A block farther on, Rodriguez heard distant screaming: a high-pitched mechanical sound that carried a hint of hysteria. He reined in his horse, looking around for the source of the sound. Just then, dozens of remote-controlled toy cars raced from a side street. Each one was the size of a large rat. They were made of brightly colored plastic, decorated with racing stripes and numbers.

His mare panicked. She reared as the screaming toys ran under her feet, zigzagging in a demented and unpredictable course. She danced and bucked, as if trying to get all her feet off the ground at the same time. Rodriguez fought to get her under control, but she ignored the bit and spurs. Around him, the other horses were bucking. The horse that had spooked earlier bolted in the direction of the baby dolls.

The cars circled once, then zigzagged down a side street. Rodriguez regained control of his horse. "Whoa there," he murmured to her, patting the side of her neck. Her eyes were wild, but she settled down.

A horse had stepped on one of the toys. It lay half-crushed on the street, twitching helplessly, still making the terrible screaming sound.

Rodriguez dismounted to examine the thing more closely. The demonic shrieking came from a device mounted on the car's back. He poked at the toy with the barrel of his rifle, then flipped it over onto its back. Its wheels spun in the air and the squealing sound went up an octave.

Someone must be controlling the toys. He glanced around. The fog swirled around the tall buildings. No people; no sound. Not far away, the spire of a concrete pagoda marked Japan Center. He knew from his map that they were about halfway to downtown.

"It's just a fucking toy," he said contemptuously. He stomped on the little car. Metal bent and plastic crunched beneath his boots, but he kept stomping until the squealing stopped. He looked up to find his men staring at him, and he kicked the remains into the gutter.

From the roof of Japan Center's Miyako Hotel, Danny-boy watched through binoculars as Rodriguez demolished the toy. "One casualty," he said. "Sorry, T.M."

The Machine was busy at the controls, directing the swarm of cars to a safe distance away from the soldiers. "No problem. There are plenty more in the toy stores."

"He looks pissed," Jax said. She sat at Danny-boy's elbow, leaning forward and staring through another set of binoculars. "Out of control."

Danny-boy put his hand on her shoulder. Her muscles were tense. "Take it easy," he said. "Just relax."

She glanced at him, then looked back at Rodriguez. "Tell it to the man who's stomping a toy to death. I'm fine."

He took his hand off her shoulder and returned to his binoculars. But he didn't believe her, not for a minute.

Rodriguez mounted and led the way down Geary Street. The fog had grown thicker. It seemed to close in behind them, absorbing the sounds they made. The hoof-beats of the horses were muffled; the jingling of the harness on Rodriguez's own horse seemed distant. Cold mist swirled around them, carried by eddies of air. "Strange wind currents," Rodriguez murmured, wanting to break the silence. "Must be the way the streets are laid out. The buildings channel the wind."

The silence swallowed Rodriguez's words. He became intensely aware of the sound of his own breathing. He still carried his rifle ready; he had not holstered it after poking at the toy car and he did not want to holster it now. He noticed that the others held their rifles ready as well. "Easy," he said to them softly. "It's just a little fog." He did not like the sound of his own voice.

They rode for some distance, and nothing untoward happened. He started to relax. Any strange city would be unnerving, he told himself. As he relaxed, the city no longer seemed as oppressive. It seemed almost welcoming. Some of the buildings even looked familiar. Then he suddenly realized that the buildings were familiar. They had just reached the turn that led back to Duff's place, and he could see the trading post in the distance.

"We must have lost our bearings in the fog." He wheeled his horse to ride forth again. They reached the corner with the baby dolls, passed the street from which the toy cars had emerged. A little bit beyond that, the buildings began to look familiar once again. And then they were heading back to Duff's.

Rodriguez swore and consulted his map. They tried again, following Balboa, a residential street that ran parallel to Geary. Somehow, in the thick fog, they found themselves back at Duff's.

And so it went, that day and the next and the day after, until at last Rodriguez returned to Sacramento to recommend that General Miles follow a different route into the city.

CHAPTER
19

The day after Rodriguez left, Jax sat on the roof of the Saint Francis Hotel, fletching a new set of bolts for her crossbow. The shaft of each new bolt was made of quarter-inch aluminum pipe, taken from a downtown hardware store. At Jax's request, The Machine had sliced the pipe into one-foot lengths and fitted each one with a sharpened stainless steel tip. The Machine had offered to fletch the bolts as well: he had some thin copper sheeting that would substitute for feathers. But Jax had declined, preferring the feathers she had gathered in Golden Gate Park. Feathers of hawks and feathers of owls—it seemed to Jax that these would make a bolt fly better than a fletching of lifeless copper. It only made sense.

The sky was a clear pale blue, washed clean by the afternoon's rain. A puddle of water had collected in one corner of the roof, and three sparrows were bathing in the water, splashing and chirping noisily.

Jezebel eyed them but did not stir from her place at Danny-boy's side. Danny-boy lay on the rooftop with one hand tucked behind his head.

Jax set a feather on the roof. With her pocketknife, she split it neatly along its quill. She trimmed the two halves to the proper dimensions.

"Why are you making those bolts of metal?" Danny-boy asked. She glanced over and found him studying her. "All your old ones are made of wood."

"They'll be stronger," she said. She offered him one of the completed bolts.

"You're making a lot of them."

"I figure I'll need a lot of them." She watched him run his hands down the metal shaft and test the point. "Ms. Migsdale thinks that we have about a month before Fourstar and his army arrive."

Danny-boy rolled the bolt between his hands. "You plan to meet him with a crossbow?"

"It's better than nothing."

He handed her the bolt and returned to his perusal of the sky. "Seems like there should be a better way."

"Yeah, maybe so." She set the bolt with the others and selected another feather. "Snake's been looking for guns, but most of the obvious places were cleaned out years ago. He found a stash hidden in a house in the Sunset, and he's looking for more. But ammunition's still a problem."

He watched her, still holding the bolt. "But one way or another, you want to kill them?"

She frowned, wondering what he was getting at. Of course she wanted to kill them. "Sure. Kill them before they kill me." She tried to slice another feather along its quill, but the knife slipped, ruining one half. His questions made her uneasy.

"Something's wrong with that," he said softly.

"Oh, yeah?" She started to trim the undamaged half of the feather, but the knife slipped again. She sheathed the knife and gave Danny-boy her full attention. "All right—so tell me what's wrong with it."

"Fourstar comes after us with guns and violence and we fight back with the same. That doesn't seem right. The gun and the knife—those are Fourstar's symbols. If we adopt his weapons, it seems like we're no better than he is. We become the enemy we want to defeat."

She stared at the half-finished bolts. She did not like this way of talking. Why would they become the enemy? "I don't know what you mean."

"We can't win by using guns," Danny-boy said. "It's not that simple." He turned on his side and lifted himself on one elbow, watching her face.

"Don't talk like that," she said. "We can win. We just need more guns. Or explosives. We could blow up the bridge before they get here."

Danny-boy shook his head. "That's the wrong approach. We won't win that way."

She crossed her arms to keep her hands from trembling. "Then what is the right approach?"

"Don't be angry," he said. "That's what I'm trying to figure out." He rubbed his chin thoughtfully. "You know, Duff once taught me to play a game called poker. And I always lost."

"So?"

"When I asked Duff why I lost so much, he grinned and told me that you can't beat a man at his own game. I think he's right." After a pause, Danny-boy continued. "You think there's only one way to fight—with guns and knives and killing. But the way I figure it—you're playing into Fourstar's hands. That's Fourstar's kind of war. That's his game, and he's good at it. We've got to get him to play our game, not try to beat him at his."

"What's our game?" she asked.

He was looking down at his own hands. Beneath each fingernail was a crescent of pale blue paint, reminders of the Golden Gate Bridge. "Our game? We're good at making traders unwilling to visit downtown. We're good at keeping farmers at Duff's and away from the rest of the city. We're good at showing people a view of the world that they've never seen before. We're good at making people uneasy. We're good at convincing people to see things differently."

"So far, those don't seem like real useful talents. Not in a war," she said.

He looked up from his hands and met her eyes. "They could be," he said. "We don't have to kill Fourstar's soldiers. All we have to do is change their minds. We just have to make them think that we could kill them at any time. That would be enough. Let's think of this war as an art project."

Jax shook her head. "No."

He didn't seem to notice her denial. "I've been talking to Books. He says that the outcome of a war depends largely

on the morale and conviction of the people who are fighting
it. He told me about this war that America fought in a place
called Vietnam. A little tiny country, Vietnam, up against
the enormous military force of America." He sat up, caught
by his own enthusiasm. "But Vietnam won. They drove the
Americans out."

"Without killing any soldiers?"

"Oh, they killed plenty—but that wasn't the important
part. What was important, Books says, was the loss of morale among the American troops. They didn't believe they
could win. And so they didn't." Danny-boy leaned forward,
holding out his hands. "Books also told me about this guy
called Gandhi. The country where he lived had been taken
over by the British. And Gandhi drove the British out by
fighting a new kind of war. Rather than attacking them, he
just got in the way. Passive resistance. The British didn't
know what to do. They didn't know how to deal with this
guy. So eventually, they left. Seems like we could manage
something like that."

Jax shook her head. "You don't understand. War can't
be art. We have to kill them."

Danny-boy reached out, taking her hand. "Look,
they're people too. You may not like them, but I don't think
we should kill them while we have other alternatives. It
seems to me . . ."

She pulled her hand away and stood up. "You don't
understand," she repeated. She turned away from him,
abandoning her crossbow and bolts, running away across
the roof and down the stairs. She heard Danny-boy calling
after her, but did not stop to listen.

Somewhere in her stomach was a knot of feeling that
she could not allow herself to touch. She could skirt the
edges of it, chart its size and location, feel it hard and heavy
in her belly. But she could not touch it. When she probed
the edges, she felt the cold sensation that comes with a great
injury, like the chill that follows the cut of a knife, just
before the pain hits.

She stood at the front entrance to the hotel. In the
center of the square, the nameless bronze lady on the pillar
lifted her trident over the rotting remnants of squash vines

and tomato plants. The rain had washed her clean, and she glistened in the early afternoon light. Like the bronze statue, Danny-boy had his eyes fixed on the sky, ignoring the rubbish at his feet. Fourstar would walk in and take over the city while Danny-boy stared up at the clouds and talked about symbols.

With no destination in mind, Jax began walking. Puddles in the street reflected the buildings of downtown. Each puddle offered a slightly different view of the city, showing it from a different perspective.

She kept walking, leaving Danny-boy behind. He frightened her. She did not understand him. The words he spoke made sense individually; together they were nonsense. But he believed his own words, and that was the most frightening thing of all.

He trusted the world, trusted the people in it—and that terrified her. He told her to relax—as if she were the one who needed to change. She told him that she was right and he was wrong, and he just smiled. He was the water in a stream, gently wearing away the rocks on the bank. Which is stronger: the rock or the water?

She kept walking, watching the reflections in the puddles. She could leave the city, she told herself. Leave before Fourstar came, and save herself at least. But she knew, even as she tried to convince herself, that she could not leave. She belonged in the city now.

After a time, she noticed that the buildings in the puddles no longer looked familiar. She had left downtown and was in a residential neighborhood. She kept walking.

The awareness of her mother's presence crept up on her slowly. She could not pinpoint the moment when she knew that her mother was leading her somewhere, but when she saw her mother's reflection in one of the puddles, she was not surprised. As Jax watched, the image of her mother caught her eyes, smiled, then vanished.

Jax looked up from the puddle. She stood in front of 738 Ashbury Street, a two-story Victorian that had once been painted royal blue with white and gold trim around the bay windows. The paint had faded and cracked over the years. A roof that extended out over the front steps shaded the trim surrounding the front door. There a spray of golden wheat stalks stood out against a cream-colored background.

It was her mother's house. Jax knew that with a strange certainty. She climbed the steps and tried the knob. The door was locked.

As she stepped back from the door, a squirrel scolded her from the branches of a camphor tree. The tree grew in a square of dirt in the sidewalk. Over the years it had outgrown its confines: its roots had cracked the surrounding cement; its spreading branches brushed against the house. Jax eyed a thick branch that passed quite near the small roof over the front door. From that roof she would be able to reach the upper-story windows.

The camphor tree had generous branches that gave her good footing. The jump from the branch to the roof was only a few feet.

White rice paper blinds hid the room's interior, but Jax could see that the window was not latched. She pushed up on the window, but it did not open. She tried again, harder this time. The frame shuddered, but remained closed. Chips of cream-colored paint flaked off and showered onto the roof. She braced herself and put her shoulder into the push. The window frame moved reluctantly, opening a few inches. Jax slipped her fingers into the gap and heaved up on the window. It slid another few inches, then a foot, a foot and a half. She pushed the blind aside and squirmed headfirst through the opening.

The air smelled of dust. She could make out the vague shapes of furniture: some bookcases, an upright piano, a sofa, two overstuffed chairs. On top of the piano was a vase that held several withered flower stalks.

The past was thick in the air around her. It crowded her, pressing close. She walked across the room, her footsteps loud on the hardwood floor. When she played a few tentative notes on the upright piano, they hung in the air, like a question she had not intended to ask.

From the mantelpiece, she picked up a photograph of a smiling family. In the dim light Jax could see a dark-haired woman, a man with curly red hair, and two young boys. The woman leaned lovingly against the man; she had her arm around his waist. Her right hand rested on the shoulder of one of the boys.

Jax carried the photograph to the window where the light was better. The woman in the photo looked very much like her mother, but she had never seen her mother smile like that. It was a happy, open smile; the woman in the photo was calm and at ease with herself. Jax peered at the faces of the man and the boys, wondering what it was about them that made her mother smile so.

She set the photo back on the mantel and prowled through the house. She was used to empty houses: shelters bounded by walls and roofs and floor, places where people had lived and died, leaving behind bits and pieces of lives. She had wandered through many houses, examining photos, books, bowling trophies, children's drawings held to the refrigerators with magnets shaped like fruit, ceramic knick-knacks of horses and dogs.

But this house felt different. These things meant something. She had lived with her mother for sixteen years, but somehow the mother she had lived with seemed like an abandoned hull, a mechanical woman. The essence of her mother was here, still in this house, still in this city, lingering here with the things that her mother had left behind.

When she was a child, she had sometimes watched her mother in secret. Once she had climbed a tree that grew by the garden. All day long, she hid among the leaves. Through the hot afternoon, she had watched her mother pull weeds and pick cutworms from the tomato plants. Late in the day, after her mother went inside, she had climbed down and noisily returned home, claiming that hunting had been bad. She did not know what she had expected to learn by watching her mother, but she could not stop herself from doing it.

One evening, when her mother had sent her out to get wood for the fire, she had stopped at the window and stared in. Her mother was reading a book by the light of the kerosene lamp. Jax remembered feeling as if her chest were being squeezed by a big hand. She had not been able to breathe. Her heart had pounded as if she had run a long way. She had turned away from the window, gotten the wood, and fed the fire, saying nothing to her mother. She had not known what to say. Exploring the house now, Jax felt as she had when she stared through the window at her mother.

In a bedroom decorated with pictures of dogs, she found her brothers, the two boys from the photo on the mantel. They lay in twin beds. Their flesh had decayed; only discolored bones remained. At the head of each bed was a miniature license plate that identified the bed's occupant. Mark lay on his back, with the covers drawn up to his chin. John was curled up on his side. On the table between the beds were medicines: a jar filled with pale blue capsules, a bottle in which cough medicine had crystallized.

Jax sat for a long time in the rocking chair that was between the two beds. This was where her mother had sat when she read bedtime stories to the little boys. Jax tried to imagine her mother, the mother in the photograph, sitting in the chair and telling a story in a low soft voice. She closed her eyes, but the only sound was the chirping of a bird outside the window.

She left the children's room and stepped back into the hall. Beside the children's room was a small study. Here Jax felt her mother's presence most strongly. She sat in the oak desk chair in front of a cluttered desk. A color snapshot was tacked to a bulletin board: her mother stood with two other women beneath a banner that read "Peace In Our Time." Beneath the photo was a political cartoon: a scruffy-looking monkey stood between two men: Uncle Sam and a portly man wearing the emblem of the hammer and sickle. Each of the men held one of the monkey's hands.

Jax examined the clutter on the desk. In the center was a folder stuffed with yellowed newspaper clippings. A rubber band was wrapped around the folder, holding it closed —as if her mother had prepared to take the folder with her, then changed her mind. The rubber crumbled into stiff pieces when Jax tried to remove it.

Jax shuffled through the clippings. They all seemed to be about the movement that Books had described, the one that had brought the monkeys to San Francisco. She flipped through them idly, wondering why her mother had bothered to clip them out. "Girl Scout Troop Raises $10,000 for

Peace Monkeys," "Zoo Director Welcomes Peace Monkeys," "100,000 Attend Parade."

Halfway through the stack, Jax found a photo of her mother, beneath a headline that read "Buddhist Activist Struggles to Bring Peace Monkeys to San Francisco."

By the dim light that filtered through the dirty window, Jax read the story. The reporter told the legend of the monkeys in much the same way Books had. The article described the movement to bring monkeys from Nepal to the United States and quoted Jax's mother at length.

" 'People say that the monkeys are just a symbol,' Laurenson says. 'I agree. But you must not underestimate the power of symbols. The Christian cross, the Star of David, the swastika—these are all just symbols. But they are symbols of great power. People have fought wars over symbols. It only seems right that we should use a symbol to bring about peace.

" 'Don't get me wrong—I'm not opposed to all conflict. Conflict is, unfortunately, inevitable—there will always be arguments, marital spats, and territorial squabbles. What I'm against is war: the institutional dehumanization of the group of people that we label the enemy. The Bible says, "Thou shalt not kill," but that refers to people, and when we're at war, the inhabitants of another nation are no longer people. They are the enemy, and therefore we can kill them.' "

Jax shifted in her chair. Reading her mother's words made her uncomfortable.

" 'Of course there are things that I would fight for: I'd fight to protect my children, my home. But I might not fight the way you expect. I think we've become, over the centuries, locked into one way of fighting: kill or be killed. That's why the British were so startled by Gandhi's approach to conflict. He came up with a new way of fighting, a method that recognized the essential humanity of the people on the opposite side. The British didn't know what to do with him.

" 'The military establishment recognizes that the peace movement has found a new way of fighting, a new weapon, in the peace monkeys. They're still trying to figure out how to deal with this movement. They've tried dismissing it, discrediting it, suppressing it. But none of their traditional tactics has worked. I can only hope they choose the next obvious tactic.' She grinned, as if at a private joke when asked what that tactic might be. 'They join us, of course.' "

Jax slipped the article back into the folder and looked quickly through the other articles. In the back of the folder, tucked behind all the rest, was the front section of a newspaper, doubled over and stuffed into the folder. Jax unfolded it carefully, trying not to crack the brittle newsprint. The letters in the headline were three inches tall: "PEACE MONKEYS LINKED TO PLAGUE."

Jax did not read the article. She put the paper back into the folder and left it on the desk. Leaning back in the chair, she looked at the snapshot on the bulletin board. Her mother was smiling. Her mother had led her here so that she could read these clippings and think about symbols and peace and the humanity of the enemy. Jax did not want to think about such things.

Jax left the study and stood for a moment in the hallway. The door at the end of the hall was open, and she stepped quietly inside. On the white wall behind the bed hung a Japanese scroll on which a rain-drenched landscape had been painted. The pastel colors of the painting were muted by a layer of dust. Except for the dust and the dead flies that lay in the corners, the room was tidy, with no signs of a hasty departure.

Jax sat on the chair by her mother's dressing table. The things on the table were covered with dust. One by one, Jax wiped them clean with her fingers and studied them. She picked up a hairclip made of enameled metal, decorated with flowers and birds. With one hand she wiped part of the mirror clean, then held the clip up to her hair and looked at her reflection: small, dirty face; ragged hair uncombed since yesterday, broken fingernails. She carefully placed the hairclip back on the table.

The hairbrush held a few dark hairs. A small cut-glass bottle still held a trace of her mother's perfume. Jax pulled out the stopper and the room was filled with fresh wild scent, like spring flowers after a rain.

Each object in the room seemed touched with power: a

hand mirror in a silver frame; a rhinestone bracelet; a crystal box that held a jumble of earrings; a silk scarf, faded from the sun; a silver pendant dangling from a silver chain.

Jax picked up the pendant and examined it. Carved on a circle of silver was a man, sitting cross-legged. He held one hand up in what looked like a benediction; the other hand pointed at the earth beneath him. His face was untroubled. A peaceful man. Danny-boy would like him.

In the distance, she heard faint sounds: the laughter of children, muffled by the bedroom walls; the sound of light footsteps coming down the hall. She clung to the pendant and closed her eyes, afraid that by looking she might break the spell.

The footsteps came closer. The room was filled with the scent of her mother's perfume. She felt a breeze tickle the back of her neck, a faint breath of fresh air. Someone reached over her shoulder and took the pendant from her hand. Still Jax did not move. She felt the chill of the silver chain against her neck, the light touch of fingers fumbling with the latch. The pendant was a cold circle in the hollow of her throat.

Jax reached up. "Wait," she whispered. Her mother's hand brushed lightly over the back of Jax's hand, an urgent caress. "I don't like this. I don't understand any other way to fight. Wait." She heard the sound of retreating footsteps.

Jax opened her eyes and she was alone in the room. Watching herself in the mirror, she touched the silver Buddha. "I don't like it," she said, protesting to the empty room. No one answered.

She fled like a thief through the open window.

Danny-boy found Jax in front of the hotel, curled up in the easy chair. She was watching the monkeys play in the abandoned cars. When he came and sat on the curb beside her, she did not speak.

"I've been looking for you," he said.

She glanced at him, but he could not interpret the expression in her dark eyes. "I found my mother's house." Her voice was rough, as if she were fighting to keep it under control. "My mother would have agreed with you."

He noticed the silver pendant hanging around her neck.

"I can't say I like it," she said. "I can't say I agree. But I'll help you fight this stupid war your way. I'll do what I can."

Her voice broke and he reached out to take her in his arms, murmuring reassurances. "It'll be all right. Take it easy."

She shook her head and pulled away from him, rubbing her shirtsleeve across her eyes. "It won't be all right. No good lying about it." She gazed at him steadily. "But I'll see it through to the end. I guess I'll stay and die with the rest of you."

"We may not die."

She shrugged, as if she had already accepted the inevitable. "Maybe not. But I'd say there's a good chance of it."

PART 3

Art in the War Zone

"In war nothing is impossible, provided you use audacity."
—General George Smith Patton,
1944

CHAPTER
20

"You'd better keep her on the leash for the first few days," Jax said, handing Jezebel's leash to Tommy. "Otherwise, she might run away."

The dog wagged her tail hesitantly, glancing from Jax to Tommy and then back to Jax. Jax avoided looking at Jezebel or Tommy. She stared across the courtyard. Duff's market area, usually bustling with traders and farmers, was nearly deserted. Word of the coming war had spread. Outsiders were staying clear of the city until the trouble was over.

On the far side of the open space, a farmer was loading Ruby's suitcases into a horse-drawn cart. Ruby, Tommy and his sister, and all the other noncombatants were being evacuated to Marin, where farmers who were friendly to the cause had agreed to shelter them.

"I don't see why Jezebel and I can't stay," Tommy said.

"Jezebel's lousy at an ambush," Jax said. "She'd run out to meet Fourstar, wagging her tail, and get her head blown off."

Recognizing her name, the dog whined deep in her throat and pawed at Jax's leg. Reluctantly, Jax knelt and rubbed the dog's ears. She understood now why Danny-boy had decided to do a final check of the barricades, and had asked her to take Jezebel to Tommy. Saying goodbye was harder than she had expected.

"But how come I can't stay," Tommy said. "My sister could take care of Jezebel."

Jax shook her head, but the boy persisted.

"I'm good at ambushes," he said. "Ask anyone. I'm real good at hide-and-seek. No one can ever find me. I'm good at sneaking up on people."

Jax stood up. "Goddamn it—this isn't like hide-and-seek. This isn't a game. You've got to understand that. This is a war. Nobody seems to accept that."

Tommy stared down at his feet, his hands twisting the leash into knots.

Jax bit her lip, immediately ashamed of herself. She had not meant to snap at him. It wasn't his fault that no one seemed to be taking this war very seriously. Sure, people had been building barricades and gathering weapons and practicing combat maneuvers, but they did it all with an air of playfulness, as if it had no more importance than painting the bridge blue or writing a good poem.

"I'm sorry," she said to Tommy. "I'm just worried, that's all. I didn't mean to . . ." She let the words trail off. "Look—when you get back, I'll teach you to shoot my crossbow, OK? You'd like that, wouldn't you?"

The boy didn't reply.

"I'm sorry," she repeated softly. "I know you're good at sneaking up on people. Give me a break, will you? You've got to take care of Jezebel for us. Danny-boy and I are counting on you."

The boy looked up and met her eyes at last. "OK," he muttered.

"You'd better get going," Jax said. "Take care of your mother and sister. They'll need you."

Tommy took a step toward the wagon, then turned back. He hugged Jax quickly, as if it didn't mean anything. " 'Bye," he muttered, then he ran toward the wagon where Zatch was hugging Ruby goodbye. Jezebel looked back over her shoulder, as if wondering why Jax didn't follow. Jax turned away, not wanting to watch them leave.

Danny-boy admired the barricade that blocked Van Ness Avenue, an elaborate construction of automobiles,

street signs, and barbed wire. The signs, which had been
taken from freeway on-ramps, all read: DO NOT ENTER
or WRONG WAY. The surrounding buildings were hung
with arrows taken from one-way streets. All of the arrows
pointed back toward the Bay Bridge.

Just behind the barricade, a trench made the street im-
passable to jeeps and cars. With a backhoe that he found on
an old construction site, The Machine had dug trenches in a
great ring surrounding the Civic Center. As much as possible, they wanted to restrict Fourstar's mobility.

Danny-boy stepped into the open doorway of an apartment building beside the barricade. He went up the stairs
and ducked through a hole that The Machine had blasted in
the wall connecting the apartment building with the neighboring office building. He strolled down the hall, climbed
three flights of stairs to the roof, then crossed over to the
roof of another building. For weeks they had been creating
and mapping circuitous routes through the city. They had
installed ladders and blown holes in connecting walls, explored the storm drains, and identified access routes to the
tunnels where Muni trains had once run. Making use of
these routes, a person could cross the city while remaining,
for the most part, under cover.

From the roof of the third building, Danny-boy looked
down onto Polk Street. Below him, he could see Rose water-
ing the plants that decorated a barricade made of wrought
iron. She wore rubber gloves and stood as far as she could
from the sprawling oak saplings. In the sunlight the leaves
glistened an attractive red, the telltale sign of poison oak. A
soldier who brushed against the colorful leaves would get a
rash that itched for weeks.

Danny-boy walked across the roofs and took a fire escape down into an alley. One block over, the Holy Family
guarded Larkin Street. Zatch had liberated cement statues
of Jesus, Mary, and Joseph from various churchyards. Half
a dozen Christs stood in the center, flanked on the left by a
dozen Madonnas and on the right by a group of Josephs.
The figures stood shoulder to shoulder, blocking the way.
With razor wire, Zatch had embellished the crown of thorns

that circled each Savior's head. The wire was looped in loose
tangles around and between the other statues.

Danny-boy was turning away from the statues when he
felt a hand on his shoulder and an arm putting pressure on
his throat. "Where's your rifle?" Jax hissed in his ear.

Danny-boy turned his head to ease the pressure on the
windpipe. "I didn't think I'd need it," he said.

"Hasn't anyone told you there's a war on?" She eased
her hold and he turned to face her. "Look," she said. "I
didn't spend weeks teaching you to shoot just so you could
leave your weapon home. I'm willing to fight this war your
way, but you've got to be prepared for other possibilities."

She studied him, her hands on her hips. She carried an
Uzi slung over one shoulder, as she had for the past two
weeks. Twin belts of ammunition crossed between her
breasts.

"I'm just checking the barricades," he said. "They look
good." He could not see her eyes behind her mirrored sunglasses.

"They'd better. We'll need them soon enough."

He reached up and took her sunglasses from her face,
folded them, and slipped them into her front pocket. She
raised her eyebrows, frowning. "The sun's almost down," he
said. "You don't need them. Besides, I like to see your eyes."

"All right," she said. "You can see them." She pushed
her hands into her pockets. When he started walking toward
Hyde Street and the next barricade, she strolled beside him.
"By the way, Tiger just finished another batch of smoke
grenades. He wants to know where to stash them."

Danny-boy thought for a moment. They had been
caching supplies and weapons at strategic locations throughout the city. "Behind the altar at Saint Patrick's Church, I
think. Ask Books to check the map to be sure."

They passed a barricade made of human bones and broken mirrors, a collaborative effort by Lily and Frank. A row
of skulls stared at them from the steps of a nearby fire escape. On the white wall beneath the skulls, someone had
painted in black: "ARRÊTE! C'EST ICI L'EMPIRE DE
LA MORT."

Danny-boy frowned at the words. "What's that mean?"

"I asked Lily. She says it means—'Stop! This is the Kingdom of the Dead.' She says she took it from the entrance to the catacombs in Paris."

"Where's that?"

Jax shrugged. "I don't know. Somewhere far away." Jax stood looking at the barricade. Danny-boy could see her face reflected in the broken mirrors that were scattered among the bones. "I don't like this one much. It bothers me," she said.

He put an arm around her shoulders. "With luck, the soldiers will feel the same way."

"Yeah," she said. "With luck." Her voice was calm, but he could feel the tension in her body. "I'm scared. I'm afraid of what will happen. I want to hurt them before they can hurt us."

"I'm scared too," he admitted.

She shook her head. "Not as scared as you should be. Not as scared as I am."

"Do you want to leave?" he said. "You could still go up to Marin. There's still time." It hurt to say it, but he had to.

She shook her head. "I'm not going anywhere. I can't leave you idiots to try to do this by yourselves. Someone has to be practical."

"You're here because you belong here," he said.

"Will you please carry your rifle?" she asked him suddenly. "I know you won't use it, but at least carry it. I'd feel better if you did."

"All right," he said. "I will."

"You know," she said thoughtfully, "we could still blow the bridge up before they get here. Or better yet, blow it up when Fourstar's on it."

"We can't do that. If we did, we'd be no better than they are."

"I am no better," she said. Then she shrugged. "I thought you'd say that. But I had to ask."

CHAPTER 21

Jax hunched her shoulders against the early morning cold. Through her binoculars, she could just make out the advance guard of Fourstar's army. She and Danny-boy sat at the top of the Union 76 tower, where they had an excellent view of the Bay Bridge. As she watched, the lead horse in the advance guard began bucking and two others bolted. At the same time, a strange screeching sound emerged from the field radio at her side.

"Must be the crickets," Danny-boy muttered. At irregular intervals along the bridge, Gambit had rigged hidden trip wires that set off sirens, alarm bells, and recordings of various sounds. Gambit's favorite was a recording of crickets mating. Played at top volume, it sounded like a train wreck.

The riders got their horses under control. Through the binoculars, Jax could see the lead horse dancing nervously. She recognized the man on its back. Major Rodriguez looked no happier than his horse.

Jax examined the procession following Rodriguez. Ten battered jeeps loaded with troops and supplies, forty or so mounted soldiers, a slow-moving transport truck, and a tank. The sun glinted on rifle barrels, but Jax could not identify the weapons at that distance. She hoped that the truck carried ammunition that the artists could use.

"About a hundred and fifty of them, wouldn't you say?" Danny-boy commented. "Not so bad."

"Only about fifty of us."

"Yeah, but we're on our home ground."

Jax didn't bother to respond. She didn't want to hear another lecture about guerrilla warfare and the advantage gained by troops on their home ground. "They've almost reached the Ambassador," she said.

The Ambassador was a mannequin that The Machine had equipped with a radio transmitter and receiver. Using the field radio, Jax and Danny-boy could communicate with the army through the mannequin.

The Ambassador was perched on an overhead sign where the freeway began to descend into the streets of the city. Lily had dressed the mannequin in a black leather jacket, a matching miniskirt, and fishnet stockings. Dangling from her ears were diamond earrings that caught the morning light; on her hands were delicate white lace gloves.

"I doubt they'll have much to say to us," Jax said.

"You never know."

"I know," she said with certainty.

The jeeps proceeded slowly over the cracked asphalt. An American flag flew from the lead jeep.

"That's Fourstar," Jax said. "Right under that ugly flag." He was staring straight ahead with fierce intensity.

"Yeah? He doesn't look very happy."

Jax shrugged. "Maybe he doesn't like loud noises."

One of the mounted soldiers spotted the Ambassador and waved to Rodriguez. The procession stopped. Rodriguez went back to confer with Fourstar, and then rode on alone.

Holding her binoculars in one hand, Jax picked up the microphone in the other. She had insisted that she be the first one to talk to Fourstar. Danny-boy had acquiesced reluctantly. "Take it easy," he advised her. She ignored him.

"Hello, Major Rodriguez," she said.

Rodriguez glared up at the Ambassador. "How do you know my name?"

"We met last time you were here. I'm Jax, remember? I wanted to warn you and your pals. The city doesn't like visitors unless they were invited. And you weren't invited."

Through the binoculars, Jax watched him frown and

study the sign's supporting structure, looking for an easy way to climb up. "You'd look pretty silly trying to get me down," Jax said. "Just tell Fourstar that I'm alone and unarmed. I'd like a word with him."

"Are you referring to General Miles?"

"We call him Fourstar," she said. "And you're in our territory now."

Rodriguez wheeled his horse around and trotted back to the jeep for a lengthy conference. Then the jeep jounced forward over the potholes in the asphalt.

Fourstar did not glare at the Ambassador as Rodriguez had. He examined her, judged her, and found her wanting. "I'm not in the habit of talking with machines," he said.

"As far as I'm concerned, we don't have to talk at all," she said. "My message is simple enough. Go home. You aren't welcome here."

He studied the mannequin calmly. "And what do you plan to do if we don't go home?"

"We'll declare war," she said. Watching him, even through the binoculars, made her uneasy. She fought to keep her voice even and confident. "Our kind of war, not yours."

"What's your kind of war?" He was studying the mannequin with tolerant amusement.

"We'll kill you." Her voice cracked a little. She felt Danny-boy's reassuring hand on her shoulder. "One by one, we'll kill you all."

Fourstar smiled and the granitic lines of his face shifted. Jax shivered and blamed it on the cold. "I don't think so," he said. "If you were going to kill me, you could have done it easily enough before now. A sniper at the entrance to the bridge, an explosive charge on the bridge itself." Fourstar shook his head. "From what Rodriguez has told me, I'd guess that you don't really plan to kill me. So I'd say that your threat is an empty one."

"You've been warned." Jax turned off the microphone and glanced at Danny-boy. "Looks like we've got a war to fight."

"We're ready for it," he said.

"I hope you're right."

She studied the army through her binoculars. Two soldiers climbed onto the sign and picked up the Ambassador. As Jax watched, the mannequin's right leg slid from its pivot, falling until the fishnet stockings pulled it up short. The leg dangled at a peculiar angle as the soldiers lowered the mannequin into the arms of the young man who was driving Fourstar's jeep. He loaded her into the back of the jeep. Through the radio, Jax heard an unintelligible command from Fourstar, and the procession moved on.

"Hey, Fourstar," she said into the microphone. "I wouldn't go that way if I were you."

No response. Just the growl of the jeep's engine and the irregular bumping of the tires over the rough pavement. She switched off the radio.

"There goes T.M.," Danny-boy said. Jax looked up in time to see the gyrocopter pass overhead. She could barely hear the distant hum of its engine. The Machine dipped low over the soldiers and dropped three smoke bombs. As they fell, they trailed colored smoke: red, white, and blue.

The horses spooked at the explosions and then disappeared behind clouds of smoke. The Machine climbed away from the sound of rifle fire. Jax watched as the smoke cleared and the army regrouped. They followed the skyway, then took the Civic Center exit, disappearing from view.

"He didn't look scared to me," Jax said, lowering her binoculars. "Not a bit intimidated."

"It's early in the game," Danny-boy said. "Wait and see."

She shook her head. "That's what I keep telling you—it's not a game." She listened to the sound of distant gunfire and wondered what the soldiers were shooting at.

Lily and Zatch lay on the roof of a warehouse, their bellies flat against the gravel and tar paper. Down below them, the army was overreacting to a work of art.

In a warehouse south of Mission, Zatch had found a couple of dozen life-sized plastic horses, intended for display at saddlery stores. He had saddled them with scavenged gear and arranged them on Ninth Avenue, facing toward the bridge. With great care he had mounted a human skeleton on each horse, wiring the bones together in lifelike riding postures.

Lily had suggested the finishing touch. Working together, they replaced the human skulls with animal skulls, taken from the back rooms of taxidermy shops and the specimen boxes of the California Academy of Sciences. With empty eye sockets, the animal skulls stared down the street: a crocodile, a wolf, a saber-toothed cat, a gorilla, an assortment of dogs, a zebra, a buck with a full rack of antlers. When the wind blew, the heads nodded, as if in solemn judgment. Like the temple guardians of some forgotten faith, the skeletal horde greeted the army. The army met them with rifles.

"Everyone's a critic," Lily muttered over the sound of gunfire.

"I hope they don't hurt that saber-toothed cat skull," Zatch murmured. "I felt a little guilty taking it."

"It was for a good cause." Cautiously, Lily peeked over the edge of the roof. Below her, the soldiers were still firing into the sculptures. The crocodile rider was down, knocked over by a spooked horse. As she watched, a man fired a burst at the wolf rider, apparently reacting to the movement of the skull in the wind. "Jesus," she said, ducking down. "These guys shoot at everything that moves."

"Don't move," Zatch advised dryly. Taking his own advice, he lay still until the sound of gunfire faded in the distance.

From a penthouse apartment in the Opera Plaza complex, Frank watched through a high-powered telescope as the army approached City Hall. Gambit sat in an easy chair beside him.

"They're coming up to Lily's sculptures now," Frank reported.

Lily had built a life-size *Tyrannosaurus rex,* constructing the giant reptile entirely of found objects: costume jewelry, high-heeled shoes, bits of linoleum, wads of tinfoil, cheese graters, wooden spoons, copper tubing, plastic toys. A twisted street sign formed its backbone and crystal doorknobs glittered malevolently in its eyesockets. Perched on a nearby lamppost was a pterodactyl made of scraps of leather and old nylon stockings, hung on a framework of human bone.

"Oh, my," Frank said. "What a pity!"

"What happened?"

"A soldier just blew the head off the pterodactyl," Frank said. "Lily will be so upset."

"Where are they going?"

"They're parking in front of that ugly concrete building on Golden Gate Avenue. They certainly don't have much taste in architecture." Frank watched for a moment longer. "I wonder where the monkeys are," he said. "Usually there are a few hanging around by the library."

"Hiding like any sensible animal," Gambit said. "No sense sticking around where people are shooting."

"They're putting up the American flag on the flagpole in the plaza," Frank observed. "You know, I'd never noticed it before, but that's a rather ugly flag."

"Possibly that's just the context," Gambit said. "In the hands of storm troopers, any flag looks ugly."

Frank nodded, still watching the soldiers in the plaza. "I suppose you're right. But it certainly is ugly."

At night the fog embraced the city like a lover. Mist from the Bay crept through the streets and alleys of the city, blending with the colored smoke that lingered from The Machine's bombs and taking on an unnatural tint and an acrid scent.

In Civic Center Plaza, soldiers huddled around their cooking fires. The fog clung to them, dampened their clothing and their spirits, hissed in the fires like whispering children. It was nasty, secretive sort of weather.

With rolls of razor wire, the soldiers had blocked off the streets nearest the Civic Center Plaza. Harsh white spotlights illuminated the barriers. Within the soldiers' camp, the generator that kept the spotlights bright growled loudly, an ugly and continuous noise. The fog drifted through the spotlight beams and glistened on the sharp barbs of the wire.

The sentry at the corner of Golden Gate Avenue and Larkin Street pulled his coat more tightly around himself and yawned. He was inside the barricade, looking out into the dark city.

Jax crouched in the shadows behind him. She had come up through the storm drains, slipping beneath their defenses. She was alone. Over Danny-boy's protests, she had insisted on working by herself. She felt that Danny-boy would be a distraction to her. She would not be able to concentrate on fighting if he were along. After much grumbling, Danny-boy had joined Snake for the first evening of fighting.

The sentry shifted his rifle, obviously bored. He tucked his weapon under one arm and fumbled in his pocket. Jax watched him roll a cigarette and light it. When the flame cast a brief glow on his face, she could see that he was no older than Danny-boy.

Jax slipped a dart into her blowgun and aimed at his neck. She had been practicing for weeks, but tension spoiled her aim. Her first shot missed him entirely. She cursed herself silently and remained in the shadows. He straightened up, listening to something—perhaps the small sound of the dart falling onto the asphalt. After a moment, he relaxed again.

The second dart struck the back of his neck, just above the collar of his shirt. He slapped at the dart, as a man might slap at an insect, then slapped again and knocked it to the ground. Jax ducked farther back into the shadows, waiting for the tranquilizer that Tiger had concocted to take effect. The sentry fumbled for his rifle, but it slipped from his hands. He fell slowly to one knee, then collapsed.

Jax ran into the light, grabbed him by the shoulders, and dragged his limp body into the shadows. Adrenalin sang in her veins and the night seemed colder than it had a moment before. Her senses were heightened: she noticed every detail of the scene. The fog made delicate patterns as it drifted through the spotlight; the cigarette that the sentry had dropped glowed like a firefly; the young soldier's chin was marked by a small nick, where he had cut himself while shaving an inadequate beard.

Working quickly, she turned him onto his back, crossed his arms neatly on his chest, and snapped open the pouch of indelible skin paints that she carried on her belt. She worked carefully, using only the red paint and the black. Simplicity, she felt, was best.

In bold letters across his forehead, she wrote "DEAD" in black. On his right cheek she signed "by Jax" in red. Between his folded hands, she placed the Death Certificate, printed by Ms. Migsdale on the *New City News* press. The paper said:

CERTIFICATE OF DEATH

Please consider yourself removed from combat.
Look at it this way—we could have killed you.
If you don't stop fighting, we really will kill you next time.

Signed,
The People of San Francisco

Danny-boy, Ms. Migsdale, and Books had argued for weeks over the wording. Jax thought this draft was fine— but she had felt the same way about the last five.

She took the sentry's rifle and stripped him of ammunition, then lifted the grating from a storm drain and slipped through the opening. Weeks before, she had loosened the gratings in strategic areas, planning escape routes through the city's subterranean tunnels. She set the grating into place above her and climbed down the rusting ladder set into one wall of the shaft. She stepped cautiously, wary of the slippery algae that coated the metal rungs. The tunnel she entered was wider than most; she could walk in a crouch, rather than crawling on her belly.

Jax liked the tunnels. There was something comforting about being completely hidden from view, contained within the city itself. The air was cold and often foul-smelling, but she was willing to accept the odor of decay in exchange for a feeling of security.

In the close darkness, she could hear the pounding of her heart. She switched on her flashlight, illuminating a stretch of pipe. Originally the cement had been gray; now it was streaked and discolored with unidentifiable stains and growths. A blue-green mold grew in irregular lines and patches, like graffiti written in an alien alphabet.

She followed the tunnel until it joined the old sewage system. On the floor of the sewer pipe, she found a dry spot where she could leave the sentry's rifle and ammunition. Then she crept into another storm drain, in search of a second victim.

The second sentry was much like the first: a bored soldier at an outlying post. She took him easily and found joy in it: a pleasure that tasted of smoke and fear and pain. Just as she was finishing her signature, she heard footsteps in the distance and ducked down the shaft. As she slipped into the storm drain, she heard a shout, followed by the screech of a whistle. She did not linger to listen.

At Market Street she emerged into the night air and stretched her cramped muscles. The wind had started to blow the fog away. Looking up, she could see glimpses of stars. She listened for a moment: in the distance, she could hear a siren wailing. A chorus of barking dogs joined the siren, coming from somewhere much closer. The barking gave way to howls, a primitive wailing that made the hair on her neck prickle. She wondered how it made the soldiers feel.

An answering howl came from a nearby alley. She peered into the darkness and saw a pair of gleaming eyes. "Good hunting?" she asked.

"Good hunting," Randall said, stepping from the shadows. Despite the cold, he wore nothing but a red kerchief, knotted around his neck. "Mercedes and her friends released the army's horses and we stampeded them. The rest of the pack is chasing them down to Golden Gate Park." He grinned. "Fine hunting."

"I'm heading for headquarters to rendezvous with Danny-boy," she said. "Want to come?"

He shook his head. "The night's young. I have time to hunt." He faded into the shadows, leaving her alone. In the distance, she heard gunfire.

"Good luck," she said to the darkness. Slinging the captured rifles across her back, she trotted in the direction of North Beach, where the artists had established their first temporary headquarters in a bar called the ChiChi Club.

The Machine was watching from the rooftop of the ChiChi Club when Jax approached. Her saw her run along the sidewalk on the far side of the street, slipping in and out of the doorways, alert to any sounds in the darkness around her.

"Jax," he hailed her softly. When she looked up, he waved. "Come up the fire escape."

She disappeared from his view, then he heard the rattle of her footsteps on the metal stairs. She climbed over the edge of the roof, setting the rifles that she carried on the tar paper and gravel covered surface. "I got two sentries," she told him, her voice low and excited. "And Randall tells me the horses are loose."

"Danny-boy told me the same thing."

"Danny-boy's back?"

"He's downstairs with the others."

"What are you doing up here?"

"I'm on first watch. Everyone else is downstairs. Rose has a venison stew cooking. You should go down."

She shook her head. "I'm not hungry yet," she said. "I'll keep you company for a bit." She sat down beside him with her feet dangling over the edge of the roof. Her heels drummed nervously against the wall.

Over the last few weeks, The Machine had grown used to having her around. When they were preparing for the war, she had stopped by his workshop often.

"So what do you think?" she asked him suddenly. "You think we have a chance?" Her shoulders were hunched forward, as if she were cold. Her right hand kept fingering the silver pendant that hung at her throat.

The Machine studied her closely. He guessed that she didn't expect much of an answer. "What do you think?" he asked.

"We did OK tonight, but that's mostly because we surprised them. I don't know how we'll do tomorrow." She rubbed her hands nervously on her jeans. "But you know what's strange? For the first time, I'm glad we're fighting

this war the way Danny-boy wanted to fight it. I was glad I
didn't have to kill those soldiers tonight. You know what I
mean?"

He nodded slowly. "Yeah, I do." Lately, working with
Danny-boy and Jax and the others on preparations for war,
he had begun to feel that perhaps people were not as bad as
he had thought. He did not trust the feeling yet, but he was
willing to admit the possibility.

Jax smiled at him suddenly, reached out, and took his
hand. He did not resist. She squeezed his hand, and for a
moment he felt happy.

On the first night of the war, the artists killed fifteen
soldiers—each one labeled "DEAD," autographed, and left
with a certificate in his hands. In addition, they acquired
fifteen rifles and a large supply of ammunition. Among the
artists, there was one casualty: a poet sprained his ankle by
tripping over the stairs on his way into the ChiChi Club.

CHAPTER
22

In the morning, Jax spoke to Fourstar by way of the Ambassador. "Hey," she said into the microphone. "Is anyone there? Can anyone hear me?"

"Yes, ma'am." The voice over the radio was hesitant. "I can hear you."

"Who's this?" she asked.

"Private First Class Johnson," said the voice.

"Glad to meet you, Johnson. Hey, do you suppose you can get General Miles over here. I want to talk to him."

She waited, lounging on a red velvet sofa in the ChiChi Club's office. She and Danny-boy had slept there for a few hours, waking only when The Machine came to tell them that it was morning, time to contact Fourstar. Jax sat up to talk to Fourstar. Danny-boy still lay on the sofa, his head on her lap.

Over the field radio she heard a door open, then close. "I told the sergeant," Johnson said. "General Miles will get the message soon."

"Good enough," Jax said. "So how'd you do last night? You still alive?"

"Yes, ma'am. I'm doing fine."

"You can call me Jax, Johnson. No need to be so formal."

"You got one of my buddies last night," Johnson said hesitantly. "Said he never saw you coming."

"Of course not, Johnson. That's the way I like it. You won't see me coming either."

A long pause. "Why didn't you kill those guys?" Johnson asked at last. "Seems kind of weird."

"Would you rather we did?" Jax asked. "We could if you'd rather."

The sound of an opening door cut off Johnson's reply. "That you, Fourstar?" she asked.

"You have something to say to me?" By the tone of his voice, Jax judged that Fourstar was not happy. She heard the creak of a chair as he sat down.

"I wanted to suggest that you leave town."

"Why would I leave now? Just because you painted on the foreheads of a few of my men?" Fourstar laughed, an abrupt, forced sound.

"We've killed fifteen of your men. At this rate, you'll all be dead in a week."

"What are you talking about? You haven't killed anyone. A little paint, that's all. This is absurd."

"I agree," she said calmly. "Fighting a war with us is absurd. You don't have a chance. On the very first night, you lost ten percent of your forces. Seems silly to stick around when you're clearly outmatched."

"You fight a stupid kind of war," Fourstar muttered.

"We've never fought a war before," Jax admitted. "We're improvising." She stroked Danny-boy's hair, and he smiled. "If you don't like the way we fight, go find yourself another war. We wouldn't mind."

"My men have real bullets, woman," Fourstar said. "When we kill a man, he's really dead."

"Are you suggesting we do the same?" She raised her voice. "What do you think of that, Johnson? You think we should really kill people? If we had decided to fight that way, your buddy would be dead now."

Johnson didn't speak.

"Would you like to answer, Private?" Fourstar said.

"No, sir."

"Have you received orders regarding communication with this device?"

"No, sir."

"That was an oversight, Private. You will not communicate with this device. Do you understand?"

"Yes, sir."

Fourstar spoke to Jax again, his voice dangerously even. "Your attempts to intimidate my men are laughable," he said. "Your war is ridiculous."

"Death is nothing to laugh at, General."

She heard the scrape of his chair against the floor as he stood. "You have nothing more to say to me," he said.

"I guess not. The war goes on." She heard Fourstar close the door behind him. "Hey, Johnson," she said to the guard. "Do you really think we should kill people?"

There was no answer, but when she listened closely she thought she could hear him breathing.

"Think about it," she said. "I'll talk to you later." She turned off the microphone. "Looks like we'll keep fighting," she said.

Danny-boy opened his eyes and smiled at her. "Just as well. It would have been a pity to waste all those great preparations."

That first morning, Jax teamed up with Snake and Old Man Hat.

"We need help carrying some stuff over to the Mission," Old Man Hat told Jax. She accepted the knapsack that he handed her. Through the strap, she could feel it vibrating slightly.

"It's humming," she said.

The redhead grinned. "Don't drop it," he said. "It's full of glass jars and the jars are full of yellow jackets. The little bastards have a nasty sting. I caught 'em yesterday, and I'd guess they're in a pretty foul temper around now." He tugged on the bicycle inner tube that he carried over one shoulder. "String this thing between a couple of poles and you got a giant slingshot. And our little insect pals are the ammunition. I figured I'd sort of distract the troops and give you and Snake a chance to pick 'em off."

Her knapsack buzzed angrily as she followed Snake to the Mission. She could feel an irregular bumping as the unhappy insects ricocheted off the insides of the jars.

On the roof of a store on Harrison Street, Old Man Hat
strung his inner tube between two ventilation chimneys. Jax
helped Snake build a bonfire in the middle of the street below. When the fire was going well, Snake added a couple of
spare tires, taken from nearby cars. The burning tires pro-
duced a stinking column of black smoke.

"That ought to get their attention," Snake said.

They waited on the roof of a furniture store across the
street from Old Man Hat. A facade that extended a few feet
above the tar paper and gravel hid them from the street.

The early morning wind had blown away the fog, and
the warmth of the sun made Jax sleepy. The previous night's
attack seemed very long ago. The Machine flew over, heading for downtown. Jax waved to him, but he gave no sign
that he had seen her. Through a drainhole that passed
through the facade, Jax could keep an eye on the street
below.

"After you get your man, take off," Snake said. "We
won't have a hope in hell of regrouping."

She nodded. "You really think they'll come?"

"Sure. They gotta investigate. That kind of smoke—
Fourstar will figure we're burning the city down." Snake's
eyes were half closed. "Just be cool. Relax—you won't get
another chance once the action starts."

"If the action starts," she said. She yawned.

"You gotta be patient," Snake murmured. "This is a
waiting game. Give it time."

When she started to reply, he motioned her to silence.
She heard the soldiers coming—the pounding of running
footsteps and the rattle of equipment. A man double-timed
it around the corner, then ducked into the cover of a doorway. He motioned the others to follow. The patrol advanced
cautiously, scanning the buildings and roofs around them.

She waited, watching the first man venture out. He
kicked a tire out of the now dying fire. "Waste of time," she
heard him say. "Nothing happening here." The other men
stepped forward to join him.

Old Man Hat hit them with three smoke bombs to provide cover, then started firing the yellow jacket bombs. She
heard the glass jars shatter on the asphalt below. There was

a burst of gunfire as one soldier shot at something, but someone was yelling "Hold your fire!" Someone else was swearing.

"Move out," Snake said. From the fire escape, she nailed a man with a dart from her blowgun. Though he had left the insects behind, he was still slapping desperately at the air around his face. He ran a few more steps before he stumbled and fell.

She marked him, working around the yellow jacket stings. Taking his rifle, she escaped the spreading smoke by climbing another fire escape. Her throat burned with the taste of smoke. The street below was still hidden by a haze of gray. She waved to Old Man Hat, gave him the thumbs-up sign, and headed out to hunt on her own.

The soldiers were accustomed to straightforward conventional warfare. Danny-boy and his colleagues did not believe in conventional approaches; their attacks were all the more elegant for being hideously unexpected.

Jax watched from the concealment of an alley as a soldier triggered one of Tiger's boobytraps. He had fallen behind his patrol, distracted by the glittering gems in the window of a jewelry store. When he stepped through the store's door, he broke a trip wire. In the darkness above the doorjamb, a large Tupperware container of cockroaches opened and upended, emptying onto the man's head. The insects scurried into his helmet, his pants legs, and his shirt sleeves, seeking refuge in any dark and private cranny. Jax smiled as the man dropped his weapon, screamed like a young girl, and slapped repeatedly at his body, dancing and yelling. While he was distracted, she caught him with a blow from behind, marked him, and left him in the doorway with the cockroaches curiously investigating his body.

She trailed another patrol, hanging back and waiting for an opportunity. The city seemed to unnerve the soldiers. They shot at their own reflections in shop windows, at pigeons, at stray cats, and at shadows. She kept her distance, slipping silently from cover to cover. It seemed to her sometimes that the city was helping her. When she needed a place to hide, there was always an empty doorway to duck into, a shadow to provide cover.

Late in the day she returned to headquarters, which had been moved to an apartment building in the Haight. There she found Lily and Gambit lounging on a battered couch in a first-floor apartment and trading information on the battle so far.

"I hear that Mercedes has been stripping 'em naked after she marks their foreheads," Gambit said. "She has three uniforms so far. Wants to stuff 'em with newspaper and hang them from the lampposts downtown."

Lily nodded. "I hear that The Machine bombed a few patrols with water balloons full of cheap perfume. Scored some direct hits, apparently. If you catch a whiff of Lily of the Valley, take cover. Some sweet-smelling soldiers are coming by."

"What's the count so far?" Jax asked. "How many are dead?"

Lily shrugged. 'You'd have to ask Books to be sure, but I'd guess it's around thirty or so. I'd say we were winning."

Jax nodded, reserving judgment. "Maybe so," she said. "But I wouldn't count on it. I'd say Fourstar hasn't really started fighting yet."

The next afternoon, Jax was in the Muni tunnel that ran beneath Market Street when she heard the first explosion, a hollow thump in the distance. The city trembled around her. Before the rumbling faded, another blast shook the tunnel. By the time the third explosion came she almost expected it, another beat in the inexorable rhythm of destruction.

She fled from the sound, heading toward the Embarcadero Station, then going aboveground and making her way toward temporary headquarters, which had moved to a warehouse south of Market Street.

She arrived just as The Machine was telling Danny-boy about the situation at the Civic Center. "I flew over as low as I dared," The Machine said. "They're shelling the buildings right around the City Hall. Looks like they're trying to clear the area. So far they've demolished a few rows of shops. But I don't think they're stopping there."

Danny-boy shook his head. He sat on an empty wooden packing crate. "I don't understand. Why would they do that?"

"Getting rid of places to hide," Jax said. "Fourstar doesn't like sneak attacks."

"I'll talk to him," Danny-boy said. "I think I should."

Jax followed Danny-boy to what had once been the warehouse manager's office. From there, Danny-boy contacted Fourstar via the Ambassador. "Ah," said Fourstar. "A new voice." He seemed at ease, pleased with himself. In the background, Jax could hear the hollow thump of mortar fire. "Who are you?"

"I'm Danny-boy. I want to know why you're destroying the city."

"So pleased to meet you," Fourstar said smoothly. "Surely you aren't surprised. If you insist on hiding, it's obvious that I must remove your hiding places. I have no choice. I don't enjoy this—it hurts me to have to demolish perfectly good buildings."

"To find us, you'll have to demolish the entire city."

"If that's what it takes, that's what we'll do."

Danny-boy shook his head, bewildered by Fourstar's response. "I don't see what you'll gain from this. If you destroy the city to conquer it, what will you have when you're done? A ruined city that's worthless to anyone."

"You really don't understand, do you?" Fourstar said, his tone that of a teacher who was disappointed by his pupil's performance. "In ruins, San Francisco will have a different kind of value. Yours will be an example that others will not want to follow. City governments will think twice before declining an offer to join our alliance."

"You'll destroy an entire city for the sake of an example?"

"For the sake of the nation, Danny-boy," Fourstar said. "For the sake of the greater good. This city is a small sacrifice. A few buildings, a few human lives—what do they matter? The nation will survive. You people just can't see the larger picture. You're trapped in your provincial view. If you could see the big picture, as I can, then you'd understand."

"So you're destroying the city to save the nation."

"Exactly. Unless, of course, you and I can come to some accommodation. If we could work out some compromise . . ."

"No," Danny-boy said.

"No possibility of compromise," Fourstar said. "What a pity." He did not sound sorry. "You leave me with no choice."

Jax heard another explosion in the background. Danny-boy switched off the radio, unwilling to listen to more. "I can't believe he's doing this," Danny-boy said.

"Believe it," Jax said. "This is war."

He walked away from her, shaking his head. For a time he stood at the window, looking out. Jax sat by the radio, wondering what to do. She wanted to help somehow, but she could think of nothing to say.

"I don't believe it," Danny-boy said again, but his tone had changed. He laughed. "I just don't believe it."

Outside the window, snow was falling: great wet impossible flakes of snow. The streets turned dark as the snow melted on the pavement. The window rattled as the wind spattered snow against the pane. The sky was gray overhead, but the clouds were darkest in the direction of the Civic Center Plaza. Jax imagined the damp snow clinging to the soldiers' boots, drenching their clothing, drifting against the treads of the tank.

"The city's fighting back," Danny-boy said. He grinned at her. "I wonder how their tank is equipped for cold weather."

CHAPTER
23

The war went on. The tank stalled in the cold, despite the best efforts of the army's mechanics. The wind and snow conspired to bury the vehicle in a drift, and after a while the soldiers quit trying to dig it out.

The soldiers supplemented their uniforms with jackets from downtown stores, and the army took on a mismatched, ragtag appearance, a mix of down parkas, flannel hunting coats, and brightly colored ski jackets.

Soldiers patrolled the streets in small nervous groups, carrying their weapons always ready. They talked in voices that seemed unnecessarily loud and spooked at the slightest sound.

Jax spent most of her time on the streets, following patrols and waiting for an opportunity to ambush an unwary soldier. The city was a big place and at one time or another everyone has to be alone. A man who lingered behind his companions to piss in an alley or pilfer a shop was fair game, she figured.

When she slept, she slept lightly, alert even in her dreams. Sometimes she holed up in temporary headquarters. More often, she slept wherever she could: on out-of-the-way rooftops, sheltered by the chimneys; in Golden Gate Park, perched in the treetops; in the tunnels, secure in the embrace of the city.

She was napping in a storm drain when a patrol stopped for a smoke by the open grating. She could hear their voices, echoing through the pipe. A man with a deep voice was razzing a soldier who had flipped out the previous night and shot out all the windows in an empty building. "Ranger, baby, you wasted that building," the deep voice said. "You nailed every damn window. And you know how the General feels about conserving ammo."

"I saw 'em out there," a young man's voice said sullenly. "Saw 'em moving in on my position." Jax could hear the strain in his voice. "Fucking ghosts. They live here."

"Can't shoot ghosts, Ranger," said another voice. "Shoot 'em and they just come back for more."

"Fucking city," Ranger muttered. "Too goddamn many shadows." Jax closed her eyes and pictured him: he was skinny, she thought, and young—not much older than she was. His hair was cut so short that his scalp showed through the stubble. When he talked, he hunched his shoulders forward as if to protect himself. His eyes had a wild haunted look. She felt sorry for him.

"You heard about the dogs?" said the man who claimed you couldn't shoot ghosts. "Wilson saw them down by the ocean. Monster dogs with glowing eyes, running along the sand."

Tiger had suggested painting Randall's pack with fluorescent dyes. Apparently he'd done so.

"Did he shoot 'em?" Ranger asked.

"Can't shoot ghosts, Ranger," the voice repeated. "I told you that already."

"You gotta do something," Ranger muttered.

"You seen the monkeys?" the first man asked. "I hear that the monkeys running around here are the same ones that started the Plague. That's what I hear. Or maybe they're ghosts too."

"You guys are nuts," said the deep voice. "Ghosts." The man put a wealth of contempt into the single word. "There ain't no ghosts. Just shadows, like anywhere else."

"Yeah, right," Ranger said in a hopeless tone. "That's why no one's ever seen Jax, or Danny-boy, or any of them."

"Hey, boy, you're just afraid that Jax is going to draw on your face."

"It's not my face I'm worried about."

Jax imagined that Ranger was rubbing his neck. She had taken to marking a broad red line across the throat of each victim—from just below the left ear, to just below the right ear. She thought the effect was quite suggestive.

"It'll take one bullet to put Jax away, same as anyone else," said the deep voice.

Jax lay on her back with one arm tucked behind her head, listening to the man talk of her death.

"Yeah, you're a hard guy, Marcos. A real hard guy. You already got the mark, man. You got no reason to talk. Why don't you go looking for Jax some night? You go looking for her and see what happens."

"Right, man," said Marcos. "You'd like that. I got no time for this bullshit."

Jax heard Marcos's footsteps walking away.

"Bastard," a man muttered. "He's already a dead man. Lot of balls he has giving the rest of us advice. I think we should blow the whole fucking place up. Burn it down."

"It's so damn cold. It just ain't natural." Jax imagined Ranger huddled in his jacket, pulling it tight around him against the cold. There was an hysterical edge in his voice. "We should leave, that's what we should do. Leave while we still can."

"Watch what you say, Ranger," the other man said softly. "The General doesn't like that kind of talk."

"Don't mean anything by it," Ranger grumbled. "I just want to go home, that's all. We don't belong here."

On the sixth day (or maybe the seventh, it was hard to keep count), Jax participated in a cooperative attack on a patrol, using a type of bomb that Tiger had concocted. Instead of smoke the bomb released jasmine-scented perfume, laced with a form of LSD. Late in the afternoon, The Machine dropped the bombs on a patrol in the Western Addition. Jax and her companions were equipped with gas masks; the soldiers were not. Jax lay low while the soldiers used up their ammunition on shadows and hallucinations. Then she helped Snake and Zatch and Gambit round up the tripping soldiers and mark them one by one.

Jax caught the last one just as the sun was setting. He

had wandered far from the site of the attack. When Jax found him he was strolling down the middle of Haight Street, singing cheerfully. He staggered now and then, but the betrayal of his legs seemed to amuse rather than distress him. He carried no weapons. When she approached him, he grinned at her like a happy kid.

"You doing all right, soldier?" she asked.

"Just fine," he said. "You know, I saw an angel flying up this way. A golden angel, flying over the city."

"I've seen the angel," she said.

"You must be Jax."

"That's right."

He laughed merrily. "You look just like my girlfriend back home." He had dark hair and brown eyes and he seemed quite pleased with himself. "You going to paint on my forehead?"

"I thought I might," she said.

"All right."

He leaned against a wall, obediently turning his head so that the fading sunlight shone on his face. Because she had the time, she embellished the word DEAD with a flowering vine growing up the E and a skull grinning from the hole in the A. As she worked, she talked with the soldier.

"What's your name, soldier?"

"Private First Class Davis," he said. "But everyone calls me Dave."

"Don't frown, Dave," she said. "You'll smear the paint."

Dave tried to stop frowning and started to giggle. He was a very happy soldier.

"So when are you going to give up this war?" she asked him. "Don't you think it's about time?"

"Oh, I'll give up," he said. "I don't care. I'll give up anytime. It's the General who won't give up. He never gives up."

"How do you know?"

"Oh, I know." He nodded solemnly. "I used to be one of his personal guards. Of course, I won't be a guard anymore. The General doesn't trust a man, once he has the mark."

"Of course not," she said, adding another leaf to the vine. "But if Fourstar won't quit, why don't you quit following Fourstar?"

He bit his lip and looked very young and serious. "The General kills deserters," he said.

"If you desert, how can he kill you? He'd have to catch you." She frowned at him. "Surely you could get away. He's just a man."

"That's not true," the soldier said. His eyes were wide and frightened. "He's more than that. He'd find me. Just like you."

"What do you mean, just like me?"

But he didn't answer. He was looking at his hand, and he seemed suddenly fascinated by the texture of his fingerprints. She heard distant gunfire and the dull explosions of smoke bombs. She finished the last letter of her signature. It was time to go. She touched his hand and said, "Goodbye. Take care." And she ran away through the streets.

CHAPTER
24

During the second week of the war, Gambit started his Automatic Bells. Before the war he had searched tirelessly for buildings with the best resonant quality and for gongs and bells with the best tone. His favorite combination was a gong that he had taken from a Buddhist temple and hung in Saint Mary's Cathedral. Every fifteen minutes, a sledgehammer struck the gong, producing a sustained middle C that could be heard for blocks. The sledgehammer was powered by the controlled fall of a safe full of sandbags, which was linked to the hammer by a complex set of pulleys. Gambit had scattered twenty-one similar bells throughout the city, setting them to ring according to a precise mathematical pattern.

Danny-boy could hear the bells even in the innermost office of the Pacific Telephone Building, which was serving as temporary headquarters. The noise jangled and disrupted his thoughts. In the brief lulls when no bells rang, he discovered he was bracing himself for the next note. He wondered how loud they were in Fourstar's rooms and he hoped that Fourstar's head ached as much as his did.

Danny-boy was trying to ignore the bells and discuss strategy with Books when Jax burst into the room. "You've got to come talk to Frank," she said. "Hurry."

"Why? What's going on?"

"Just come on."

She would not stop long enough to answer his questions. She grabbed his hand and dragged him out the door. Without the building to muffle the bells, each low note vibrated in his bones. He gave up trying to question Jax and simply followed her, running along alleys and over rooftops. She led him to the Garden of Light. Or rather, to what was left of the Garden.

The framework of the mirror maze still stood, an elaborate structure of crisscrossing metal strips. A few of the mirrors had remained intact, but most were broken—peppered with bullets, shattered by a kick or a blow from a rifle butt. Jax led the way. The broken glass crunched beneath her feet. Danny-boy followed, staring at the destruction with horror.

"He won't move," Jax said over her shoulder. "I couldn't convince him."

Frank sat beside the remains of the stained glass window. Shards of colored glass and fragments of mirrors littered the pavement around him. Someone had used the window for target practice. The top half was gone. The bottom half was riddled with holes. Frank did not look up as they approached.

Danny-boy squatted beside Frank, putting a hand on the old man's shoulder. Jax hung back, scanning the street for signs of Fourstar's men.

"Frank!" Danny-boy had to shout to be heard over the bells. "We've got to get under cover. It's not safe here."

The old man looked up and Danny-boy saw what he was holding. The Virgin Mary's face, still miraculously intact, smiled from Frank's hands.

Frank said something, but Danny-boy caught only a few words between one bell and the next. "I just don't understand. . . ."

Danny-boy felt disoriented. The bells pounded in his head. Frank had worked on the Garden of Light for years, and Fourstar had destroyed it in a day. "You're right," he said. His voice sounded odd, like someone else's voice. "It doesn't make sense." He had nothing more to say.

People expected him to have words to say. Ever since he had proposed the plan to fight the war, people had been looking to him for words. But he had no more words. He groped for things to say and found a hollow place where words should have been. He looked down, afraid to meet Frank's eyes, afraid to look at Jax, afraid to catch a glimpse of his own face in a mirror.

"Talk to him," Jax said. "You've got to talk to him."

Danny-boy shook his head. The bells filled the silence.

"So it's broken," Jax said suddenly. Her voice was loud enough to carry over the bells. "Big deal. You can build it again, after all this is over. It's just a lot of glass, Frank. You know that. It was wonderful, but that's all it was: a lot of glass. You can do it again. Or do something better."

She grabbed Frank's shoulder and shook him a little. For a moment the bells had fallen silent, in one of the unpredictable rests that were a part of their pattern. "Suppose I gave you a choice. You could have saved the Garden by giving Fourstar the city. But if Fourstar took the city, then he'd never let you build anything new. What would you choose—the Garden that was, or all the Gardens you have yet to build?"

Frank studied her face. "Not a fair question," he said softly.

"I don't have time to be fair," she said. "If anyone comes along now, we're dead meat." She glanced at Danny-boy. "Someone told me once that making something beautiful changes who you are. Even if what you make lasts for just a day, you're a different person because of it. Making the Garden changed who you are, and they haven't broken that." She shook her head and glanced at Danny-boy again. "I'm saying it all wrong. I don't know the right words."

Frank looked at the face in his hands and then at Jax. "Of course I would choose the Gardens of the future. There's no choice there. I just wish it could be different."

"Come on," Jax said. She held out her hand and helped him up. "You too," she said to Danny-boy. Her voice was uncharacteristically gentle. "We'd better get back to headquarters."

A single bell rang with a low deep note; then the others started, and an avalanche of music pursued them through the streets. At the Pacific Telephone Building they turned

Frank over to Tiger, though the old man was already protesting that he was fine, just a momentary shock.

"Thanks," Danny-boy said to Jax. "I didn't know what to say. It was because of me, because of my plan, that the soldiers destroyed the Garden. If I hadn't . . ."

"Don't be stupid," she interrupted. "Blame Fourstar, don't blame yourself. And I didn't say anything that you haven't said to me." She studied his face. "When was the last time you had something to eat?" she asked him.

He shrugged. "I don't know. A while, I guess."

She shook her head. "Come on."

Rose had set up her field kitchen in the employee cafeteria. Jax got him a cup of hot soup to drink and he took it, though he didn't really feel hungry. He couldn't remember the last time he had eaten. Maybe breakfast—he seemed to remember eating toast. His body ached, but he didn't really feel tired. He couldn't feel tired; he had to keep fighting. The war was his responsibility, and he could not rest.

The only light was sunlight shining through dusty windows. People moved through the gloom, talking quietly. He sat at a table with Jax and some of the others. Jax smiled and touched his hand. In the dim light, she seemed less than real. He could almost believe that she was a ghost, that they were all ghosts, nothing more than dreams of the city.

"The ghosts were out in force today," Zatch said, as if echoing Danny-boy's thoughts. "I saw the Chinese New Year's parade going down Market Street this morning. An army patrol practically got run down by a couple of lion dancers. The soldiers really freaked when the firecrackers started going off."

"The city's doing what it can," someone else murmured. "I saw a stampede of buffalo heading for City Hall. Must have been a hundred of them, charging down Fulton Street."

"Those were real," Jax said. "Randall's pack chased them from the park, nipping at their heels the whole way."

"I hear a couple of soldiers tried to stand their ground and just about got trampled." Danny-boy recognized Snake's voice, though he could not make out his face in the dim light. "That's the bit I like. When they decide that something must be a ghost and it turns out to be real."

"Most of them are shooting at everything now. If it moves, they shoot it," Jax said. "Gotta watch your ass."

"True enough. But that has a fortunate side effect: sometimes they shoot each other." Snake's voice was filled with black amusement.

"Any fatalities?" Jax asked.

"Not yet. Unfortunately, they're lousy shots."

"Too bad," Danny-boy said. He heard a hard edge in his own voice.

Jax glanced at him, frowning. "You all right?" she asked softly.

He shrugged. "Sure. Just a little tired."

"You need to get some sleep."

He shook his head. "Can't sleep with those bells ringing."

"Yes, you can. Come on." She took his hand and led him away from the cafeteria, down one flight of stairs to a sub-basement. There was a mattress and a few blankets on the floor. He could still hear the bells, but they were a distant annoyance now. He lay beside her and put his arms around her. He thought he felt her trembling, but after a moment he realized that his own arms were shaking with fatigue.

"What's the matter?" she asked him. "What's going on?"

"I'm just tired," he said. "Very tired."

She kissed him gently. "Go to sleep. We're safe here." She held him until he fell asleep in her arms.

CHAPTER
25

The war went on.

The Machine, flying out of rifle range as always, towed a banner that said SURRENDER NOW. Ms. Migsdale began a series of propaganda broadcasts through a system of speakers that The Machine had rigged up in the Civic Center Plaza before the war. She played a recording of Ruby's sweetly chiding voice. "Soldiers," Ruby's recorded voice said. "Why do you keep fighting? There's no need for that, no need at all. Put down your weapons and join us. We'd be glad to have you. Don't you understand that you're free men?" By the end of the second day of broadcasting, the soldiers had found all of the speakers and destroyed them.

There were rumors of strange happenings. Hundreds of rats swarmed under the razor wire and into the enemy camp. The sentries shot at them, but hit only one in ten. The rodents overran the field kitchen, fouling the food and terrorizing the cooks. The soldiers shot the rats, stamped them beneath their feet, attacked them with meat cleavers. The grass beside the kitchen was piled high with dead vermin. The cooks scrubbed their pots repeatedly, but still dared not eat the food.

A rain of frogs fell on the Civic Center Plaza. They were tiny tree frogs, no larger than the last joint of a man's thumb. They clung to the trees, to the tents, to the men's helmets, and they sang in sweet high voices. Wherever the soldiers walked, they crushed the small animals underfoot.

The air reeked of smoke and the fog was constant.
Sometimes, late at night or in the early hours of the morning, when the fog glowed faintly with dawn light, Jax began
to believe that she might be a ghost after all. It was difficult
to believe in the sun—she had not seen it for so many days.
And if the sun were not real, perhaps she had imagined all
the rest as well. Perhaps the angel had taken her when she
arrived in the city, and all the memories since that time were
just fever dreams, adrift in the multicolored mist.

It was easy to get lost in the fog. Jax found her way by
scents and sounds: the reek of gunpowder, the tang of the
sea; the cooing of pigeons, the crying of gulls. Once, she
heard the voices of soldiers, passing just a few feet away.
"Saw an angel," one said. "Its face was a mess, but it had
wings of pure gold."

"You're nuts," said another. "Next thing, you'll be
claiming you saw Jax herself."

"Nobody sees Jax," said the first.

She ran away, looking for familiar faces. Temporary
headquarters had moved to the Palace of Fine Arts, a cav-
ernous structure built for a long-past exposition. To reach it
she climbed the Divisadero Street hill. For the first time in
days she left the fog behind, breaking out into the sunshine.
From the top of the hill she could see the gray dome of the
Palace's rotunda, surrounded by a jungle that had once been
a city park. She walked slowly toward it, relishing the
warmth of sunlight on her face.

Up close, she could make out the Palace's Roman col-
umns and elaborate carvings, now covered with clinging
vines. She made her way along a narrow track, shaded by
the trees, and entered through a door marked "Staff Only."

She found Danny-boy sitting in what had once been an
office. He looked up when he heard Jax's footsteps. His eyes
were bloodshot and he looked very tired. His hands were
empty and the desk in front of him was clear.

"What are you doing?" she asked him.

"Thinking." His voice was hoarse.

"Thinking about what?"

He looked down at his hands. "Have you been out in

Golden Gate Park? There are some soldiers living there. They've run away from the fighting."

"I heard," she said. "Randall told me."

He nodded slowly. "Have you talked with them?"

She shook her head.

"I talked to them," he said. "Do you know—they're as afraid of Fourstar as they are of us. They say that he kills deserters. They say he will never give up."

"I know," she said.

"We have to get to Fourstar," he said. "We have to do it."

"We have to kill him," Jax said.

Danny-boy nodded. "I think you're right."

"No," Jax said, "not just label him dead. We really have to kill him." She was not surprised when he shook his head.

"He just needs to know that we can get to him," Danny-boy said.

"You know better than that. He won't scare. That won't work. Not with Fourstar."

Danny-boy shook his head again. "If we mark him, his men will know that he is just a man. Then they will be able to leave. They won't be afraid."

"It won't work," Jax said.

"Why are you so sure? We can try it and see. We'll mark him and watch the results."

"Have you forgotten, Danny-boy?" She could not keep the edge out of her voice. "They use real bullets. And Fourstar stays in the most heavily guarded areas."

"I've been out there," he said. "I remember."

"Sometimes I think maybe you've forgotten. Or maybe you've started believing the stories that the soldiers are telling. Maybe you think you're a ghost and you can't be hurt."

"I don't believe that."

"You think this is a game. It isn't."

"I know it's not a game."

"Then what is it? Why shouldn't we kill Fourstar?"

He would not look up to meet her eyes. "You've got to realize that violence and death aren't the only forces that can change the social order."

She shook her head, started to speak, then shook her head again. "I don't have to realize that. I don't have to realize anything. Don't you understand? This is real."

"We started this way, and we have to keep going or it's all for nothing." His voice was flat. "If we kill him, that won't end it. We need to make him run. We have to play by the rules we set up. We have to warn him, and then, if we must, we can kill him." He spoke as if he were trying to convince himself. "It's my responsibility. I'll go in after him."

"You wouldn't make it past the first sentry," she said.

"I might surprise you."

"Yeah, you might make it to the second sentry." She reached across the table and took his hand. She would protect him from his own folly, whether he liked it or not. "You can't go. You've got a war to run. I'll go. I'll help change the goddamn world."

"No," he said. "This is my war."

"Forget that, Danny-boy. This isn't just your war. This is my city and this is my war. You understand?"

"I won't let you go," he said.

"You've got to," she said. "I'm the only one who stands half a chance of getting through." She turned and ran from the office before he could protest again.

She walked out through what had once been the museum's exhibit floor. Sunshine filtered through skylights, creating patches of brightness in the dark interior. In one such patch, she found The Machine, adjusting the valves on his gyrocopter. She sat beside him on the asphalt floor and watched him work.

"So how does the war look from up there?" she asked him at last.

He shrugged. "Small. Everything looks small from up there."

"Yeah, I guess so."

"How does it look from down below?"

She looked at her hands, clasped quietly in her lap. "A little too big, I think." She could hear pigeons cooing in the rafters overhead. The Machine waited calmly for her to speak. "I'm going to try to mark Fourstar," she said.

"That won't be easy."

"I know." She found herself fingering the silver pendant that hung around her neck. She released it and returned her hands to her lap.

"Do you think marking Fourstar will end the war?" The Machine asked.

"I don't think so. But I have to try. If I don't, Danny-boy will." She stopped abruptly.

"You don't want him to."

"He doesn't have a hope in hell of getting through. He'd get himself killed for sure. I have a better chance." She shook her head and spoke softly, half to herself. "I've got to do it."

She was staring down at her own hands. She heard The Machine set a tool on the asphalt floor, then felt his hand touch hers. For the first time since she'd known him, he reached out and touched her—a gentle, hesitant pat of reassurance. "I'll help," he said.

Her mother would have approved, she thought, as she ran through the streets of the fogbound city. Her mother would have agreed with Danny-boy. But her mother did not have to find a way to get to Fourstar.

It wasn't hard to find the camp where the deserters were living. She could smell the smoke from their campfire. They had taken shelter in a picnic area, where a grove of trees sheltered them from view. But she could see their boot prints in the grass, a clear trail leading to their refuge. She climbed an oak tree a short distance from their camp and relaxed, leaning against a broad branch. From there, she watched soldiers pass by, going out to get firewood and water, returning from hunting with rabbits or quail. She waited until she saw one that she recognized.

Dave was returning to camp with an armload of firewood. As near as she could tell, he was unarmed. She dropped from the tree to the trail in front of him.

"Hey, Dave—seen any angels lately?" she asked him.

He eyed her, still clutching his armload of wood. "I deserted, like you said," he told her, speaking quickly. "I want to leave the city, but the General's guarding the bridge. All the guys here—we all want to leave."

"No problem, Dave. Relax. Come here." She jerked her head in the direction of a fallen log, just off the trail. She sat on it and patted a place beside her. He glanced longingly in the direction of his camp. "I'll catch you if you run," she said, and he sat on the log.

"You were a lot more relaxed last time we met," she said.

"When you've seen an angel, a few ghosts don't matter," he muttered.

"I'm not really a ghost."

He glanced toward the trail.

"Look—I didn't hurt you last time, I won't hurt you now. I just need some information. I'm looking for a way into Fourstar's quarters. And it can't involve walking through walls or becoming invisible."

"You going to kill him?"

"You think I should?"

He nodded slowly. "If you kill him, we can go home."

"I'll mark him the same way I marked you."

He shook his head. "You should kill him, really kill him. If you can."

"Do you know the sentry posts around his quarters?" she asked him. "Can you help me find a way in?"

With a pointed stick, he drew in the dirt, diagramming the floor plan of the house where Fourstar slept. He made X's where guards were posted. "The guards change at three in the morning. It's pretty slow around then. No one's paying much attention. That might be a good time."

Jax listened carefully and studied his map. She made him mark all windows and doors, point out the location of the fire escapes and emergency exits. "Looks good," she said at last. She reached over and touched his hand. "Thanks."

"So you're not a ghost," he said, watching her closely.

"Not yet," she said. "If this information is wrong, I may become one."

"It's right," he said. "Good luck."

Then she ran away to kill Fourstar.

CHAPTER
26

The Machine checked his watch. Midnight exactly. He circled once, then swooped low over the Civic Center Plaza to dump his load of water balloons. They were filled with a synthetic stench that smelled remarkably like skunk. Working in an isolated house on the edge of town, Tiger had concocted the scent and loaded the balloons.

The Machine climbed steeply, leaving the shouting and gunfire behind. The half moon hung over the bay, casting just enough light to let him see the sharp-edged skyscrapers. The moonlight reflecting from the snowdrifts in the Civic Center Plaza made them glow as if lit from within. He watched the soldiers running, trying to leave the stench of his bombs behind. They took cover in City Hall and in the library, and he smiled, hoping that they would stay inside long enough for Jax to get in and out.

He had accomplished his mission and he could return to headquarters, but he decided against it. It was a lovely night for flying. He circled, climbing higher. As he passed over the Holiday Inn on Eighth Avenue, he caught a glimpse of Danny-boy and Snake, waving to him from the roof.

Looking back, he saw the first of the fireworks that Danny-boy and Snake were setting off to draw attention away from the Civic Center Plaza. A brilliant burst of colored light bloomed in the darkness like a luminescent flower.

* * *

Jax went in through the tunnels, crawling along a storm drain. By flashlight, she checked the time on the delicate gold wristwatch that Ms. Migsdale had given her to use on this operation. At a few minutes to midnight, Jax emerged from the storm drain into an alley behind the house where Fourstar slept.

Dave had assured her that no sentry was posted in the alley. She was relieved to learn that he had been telling the truth. She climbed up through the storm drain and waited, resting in the shadows. In the narrow strip of sky above her, the stars seemed very cool and distant. The stench of skunk made her eyes water.

She heard a distant explosion and saw a burst of colored light in the sky overhead: brilliant red sparks spiraled madly in all directions, whistling as they went. Then there were three more muffled explosions, and simultaneous bursts of green, silver, and gold.

While the fireworks were exploding, Jax climbed the fire escape to the fourth floor. The sentries were at the far end of the hall, watching the fireworks through an open window. "Never seen anything like it," one young soldier was saying to the other.

Jax slipped behind them and let herself into Fourstar's room, quietly closing the door behind her. She stood perfectly still in the darkness, listening to the steady rhythm of Fourstar's breathing. Silently, she crept closer and looked down at the sleeping man.

He looked older up close than he had from a distance. His gray hair was rumpled; his skin was slack and wrinkled. He frowned, even in his sleep. She wondered what he was dreaming about.

She took a deep breath and pulled an ether-soaked cloth from a plastic bag. As he finished exhaling, she gently placed it over his nose and mouth, so that his next breath was laden with ether. He grumbled in his sleep and moved his head restlessly. She followed the movements of his head with the cloth, staying with him. His eyelids fluttered and then he lay still again. His breathing eased, returning to the steady rhythm of deep sleep. His face relaxed.

When she was sure that he was out, she sealed the cloth back into its plastic bag and opened the window, letting in a gust of fresh air. She took a deep breath and shook her head to clear away dizziness. Then she returned to the bed where Fourstar lay sleeping.

In a gesture that felt strangely intimate, she smoothed the hair back from his forehead. It was difficult to think of him as dangerous now. He was just an unhappy old man. She looked around the room at his things. His uniform was laid neatly across the chair; his hat hung from a corner of the chair back. A bottle of pre-Plague whiskey stood on the table. A paperback book—it looked like a spy novel—lay open on the bedside table.

With the red paint that had become her trademark, she carefully marked DEAD on his forehead and signed BY JAX on his cheek. When he moved restlessly beneath the brush, she held the ether-soaked kerchief to his nose. As she worked she could hear the explosions of the fireworks. Now and then there was a burst of answering gunfire. She did not let the sounds distract her; she worked steadily. When she finished, she tucked the Death Certificate into Fourstar's hands.

She went to the open window and glanced out. As near as she could tell, the street below was empty. The Federal Building blocked the moonlight, leaving the side of the building below Fourstar's window in dense shadow.

Jax tied one end of her climbing rope to the iron bedstead, dropped the other end out the window, and rappelled down the side of the house, moving quickly and trying to stay in the shadows. Above her the fireworks continued, painting the night sky with brilliant colors.

Just as she reached the ground, she saw a soldier step into the alley. She flattened herself into a window alcove, trying to blend with the shadows, but she was sure he had seen her. He ducked for cover, crouching behind a parked car.

For a moment, he did not shoot. In the darkness she could hear him breathing, almost hear him thinking. He had shot at so many shadows. Was this another of the city's tricks? Or was this one real?

She pressed herself deeper into the alcove: there was no better cover and she knew that any attempt to run would only convince him to fire. She breathed softly, fighting the urge to panic and run.

She saw a movement on the far side of the street. She caught the scent of burning marijuana. And suddenly the street was crowded with people: men and women walking arm in arm. Their faces seemed to glow in the darkness. Some carried signs—"U.S. out of Central America," "No Contra Aid." Three women carried a long banner that said "NO MORE WAR." In the distance, Jax heard the murmur of an enormous crowd, a great restless rumbling that blended with the chanting of the marchers: "No more war. No more war."

The soldier behind the car fired a burst across the crowd, but the people didn't notice. The chanting continued. Jax saw the soldier turn and flee.

She stepped from the shadows and made her way through the crowd to the storm drain from which she had come up. People smiled at her as she slipped among them, and she felt the heat of their bodies around her. She lifted the manhole cover and looked up once more. One of the women smiled and waved and Jax recognized her mother in a happier time. Jax waved back and slipped down into the tunnels.

In the darkness beneath the city, she felt warm, as if the phantom sun of that long-ago afternoon still shone on her. For a time she could hear the voices of the marchers echoing through the tunnels: "No more war." She hurried back to headquarters, filled with the hysterical joy that often follows a narrow escape. Even in the tunnels she could hear the marching ghosts, catch the distant rumble of their chanting.

The Machine was on his way back to headquarters when he saw a flash of golden light in the darkness below. For a moment he took it for a fire, ignited by a spark from the fireworks, and he swooped low to check it out. For a moment, he lost sight of the light; he could not see it anywhere on the ground beneath him. He glanced upward and saw the angel flying above him.

He could not see it clearly—just a spark of light from a glowing eye and the reflection of moonlight on burnished wings. But he felt its presence with a jolt as sharp and clean as an electric shock. It had come for him.

He followed, even when the angel dove low, dodging through the twisting streets. He was caught by a feeling of impossible rightness. Ah, the glory of the angel. The beauty of a polished gear neatly meshing with another, so perfect and inevitable. The satisfaction of a ball bearing, rolling in its track without a catch or a moment's hesitation. The wonderful intricacy that added up to such complete simplicity, like the complex mechanism of a ticking clock.

In pursuit of the angel he plunged into the canyons of downtown. The tips of his rotor passed within inches of the buildings, but he did not pull up. He could not pull up without losing his quarry and he would not allow that.

Beneath him, he heard the rattle of gunfire. For a moment the sound drew his attention to the street. A group of soldiers was firing at a parked car. In a tiny sliver of time, a crystalline shard broken from eternity, he saw Danny-boy and Snake taking shelter behind the vehicle. He saw the patrol closing in.

It all happened very quickly or very slowly. He did not know which. It did not matter. He saw everything: Snake's hand, reaching for his rifle; Danny-boy's face, smudged with soot from the fireworks; the soldiers' eyes, wide and frightened in the darkness.

He knew the proper course to follow. He understood why the angel had led him to this place. He cried out and his voice blended with the engine as he twisted the throttle to give the gyrocopter more gas.

Ah, it was a beautiful night. He had never felt air as cool and pure as the air that caressed his face as he dove. It filled his lungs and made his heart beat faster. His heart—he could feel it beating in his chest and with each beat the blood surged in his body.

He laughed out loud and rushed down to meet the soldiers.

* * *

Jax was the first to reach headquarters, now in a Pacific Heights apartment building with a view of downtown. "I got him," she told Lily, who met her at the door. "I got him and escaped. No problem." Her hands were shaking and she could not make them stop. "Where are the others? Aren't they back yet?"

"Not yet." Lily's voice was strained. Jax could not see her face in the darkness of the lobby. "The fireworks stopped half an hour ago, but there's no sign of them yet." She put her hand on Jax's shoulder. "You're trembling."

"I'm OK." But she could not stop trembling, even when Lily draped a blanket over her shoulders. Lily urged her to go up to the penthouse apartment, where some of the others were watching for more fireworks, but Jax refused.

"I've got to talk to Fourstar," Jax said. "That's what I should do. He's got to know that I can get to him. He's not safe from us."

She got the field radio and sat on the front steps with Lily. "Hey, Johnson," she said into the microphone. Since the other guards would not tell her their names, she called them all Johnson, after the first one to talk to her. "Get Fourstar, would you? I've got to talk to him."

Lily pulled the blanket around Jax's shoulders and put her arm around her. The shaking was easing somewhat. Jax felt better now that she was doing something. From the steps they could see all the way down the hill to the Civic Center Plaza, where spotlights still blazed. It took a while for Fourstar to come to the microphone and when he greeted her, he sounded groggy.

"Are you ready to give up?" Jax asked.

Through the radio, she heard a chair creak as Fourstar sat down. She imagined him—he was wearing his jacket and leaning forward a little. His hair fell across his forehead, but the lettering on his cheek was clear.

"I don't give up," he said. "I don't know how."

"You can't win. This place belongs to us. We belong to the city. You'll never win."

A long pause. She could hear him breathing.

"That was a clever trick you used to get away," he said softly.

"That wasn't a trick. The city rescued me. Those were ghosts from the city. They live here."

"I don't believe in ghosts. I don't believe in spirits. I believe in things I can touch." He sounded, just for a moment, like he was trying to convince himself. Then the doubt slipped away and his tone of certainty returned. "You know, when I catch you I'll have to kill you."

"Why?"

"To prove that you're a woman, nothing more. My men think you're a ghost. Some of them fear you more than they fear me. So I'll have to kill you." She heard his chair creak as he leaned forward. "I think you understand the need for blood and the need for fear."

"You won't catch me."

"You sound so sure." His voice was just a little slurred from the anesthetic, but he spoke with confidence. "Maybe you're starting to believe your own legend. Maybe you think you can't be killed. Do you think that?"

Jax said nothing.

"You're wrong if you do." Fourstar's breathing was labored. "My men once thought that I was more than mortal. They know better now. But even when they believed that I was more than a man, I never made the mistake of agreeing with them. I always remembered that I could be killed. You must always remember that. Remember I can kill you."

"You won't catch me." Jax turned off the microphone.

"I hear someone coming," Lily said suddenly. She stood up and looked down the hill. Jax let the blanket slide from her shoulders and picked up her rifle. She slung it over her back as Danny-boy and Snake approached.

Danny-boy stopped at the bottom of the steps. She went to meet him. She put her arms around him, but his body felt stiff and wooden in her embrace.

"What's wrong?" she said. "You're back. You're OK. What's wrong?" She pulled back to look at him. Tears had traced meandering lines through the soot on his face. "What is it?"

He shook his head, but said nothing.

She put her hands on his shoulders, staring into his face. "Tell me what happened."

Still, he was silent.

"The Machine's dead," Snake said. "A patrol was after us. He crashed his 'copter into them. He couldn't have survived."

"Dead?" she said. "He's dead?" She was shaking again. The vibration came from deep within her and she knew that it would not stop this time. "I should have killed Fourstar. Then The Machine would have died for a reason." She did not know she was crying until Danny-boy brushed a tear from her cheek. She backed away from him. He watched, his hands open at his sides.

"Jax," he said. Then he stopped, as if he did not know how to continue. He held his arms out to her, and she took another step back. "Where are you going? Don't go."

She walked away. When she reached the end of the block, she was surprised to find Danny-boy still at her side. He took her hand. She stepped back, jerked her hand up and out to break his grip. Her hands were in fists. "Don't get in the way, Danny-boy," she said. "You grieve your way, and I'll grieve in mine. Don't get in the way." She turned from him and ran down the hill.

Fog and smoke filled the streets. She heard Danny-boy calling after her, but she ran from the sound. All around her there was gunfire, always distant gunfire. The darkness around her seemed like the darkness of a dream, where some things are very clear and others are vague and ill-formed, as if only half imagined. A streetlight with a woman's face; the howling voice of the wind, singing across the mouth of an open pipe; a department store window filled with skulls.

She did not know where she was going. She was going away, that was all that she knew. Somewhere in the darkness she would find what she needed: a quiet place where there were no friends and therefore no pain. Love caused pain—she knew that now and she wanted no part of it. She was very tired and the shadows seemed to shift and follow her. Faces watched her from the windows of the houses.

Overhead, she heard the thunder of wings. Through the

fog she saw the glint of gold, like the sun on burnished metal. She lifted her rifle and fired at the angel. The fog spoiled her aim—at least, she blamed it on the fog, rather than the tears that blurred her vision. She followed the sound of wings as she ran through the alleys and streets. She fired until she ran out of ammunition, and then she discarded the useless weapon.

The streets took her deeper into the darkness. She did not care. In the darkness, she knew she would find the angel.

She found a soldier instead. She ran from the fog and saw his face, a pale oval in the darkness. She dodged him and started to run past, still chasing the angel. But the man called out and the rest of the patrol caught her. A young man brought her down with a flying tackle and held her. When the sound of the wings faded, she stopped fighting.

Suddenly calm, she looked at them. Five young men, three of them DEAD. Two held her arms; the others stood a respectful distance away, holding their rifles ready. They searched her for weapons and took her knife, her paint kit, her smoke grenades.

When she rubbed her forehead, her hand came away streaked with blood. Her other hand ached. When she opened it, she found that she had gashed the palm. She had a vague memory of falling and catching herself with that hand, but she could not remember when or where. She rubbed at the cut, trying to rub some of the blood away, and she was surprised to feel pain.

The soldiers marched her through the streets, past the razor wire and the spotlights. "We have a prisoner," they called to the sentries on duty. "A prisoner." The sentries stared at her curiously. The rising sun touched their faces with pale light.

"She's too small," one of them called out. "She can't be one of the artists."

Her guards did not stop to answer; they headed directly for the building that housed Fourstar. From the trees in the plaza, she heard the high sweet peeping of the tree frogs. She glanced around her, seeing the Civic Center Plaza in daylight for the first time in weeks. Dirty snow filled the gutters.

The air was cold, and the men who stood near the kitchen tent looked tired and dirty. "A prisoner," she heard them saying. "One of the artists."

The soldiers took her directly to Fourstar. While she waited in the lobby, soldiers crowded around her, but her captors kept them back. Faces marked DEAD stared at her. She looked past them, meeting no one's eyes. The guards brought her to another room, where Fourstar was waiting.

His gray hair was rumpled, as if he had been asleep. His shirt was wrinkled and one cuff was marked with a coffee stain. He looked tired.

"Can you speak?" he asked her.

"Yes."

"Make that 'Yes, sir.' "

She studied him for a moment, considering her options. "Why?"

Smiling, he reached out and slapped her across the face. She did not dodge far enough to avoid the blow.

"Don't be stupid. You're unarmed and my soldiers are all around you. Say 'Yes, sir.' "

She regarded him steadily. "Yes, sir."

"Good," he said. "Very good. What's your name?"

She realized suddenly that she could lie. She could disown her name and he would never know. She hesitated, studying the signature on his cheek. He stood with his hands locked behind his back. It seemed important that he know who she was. She wanted him to know.

"My name's Jax," she said.

He studied her for a moment. She stared back, her face carefully neutral. "I see," he said. "When I said we would capture you, I didn't think it would be so soon."

She shrugged wearily.

"She's unarmed?" Fourstar asked.

"Yes, sir."

"Good. Leave her then," he told the guards. They seemed glad to leave. "Post a guard at the door."

"Yes, sir."

The soldiers left and he studied her face. "Sit down," he said, gesturing at a chair. She sat. He sat in another chair and continued watching her. His eyes were shrewd. "I realize, of course, that you could have killed me last night," he said at last.

She nodded. "That's so."

He nodded, his hands forming a steeple in front of his chin. "You should have. Because if you think that I'm grateful that you spared my life, you're wrong."

She said nothing. She had no expectations.

"Why did you come here? You've been so clever for so long that I can't believe you'd simply run into a patrol by mistake."

"I was following the angel," she said.

"The angel?"

"The angel. I heard his wings and I was following the sound." She felt empty and cold. Her own words seemed to come to her from a distance, as if they were echoing through the tunnels beneath the city.

"So you followed the angel to me," he said. "The angel of death, maybe? That seems appropriate." He leaned forward and poured two drinks from the bottle on the table. He gave her one and took the other himself. She sipped from the glass: it was whiskey and she winced when it touched a cut on her lip. "I have no qualms about killing."

She said nothing.

He sipped his whiskey. "I've been wondering when my luck would turn. It seems it finally has. Now the question is: What will I do with you?"

"I thought," she said slowly, "that we talked about this once before."

He nodded, obviously enjoying himself. "We did. But that was a different situation, wasn't it? You would never have said 'Yes, sir' then."

"True."

"Make that 'Yes, sir,' " he said.

"The soldiers aren't here," she said. "Why put on a show?"

His grin broadened. "Perhaps for my own amusement?"

His grin penetrated her weariness. "If you're going to kill me anyway, I'd rather not amuse you first." She knew that he could order the soldiers back to beat her, but she did not care.

He laughed and slapped his hand against the arm of his chair. "I like you, Jax. So angry, so arrogant. You know— it's possible I might not kill you at all."

She kept her face still, hiding her surprise. How strange, she thought, how very strange. An option she had not considered.

"I need some information," he said. "For a start, you can tell me where your headquarters are."

She shrugged. "Headquarters change from day to day. They've moved by now."

"Where were they?" He stood up and moved a little closer. "Where were they last?"

When she did not speak, he smiled and calmly slapped her across the face. She could feel the pain, but it was distant, as if it had happened to someone else. She shook her head, trying to clear it of the pain. She spilled her drink; she could feel the cold whiskey soaking her leg.

"I thought we'd gotten past that," she said.

"Just a reminder," he said. "Now, you were going to tell me about your headquarters."

"There's nothing for you there," she said. "I can't tell you anything of value. Temporary headquarters can be any-where. We carry our weapons with us. Even if I told you all I know, you'd learn nothing of value."

He returned to his chair and leaned back in it. "Unfor-tunately, I suspect you're telling the truth. I could make you answer, but the information you gave me would be worth-less by the time I got it. Would they ransom you, I wonder? What would you be worth?" He rubbed his chin thought-fully. "Or maybe I could persuade you to work for me. Suppose I sentimentally spare your life. You could surrender publicly and swear allegiance to me. What do you think?"

She licked her lip, tasting blood. She studied his face. He did not frighten her anymore. He was willing to bargain with her, like a trader in the market. "If I said yes, what then?"

"You'll tell me all that you know. And then I will assemble the troops and you will vow allegiance to me."

"And if I don't."

"In that case, I think we will have a public execution. A hanging on the steps of City Hall."

She liked living. She sipped her drink and the whiskey tasted good. She could hear one of Gambit's bells ringing in the distance, but the sound did not touch the silence in the room. What difference would it make if she pledged loyalty to Fourstar? None. It would mean nothing. The words would just be words, words like "Yes, sir." She liked living. She swirled the whiskey in her glass. Danny-boy would say that the words were symbols. They were fighting a war of symbols. Danny-boy was crazy. He was wrong. She liked living.

"Hanging is, I think, one of the most dramatic ways to execute a prisoner. It's really ideal. There's the anticipation while the stage is set—the men build the scaffold in a central place and everyone watches it take form. There is the execution itself—the moment of silence when the prisoner is led forth, the touching ceremony when the blindfold is offered, the brief delay while the noose is adjusted around the prisoner's neck. Then the sudden crack when the trapdoor opens and the moment of heart-stopping pathos when the prisoner dances in the air, struggling against death and losing. And after the event is over, the memory lingers. The shadow of the scaffold stretches across the plaza, the body sways in the breeze, a constant reminder of death. Of course, I'll leave your body hanging until the war is over."

She stared at him, not really listening.

He smiled and nodded. "Dramatic," he said. "And effective. You could learn a little about dramatic staging, you know."

"I should have killed you," Jax said dispassionately. "Danny-boy was wrong."

He shrugged easily, leaned forward, and filled her glass again. "Yes, you should have. You know, in some ways, I'm disappointed in you people. I had heard you were artists, but you don't take this art business far enough." He sipped his whiskey and nodded slowly. "You take the easy way. You don't risk enough."

"What the hell do you know about it?"

"I know you draw foolish lines. You're willing to die for art, but you aren't willing to kill for it." He leaned forward to rest his elbows on his knees. "A good death can be a work of art. So can a good execution. You should learn by my example."

"I don't believe I'll have a chance," she said coldly.

He nodded. When he smiled, the signature on his cheek wrinkled. "True enough. You'll die tomorrow."

CHAPTER
27

That night, she dreamed of dark rooftops and empty streets. She rode a horse through the city, and Fourstar rode beside her. Somehow, in the dream, she did not know if she was fighting with Fourstar or against him. As they rode, Fourstar kept lecturing her about the nature of art and death.

She dreamed of darkness and the smell of smoke. Danny-boy was with her in the windowless room where she was imprisoned. "I guess I'm going to die," she told him. He handed her a red rose and smiled. "Do you know how to tell if a work is art?" he asked her calmly. "True art changes the artist. The artist puts something into the work and he changes. That's how you tell." He smiled and vanished in the smoke.

She woke to a rhythmic pounding, like the hoofbeats of running horses. In the thin light of dawn, hammers pounded as soldiers built the scaffold where she would die.

They did not come for her until noon. The guard at her door brought a basin of water, a bar of soap, and a towel so that she could wash herself. He was a tall young man with red hair, and his cheek was signed by Snake.

She was done washing when he knocked again, bringing her a bowl of canned fruit cocktail for breakfast. He stood uneasily in the room, watching her as she ate. She suspected by his expression and by the way he kept glancing toward the door that this breakfast had not been ordered by Fourstar.

"What's your name, soldier?" she asked him.

"Dan."

"Glad to meet you, Dan," she said. "You know, Snake is an excellent artist. You should be honored that you wear his name. He painted most of the graffiti in the Haight."

The soldier nodded. He seemed uncomfortable, but he clearly wanted to continue talking with her.

"What do you think of all this?" she asked him. "What do you think of this war?"

He shrugged. "I'm sorry you have to die, ma'am."

"Yeah? Why's that?"

"You didn't kill anyone. It doesn't seem fair." He hesitated, and she knew that he wasn't done.

"What is it?"

"I hope that your friends save you, ma'am. Good luck."

She smiled and gave him her empty bowl. "I wouldn't count on that. I wouldn't count on that at all."

Five soldiers came for her. All of them were DEAD. They bound her hands behind her back with surprising gentleness. Dan stood to one side, his expression carefully blank. She smiled at him as she walked by. She went with the soldiers willingly. She saw no point in struggling. Not now.

The plaza was quiet except for the chirping of the frogs in the trees. The soldiers stood in formation before the scaffold, and her guards escorted her up the aisle between the ranks. The soldiers stood at attention. Though they did not turn their heads to watch her pass, she could see their eyes straining to see her. She felt very old and they all looked very young. She was glad that she hadn't killed them.

The sun shone dimly through the haze of smoke and fog. She could feel the breeze on her face. Bright banners flew over the plaza, snapping in the breeze. She had helped put them up before the war began. Now they were smudged with smoke and a little tattered. Even so, they were a fine, brave sight. The city was a beautiful place, she thought, such a beautiful place.

Her guards waited below as she climbed the crudely made steps to the wooden platform. Fourstar stood on the platform beside her. Strangely, she did not hate him. He seemed so much smaller now. She had seen the coffee stain on his cuff, seen his face when it was relaxed in sleep. She did not hate him.

Fourstar made a speech, but Jax was not listening. While Fourstar spoke of her crimes and of the glorious future of America, she admired the way that the light played on the trees. She savored the touch of the breeze on her face.

Too soon, Fourstar offered her a blindfold. She refused. She wanted to watch the banners fly over the gathered soldiers. As she watched, a man in the ranks crossed himself.

Fourstar put a rope around her neck and adjusted the knot. He raised his hand, ready to signal to the man who would pull the rope to release the trapdoor and kill her.

She saw a movement on a roof to one side of the plaza. She heard the sound of a single rifle shot. She saw a blossom of blood on Fourstar's forehead; he swayed, then fell. The stiffness went out of him as he fell; he crumbled, folded. His body struck the steps and rolled down. Rolled more like a sack of old clothes than a man.

Jax looked up to see the assassin. Danny-boy stood above the crowd on the edge of the roof. Sunlight glinted on the barrel of his rifle. He was too far away; she could not make out his expression. For an instant, the world seemed frozen. The colored banners stood still; the smell of smoke hung in the air.

A soldier fired quickly, and Danny-boy jerked. He fell against a stone carving on the building's facade, clung for a moment, then fell to the ground below. She watched from so far away, unable to move. The soldiers reacted then—some running to Fourstar's body, some to surround her, others ducking for cover.

"Gentlemen," Ms. Migsdale's voice boomed from a speaker that was hidden somewhere in the plaza. "The ground where you stand was planted with explosives before your arrival. The charges are wired to explode at my signal. We had hoped to avoid this necessity."

It was a lie, of course. But Ms. Migsdale lied well, and the soldiers were ready to believe in any lie that would let them leave, free them from the war that they were tired of fighting.

"If you lay down your weapons, no one will be hurt. We will welcome those of you who wish to join us, and escort the others over the bridge. Please put down your weapons. Now." The last word was delivered with uncharacteristic force.

The soldier who had shot Danny-boy was the first to put down his rifle. The plaza was quiet. Danny-boy lay where he had fallen. His head lolled back and the hole in his chest was a deep rich red.

Fourstar lay tumbled at the bottom of the steps. The hole in his forehead was the same red.

Jax remained on the scaffold. The soldiers laid their weapons at her feet, then backed away as if frightened. She stood, swaying a little. Her hands were still bound behind her. The numbness that had sustained her was gone, and her wrists were starting to ache. "Well," she said to the soldiers. "Who won?" She looked at Danny-boy and at Fourstar. "They're both dead, so who won?" She stopped for a moment, staring across the plaza. "A good death," she said to no one, "is a work of art." She started to laugh, but the sound caught in her throat.

The banners fluttered and snapped in the afternoon breeze. The sun broke through the fog and warmed her face. The clip-clop of hooves on pavement echoed across the plaza. Snake rode a horse through the open space. He stopped in front of her and she studied him for a minute, wondering if he were a part of the long dream from which she was emerging.

He swung his leg over the horse's back and slid to the ground. When he untied her hands, she smiled with unaccustomed sweetness. "It's over," she said. And then her knees gave way. He caught her and helped her to the edge of the platform. She took his hand and held it in hers.

Zatch, Lily, Frank, Tiger and the others moved through the crowd, dividing the soldiers into groups: men who would stay; men who would leave. Jax shivered and Snake draped his jacket over her shoulders. "We spent last night talking about it," Snake said. "Danny-boy insisted that he would be the one to do it."

She looked out at the flying banners and the horse. The horse's harness jingled when the animal moved its head, searching for a few blades of grass. Most of the grass had been trampled, and little was left. She looked over at Fourstar. Through the blood on his forehead and cheek she could still read the words "BY JAX."

CHAPTER
28

In an isolated valley high in the Himalayas stood a stupa, a great white-washed dome topped by a gilded tower. From each side of the tower, painted eyes stared out at the snow-capped mountains, eternally watching over the followers of Buddha. On ropes that stretched from the tower top to the base of the dome, brightly colored prayer flags waved in the breeze.

The Rimpoche, head of the monastery that cared for the stupa, gazed from the window of his study. From the temple below, he could hear the monks chanting their prayers and the chiming of the windbells that hung from the eaves. It was late afternoon, and most of the monks had returned from the fields for their afternoon prayers.

As the Rimpoche watched, a young monk hurried into the courtyard, his red robes fluttering as he ran. He carried a bowl of rice and a handful of flowers. Following close behind him were three of the sacred monkeys that lived around the stupa.

The young monk set his offering before the shrine of Ajima, the goddess of health. As he prostrated himself in devotion, the boldest of the monkeys snatched a handful of rice and leapt to the lowest roof of Ajima's pagoda to eat. Before the young man could finish his devotions, the bowl was empty. The monkeys perched on the roof of the pagoda, pelting the monk with flowers that they had taken from the offering and found to be inedible.

The population of monkeys was up to its former levels. The Rimpoche regretted that the Americans would not be back to take more of the beasts away. He smiled and rubbed his bald head, thinking of the Americans. He had liked them enormously—they were so intense and impatient and convinced of their own importance. So much like children. The Rimpoche was fond of children.

The Americans had come to him to confirm a legend that they had heard about the monastery's monkeys. With the help of a Peace Corps volunteer, he had told them the story. Yes, the monastery was called the Mountain of Peace. Centuries ago, a powerful warlord had brought his army to the monastery. The warlord had acquired many lands by conquest, but he was weary of fighting and wanted to maintain his kingdom in a peaceful time. He had demanded that the Rimpoche bring forth the secret of peace.

"I bowed respectfully and declined," the Rimpoche had told the Americans. "Peace is not something that can be taken by force."

The Americans had nodded, exchanging glances of wonder and doubt. The Rimpoche knew that they did not believe that he was the reincarnation of the Rimpoche of that time, but they did not speak of their doubt.

"The warlord offered silver and gold for the secret of peace, but I refused again. Peace cannot be bought for money. Finally, he drew his sword and threatened to cut off my head unless I told him the secret. I asked for seven days to consider the matter, and he agreed." The Rimpoche glanced around at the serious young faces as the translator relayed his words. "On the seventh day, I met with the warlord again, and told him that I could not be forced to give him the secret. He raised his sword to behead me, and something very strange happened. As he raised the weapon, he stumbled and closed his eyes. Right there, he fell asleep, collapsing to the ground at my feet. All around us the soldiers fell, unable to lift their weapons. Peace came to them, whether they would have it or not."

The Americans nodded eagerly as the translator passed on his words.

"The monkeys laughed and chatted from the temple

roofs, and the soldiers did not fight. The monkeys, you see, are the keepers of the peace. If they were to leave the monastery, peace would come to the world. Though it might not be the peace you expect."

The Americans had been happy with the legend. They had smiled at each other and had spoken quickly among themselves. The Rimpoche smiled, remembering their enthusiasm. They had asked his permission to capture some of the monkeys.

"You wish to bring peace to your country?" he had asked them, and they said that of course they did. They told him, through the translator, of what the monkeys would mean to the world, what a powerful symbol they would be.

"It will change your country," he had advised them. "It will change the world."

They had smiled and nodded. "Yes, yes. It will be a wonderful thing."

In the end, he had granted his permission willingly. Keepers of the peace or not, the monkeys were mangy, ill-tempered beasts and the stupa had entirely too many of them. If the Americans wanted to bring peace to their country, they could take them.

Zoologists had come with nets and cages. They had captured dozens of monkeys and taken them away. After they left, the Rimpoche had never heard from them again. From a traveler who had come to the monastery from Katmandu, the Rimpoche had heard about the Plague that struck in San Francisco, Moscow, Washington, D.C., Tokyo, London, and all the other places that the monkeys had traveled.

The Plague had not affected the monastery. The monks still grew barley and corn in their terraced fields. The wedding of a woman in a nearby village meant more than the deaths of thousands in America.

Sometimes the Rimpoche wondered about the Americans. Had they understood what they were doing when they took the monkeys away? Certainly the legend was clear. He had told them that the world would change, and it had.

He turned away from the window. On the altar, a golden statue of the Buddha stared serenely over his head.

Taking an orange from the bowl on the table, he placed it on the altar. An offering for the Americans, he thought as he placed it beside the flowers and food left by the other monks. He hoped that all was well with them.

EPILOGUE

"Gone. Gone. Completely gone. Gone on beyond. Enlightenment. So be it."

—Prajapramita Hridaya Sutra
(*The Heart of Perfect Wisdom* Sutra)

Fourstar, Danny-boy, and The Machine were buried in the Civic Center Plaza, and their graves were surrounded by memorials.

Zatch and Lily, with the help of some of the soldiers who had stayed behind, constructed the Arch of Peace from weapons that they had taken from the army. The arch was wide enough to accommodate four people walking arm in arm, tall enough so that someone on horseback could ride through it without stooping.

Ms. Migsdale wrote an official account of the war and published it in a very limited edition. On the white wall of the house where Fourstar had lived, Books painted the story of the war in Egyptian hieroglyphics. Danny-boy was Ra, the sun-god; Jax was Isis; Fourstar was Anubis, the jackal-headed god of death.

Rose Maloney buried the army jeeps and the tank up to their bellies on the open lawn, then used them as planters for flowering vines. The camouflage patterns blended with the leaves. Finches came there to nest and sing.

Gambit dug through the debris left in the army camp and used the objects he found to build a singing fountain. He strung thousands of empty cartridges together in loose strands. When the water flowed over them, they rattled together like teeth chattering.

In a tree near the graves, Frank hung a half-silvered mirror that he had found in a warehouse years before. The image in the mirror changed as the light shifted. Sometimes the glass acted as a window, showing the scene on the far side clearly. Sometimes it was a mirror, reflecting back the image of the person looking into the glass. And sometimes it was both: if two people stood on opposite sides of the mirror when the light was just right, the image that they saw was a blend of both their faces, borrowing something from each person's features to create a composite of the two.

Jax did not help with any of these projects. She felt restless, unsettled, uneasy. She remained in the rooms she had shared with Danny-boy, but she did not sleep well. She would wake up at night, peering into the darkness and listening for the thunder of wings. By day she wandered the city, searching for something that she could not name. People tried to take care of her: Snake tried to interest her in graffiti art. Randall showed her secret glens in the park, where ghostly white deer mated and played. Tiger offered to tattoo her back. Ruby baked her cookies and tried to comfort her. Jax was oblivious to their attentions.

Ms. Migsdale insisted that Jax come to her house for dinner and tried to talk to her. They ate together in Ms. Migsdale's small kitchen, but Jax would not sit still. She kept wandering to the window and staring out. "Seems so quiet now," she said.

"It's hard to get used to Danny-boy being gone," Ms. Migsdale said, approaching the matter directly. "We all miss him."

"I wish I could tell him that I think he was right about the war," Jax muttered, peering out at the darkness. "Do you think he knows that? I wonder sometimes why he didn't duck for cover after he shot Fourstar. Seems like he had time. I think maybe he chose to die. I think maybe he felt he had to."

Ms. Migsdale watched Jax, wishing she knew what to say. "I don't know. I think he'd be happy with the way it all worked out."

"Oh, I know that," Jax said impatiently. "I just wish I could tell him that I think he was right. We argued, right at the end, and I never got to tell him." She wandered back to her seat by the fire. "I get the feeling sometimes that he's

just around the corner. He and The Machine—they're still
in the city somewhere. But I just can't find the right place to
look." She shook her head. "But it's not over yet. I know
that for certain. I just have to find the right place."

Tommy had better luck talking with Jax. He demanded
the crossbow lessons that she had promised him, and they
spent an afternoon in Union Square, shooting at a target
that Jax hung on a telephone pole. Jezebel came with them.
The dog seemed torn between Tommy and Jax: sometimes
she sat at Tommy's feet, and sometimes at Jax's.

"If I were to go away somewhere," Jax said, "you'd
take care of Jezebel, right?"

"You going somewhere?" Tommy asked. "Where are
you going?"

Jax shook her head. "Nowhere. I was just asking. Why
don't you just keep on taking care of her. She likes you. And
you need a dog."

"OK, but you aren't going anywhere, are you?"

Jax shrugged. She handed him another bolt for the
crossbow. "Here, try again." He loaded the bow, aimed, and
fired, hitting the telephone pole but missing the target.

"Not bad," she said. "Try to relax your shoulders.
You're still too tense."

He tried again.

"Better. A little more practice and you'll be fine."

At the end of the lesson, he handed her the crossbow.
"Will you help me make a crossbow?" he asked her. "So I
can practice on my own."

She hesitated, holding the weapon, and then held it out
to him. "Take this one," she said. "I don't need it."

He shook his head. "What do you mean? That's your
crossbow. Sure you need it."

"Take it." She put it in his hands. "I won't be using it
again."

Before he could reply, she ran away. He chased her, but
she lost him in the twists and turns of the downtown streets.

Jax explored the city's high places, climbing Telegraph
Hill, Mt. Sutro, Mt. Davidson. In the Sunset District, she
found a high hill so steep that houses had never been built

there. The soil was dry and sandy; only a few stunted pine trees clung to the slope.

The moon was three nights from full when she found the hill. With her bare hands, she scooped out a small depression in the loose soil and there she waited. She fasted, drinking only the clear water that she had brought with her. At night the stars came to see her, and the moon passed calmly overhead. The air held the clean sharp scent of pines, and the animals that shared her hilltop went about their business. The fox that lived in a burrow among the roots of the largest pine looked at her curiously, then went to hunt for rodents. An owl soared silently overhead. Three monkeys that had followed her to the hilltop huddled by a tree, staring at her with curious yellow eyes.

The moon was full on the third night. She had given up sleep as well as food, and her senses had grown more acute. She could smell the distant wood smoke of someone's cooking fire in the city, hear the delicate rustling of twigs as the fox crept down the hill. She heard the gentle sound of her mother's breathing and felt the warmth of her body nearby.

"You've been looking for me," her mother said.

"Sometimes."

"Peace comes hard," her mother said. "I should have warned you about that."

Jax looked at her mother's face. Her mother was a young woman now, just a little older than Jax. Her head was tilted back and the pale moonlight shone on her face.

"Peace has a price," her mother said. "It always does. When you start, you don't know what the price will be."

"I understand," Jax said. She looked past her mother and saw Danny-boy and The Machine standing together in the moonlight.

The angel came to her then, its wings rustling softly. Jax smiled at its ravaged face. It was not so frightening now.

"I guess I belong here," Jax said, and she took its metal hand in hers.

Late at night, when people tell stories, the artists who live in San Francisco talk about the war. Tommy, now an old man, remembers that time and speaks of Danny-boy,

The Machine, Ms. Migsdale, Books, Snake, and—most important of all—Jax. He describes her for the others: a stranger who came to save the city, a wild woman with dark eyes and a quick temper. Some of the young people have their own stories of Jax—they have seen her in the early morning fog, appearing briefly and then vanishing into the mist.

The artists say that if the city were ever invaded again, Jax would return, accompanied by Danny-boy and The Machine, to defend her home. But the legend has never been put to the test. The city is a peaceful place. The monkeys sleep in the trees of the Civic Center Plaza and the pigeons nest between the feet of the statues on the library facade. On market day, Marin farmers cross the brilliant blue bridge to trade at Duff's. Despite the passage of time, its color has not faded. And sometimes, though rarely these days, it rains flowers.

ABOUT THE AUTHOR

Pat Murphy lives in San Francisco, where she edits the *Exploratorium Quarterly,* an idiosyncratic magazine of science, art, and human perception.

In 1987 she won Nebula Awards for both her novel *The Falling Woman* and her novelette "Rachel in Love." Her short fiction has appeared in many magazines and anthologies.

Her cat is named Potato and her favorite color is ultraviolet.

AFTERWORD

Back in 1983, I wrote a story titled "Art in the War Zone," which appeared in *Universe 14*. In the story, a group of artists has taken over San Francisco. Over the years, they have remade the city as a sort of an art project. Invaded by an army from Sacramento, the artists fight back using art.

Sometimes, when I finish a story, I am done with it. At other times, I find myself haunted by the characters long after the story is done. In the case of "Art in the War Zone," I kept on thinking about Jax and Danny-boy, the two main characters. It seemed obvious to me that they had led rich, full lives before I started writing about them. Jax in particular had gone through some hard times.

Eventually, I was compelled to return to Jax and Danny-boy. I needed to know more about where they came from. I wanted to know how Jax, a tough practical-minded young woman, had fallen in with these wildly impractical artists. I was curious about how Danny-boy had decided to paint the Golden Gate Bridge blue. To find out, I had to write this novel.

While I was thinking about the novel, I started working at the Exploratorium, San Francisco's internationally known museum of science, art, and human perception. The Exploratorium's exhibits are interactive, requiring visitors to fool around and make discoveries for themselves. Journalists writing about the Exploratorium have compared it to a county fair, a mad scientist's basement. I edit a magazine for the museum: *Exploratorium Quarterly*, an idiosyncratic publication that reflects the attitude and approach of the Exploratorium.

In many ways, the community of artists in *The City* reflects the sensibilities of the Exploratorium. In addition to being a museum, the Exploratorium is a community of creative individuals: artists, scientists, teachers, writers, poets, and people who just like to tinker with stuff and see what happens. It's an odd sort of place, difficult to describe in the limited space I have here. The people who work here are, for the most part, renegades, iconoclasts, the kind of folks who ask too many questions and won't rest until they have too many answers.

That attitude was typical of Frank Oppenheimer, the creator and founding director of the Exploratorium. I remember one meeting at which a staff member chided Frank for thinking that the museum could do something or other. I don't remember what it was—something vaguely outlandish and improbable, I expect. The irate staffer said, "Come on, Frank. We can't do that. We live in the real world, after all." Frank shook his head. "No we don't. We live in a world we made up."

Frank was right. We live in a world we made up—one that we're still making up, day to day. In *The City*, Duff, the innkeeper who lives on the outskirts of San Francisco, accepts the real world, working within its constraints. The artists, on the other hand, are making up the world as they go along, questioning, changing, exploring different ways of approaching the problems they confront.

When *The City, Not Long After* came out in hardcover, some reviewers criticized it as a return to "sixties sensibilities" and "flower power," as if peace and pacifistic attitudes are now passe. We did that once—no need to do it again. The implication was that such attitudes are not realistic, unsuitable to the real world in which we live.

I am dismayed by the notion that some seem to think that there is no need to consider other ways of living. Needless to say, I disagree. For me, the concerns and sensibilities expressed in *The City* are not those of the sixties, but rather those of the present.

But hey—to be honest, I wasn't really setting out to write about grand themes. I set out to write about Jax and Danny-boy, two people living in a difficult and complex world. I wanted to learn more about them, get to know them a little better.

—Pat Murphy

SPECTRA
SPECIAL EDITIONS

Bantam Spectra Special Editions is a program dedicated to masterful works of fantastic fiction by many of today's most visionary writers. Don't miss them!

"Dan Simmons is a breathtaking writer."
— Harlan Ellison

Hyperion
by Dan Simmons

On the eve of invasion by intersteller barbarians, seven citizens of the Human Hegemony have come to Hyperion on a pilgrimage toward almost certain doom. They travel to the Time Tombs within the realm of the Shrike, whose powers transcend the boundaries of space and time, sharing their incredible stories in the hopes of unraveling the mysteries of the Time Tombs, of the Shrike and of Hyperion itself.